DISHONORED

BETHANY-KRIS

Published by Bethany-Kris

BK

www.bethanykris.com

eISBN 13: 978-1-988197-65-4

Print ISBN 13: 978-1-988197-66-1

Cover Art © London Miller

Editor: Elizabeth Peters

For K. You know why.

CONTENTS

ONE

THERE WAS NOTHING that made Caesar Accardo happier than coming home to Philadelphia after fucking with another one of his father's plans for him. This time it was a failed marriage arrangement between him and a daughter of a New York family. He'd hoped to have a bit of his own brand of fun—fucking up people's lives in a way only he could while he was there—but he ended up having other things to focus on.

Like *not* getting married because his father told him to.

His father hadn't stopped to consider that the Gallucci Cosa Nostra out east would have their own giant pile of steaming shit they were currently dealing with—a pile of shit that worked to Caesar's benefit in more ways than one when it came to getting him out of the whole marriage *deal*.

Marriage was not for him.

Not one he chose.

Not one arranged.

It just wasn't in his cards.

Honestly, this wasn't the first time Angelo tried to pull this trick on his son. It probably wouldn't be the last, either. Caesar was starting to believe he should wear a fucking sign on his back that simply read: *Lucky little shit*. If nothing more than for the amount of times he managed to somehow screw up everything his father planned for him.

As soon as the plane had taxied to the gate, the passengers in coach wasted no time standing, and getting their bags down from the overhead bins. They crowded the aisle soon after even with the cute flight attendant asking them all to remain seated for another few minutes.

Caesar didn't even bother to stand.

What would be the point?

He was not like the rest of these people—he rushed for nothing, and no one. He didn't push and shove to get what he wanted, or to be at the front of the line. That looked good on no man, but especially not one of his status.

His life had allowed him that privilege, and status. His appearance was everything and nothing all at once; sometimes he cared to indulge in maintaining his appearance, and other times, he preferred to stain it with just about everything he could.

The dark urge came on like an itch he couldn't scratch. A whispered voice in his ear demanding he feed the shame that was ever-present in his mind. Like fingernails digging into his back, and pushing him into something *awful*.

And yet, it always made him feel better.

Never failed.

Funny how that worked.

He mulled over his shitty decision to take the earliest flight out of New York—which just happened to be a seat in coach instead of the first class he would usually fly. Soon enough, coach had been deplaned, and Caesar decided it was time for him to move his ass, too.

Maybe it wasn't only flying coach that had him in a mood. After all, pretty soon, he was going to need to face his father, and let Angelo Accardo know that—*yet again*—Caesar didn't follow through with one of his demands and plans.

Not that *telling* him would be the problem. Caesar would greatly enjoy that part—he always took pleasure out of upsetting or angering his father by doing exactly the opposite of what Angelo wanted. He'd always been a disappointment to his father, anyway, so he got his thrill from proving that theory exactly right.

Living up to my birthright, Papa.

That had never changed in all his twenty-seven years.

It was what might come after that concerned Caesar. His father was predictable in that way when it came to his son. Angelo only settled himself on working that much harder to put Caesar in his place, or to take him down a couple of notches.

To his father Caesar was … too arrogant.

Too undisciplined.

Too *wild*.

Too fucking everything.

And nothing a made man living the life of Cosa Nostra should be. Anyone who was asked would say, Caesar had no morals, zero honor, and a severe lack of care when it came to their life, traditions, and rules.

They would be right, too.

That was the whole problem, though—Angelo wanted Caesar to be something he couldn't be. His father wanted his son to be *him*.

Twenty years ago, when Caesar was just a boy still, he would have been happy and pleased to be compared to his father. He wanted to emulate Angelo in every single aspect of his life. Except … he had been just a boy then—stupid, innocent, and naive.

He was none of those things anymore.

Someone had taken it away from him.

It all started and ended right there.

Tossing the leather messenger bag over his shoulder, Caesar headed down the plane for the exit, and gave the flight attendant a wink as he passed. The reddish tint that instantly colored up her cheeks at his gaze drifting over her pencil skirt and then lingering on the top two buttons of her unbuttoned blouse made him grin—*satisfied*. Had he been in first class, and she paid more than twenty seconds of attention to him during the flight, he might have seen just how long it would take before she snuck him into the bathroom to get a hand up that tight skirt of hers.

Another thrill of his.

Women, that was.

Caesar didn't have much of a preference when it came to females, but he did have a kink, of sorts. Or that's what his friend—his *only* friend—liked to call it. As if calling it a kink somehow made it slightly less unappealing or *wrong*. Married women, or those he shouldn't be fucking with for one reason or another, were a particular favorite of his.

Maybe it was the shame they would feel after …

Or the forbidden that got his dick hard …

It could be any number of things.

It didn't matter.

That's what he liked.

Not today, though.

He gave the flight attendant another look—including the wedding band on her finger—and forced his gaze away before he disembarked the plane. He had other things to handle before he could worry about sticking his dick into something warm and wet.

Things like his father.

And his family.

Speaking of which …

Caesar had just come down the escalator at arrivals when the sight of someone waiting for him down below had his rage simmering damn near instantly. Of fucking course his father wouldn't let Caesar come home to no one waiting for him.

He should have known better.

But *shit*, he was surprised to see the man who his father did send to wait for him. His half-brother—Daniele.

Was Angelo trying to start a war?

Because Daniele looked ready for it.

Caesar found that amusing.

That was half the problem.

"Caesar," Daniele greeted when Caesar stepped off the escalator.

The hatred dripped from his half-brother's tone. It almost made Caesar giddy—yet another person in his life that he had ruined in one way or another. Really, what Caesar had done to Daniele was just a by-product of someone else's doings to *him*.

So was Caesar's circle.

3

Vicious.

Cold.

And far too wide.

Everyone got caught in it.

Eventually ...

"Papa sent you?" Caesar asked.

"Why else would I come? Others were busy."

Or they made excuses.

"And you couldn't be busy, too?" Caesar asked.

"I was told to get over what happened, and that starts with this."

Right.

His half-brother was never going to get over what happened. Daniele was never going for forgive Caesar for what he did, or forget it. That was kind of the point, though. That was exactly why Caesar did it. He *needed* his brother to remember what he had done, and that he could do it again in a second.

Hell.

Maybe he would do it again.

Daniele's gaze blazed with his blinding rage. "And unlike you, I make an effort to follow the rules our father sets out for us."

Sure he did.

That's why he was the favored one.

The golden Accardo son.

The honored.

The loved.

The perfect made man.

And Caesar?

He was the dishonored.

The despised.

The shamed made man.

And he fucked his half-brother's wife just because he could—because like his father, Caesar enjoyed taking people down a peg or two, also.

He humbled people in a different way.

Caesar liked this way better.

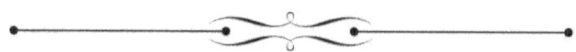

The Accardo estate was set in a private, gated community just outside the Philly city limits. It was almost disconcerting how one could go from the hustle and bustle of cement and steel—something he preferred—to the quiet stillness of a rich suburb.

Most people tended to feel comfort, warmth, and nostalgia when they came back to their childhood home, but Caesar was not one of those people. He felt everything *but* those things, and all of it was negative.

Most notable was the anxiety that was ever present from the second he drove into the large circular driveway. He hid the slight trembling of his hands by shoving them into the pockets of his slacks. His clenched jaw couldn't be contained, but his father was so accustomed to seeing Caesar in some form of scowling or displeasure that he probably wouldn't even notice.

Inside the three-level, two-wing monster of a home, Caesar became slightly more agitated than before. His gaze was drawn upward—to a place that left him most haunted whenever he was forced to come here, and stay for longer than a breath.

Monster was a good word for this place, as it certainly felt like it could be a living, breathing *thing*. A tangible horror he couldn't escape from that left him feeling tainted in far more ways than one.

Much like the people inside.

Or *because* of the people inside.

It was all the same now.

Daniele broke away from Caesar the moment he could, and without a goodbye. Likely to find his mother—a woman, Martina, Caesar's father had married shortly after his mother died when he was only four. Soon after, Daniele came along.

Caesar remembered that day *vividly*.

And the years that followed.

All those fucking *years*.

His jaw clenched harder, and he felt the pain throbbing in his molars from the action. It was his go-to move to get the hell out of his thoughts and memories—pain, or *sex*. One or the other, because he wasn't fucking picky.

Either one would do the deal.

Get it over with; see him, and get out.

His thoughts had the right idea, so he went in search of his father in the large mansion. Unsurprisingly, he found Angelo in his large office sitting behind his domineering oak desk. He never understood the need for a man to have a desk that size other than to show off wealth, or intimidate a man standing on the other side of it.

But who was he to say?

Caesar stood in the doorway until his father *pretended* like he noticed his waiting presence. Angelo knew his oldest son was there from the moment Daniele drove them through the gate. That's what the half of a dozen fucking guards were for.

"There you are," Angelo said, sitting straighter in his chair, and folding his hands on the desk. "Give me the good news, son."

Yes, the *good news*.

That the marriage would happen.

That all was well.

That Angelo got what he wanted.

Caesar shrugged, and felt the tension in his shoulders loosening a bit at the promise of what was to come when he said, "A bit of a change in plans, I guess."

Instantly, the happiness in Angelo's expression fled. "How so?"

"New York had to back out for … *reasons*. Seems their daughter somehow got back to her Russian husband, and well, our marriage won't be going ahead."

It took a second.

Then, *two*.

Caesar waited with a small smile that he couldn't be bothered to hide.

And then there it was.

Molten red dotting his father's cheeks. Narrowed eyes as Angelo took Caesar and his gleeful disposition in all over again.

Rage.

Disappointment.

And for him?

For Caesar, it all spelled his *triumph*.

"What happened?" his father hissed.

"I just told you."

"Did you help the girl get back to her husband?"

"Why would I do that?" Caesar asked innocently.

But *yes*, he had.

And he would do it again.

Angelo was quiet for a long time, and it gave Caesar the chance to observe his father more studiously while he was distracted by his thoughts. His father was all meat and girth—something Daniele had taken from the man. Dark hair, rounded face, and brown eyes.

Caesar, on the other hand, was grateful to have taken his features from his dead mother's side of the family. From their strong jawlines, to the blond wavy hair that he kept a little too long for his father's liking, and even the steel-blue eyes. Standing next to his father, Caesar's lean runner's form was a bright contrast against the Italian girth his father sported.

He liked the differences.

Liked that he was different from them.

He didn't want to be the same.

"This is what, the fourth marriage you've somehow found your way out of?" Angelo asked. "I am catching onto your schemes, Caesar. You cannot ruin every single marriage arrangement I make for you—mark my words, one will go through."

"Actually, it's five," Caesar said, "if you include the poor girl that took her life two years ago."

By jumping off a goddamn bridge.

She had not wanted to be forced to marry.

Caesar understood that feeling well.

"Yes, well, you didn't have any hand in foiling that one," his father muttered heavily. Then, his gaze lifted to find Caesar in the doorway, asking, "Or did you?"

"I am not that kind of monster, Papa."

"Hard to tell sometimes with the shit you do, *figlio*."

"So says you."

Angelo grunted, and slumped a little in his chair. "That ... *that* right there, Caesar."

"I beg your pardon?"

"You have an attitude problem, and I will be damned if I don't find a way to correct it before I have to kill you for it."

He'd once been his father's favorite.

He'd lost that when he fucked his brother's wife.

Caesar lifted a brow, uncaringly. "I don't have an attitude problem."

"Oh, no?" Angelo laughed darkly. "How do you figure? Indulge me, son. Name one other man who would think your attitude is in any way acceptable for a made man in Cosa Nostra?"

"My attitude is fine. I rather like it. It's you who has a problem with it. That kind of sounds like a *you* problem, and not a me problem."

Angelo quieted.

A tic showed in his jaw.

Yes, this was making Caesar feel *much* better.

Soon, he would be gone, too.

All good things.

"Until I figure out what to do with you," Angelo grumbled under his breath as he scrubbed a hand down his jaw, "things have changed here since you were in New York."

That piqued his interest.

"How so?"

"The Camorra family on the west end—they've begun moving into our streets."

Caesar nodded appreciatively. "Someone has big balls."

Because the Accardo family was a force to be reckoned with in Philly. They were too large, and had far too much control of the area to be challenged by a rather small Camorra clan when put in to comparison. And the two criminal organizations were a world apart from one another despite both being Italian based.

One, structured like a pyramid.

The other, structured more like a horizontal line.

And when a family took one clan down, five more might pop up from the ruins because of their structure. Caesar had to give them that—Camorra clans were fucking resilient. That was just about all he knew regarding them, though.

Cosa Nostra was his thing.

Very little else.

"Yes, well, balls or not," Angelo said, anger coloring his tone again, "they need to go. I won't have them causing me these kinds of problems regardless of what they want. And until things are settled here—your brother and the rest of my men are still a bit sour with you from all the shit you pulled a few months back—you're handling that issue."

Caesar stiffened. "What, the Camorra clan?"

"Yes, get rid of them. Make them a deal. Wipe them out. Just … *do something*, Caesar. Be useful for once."

He brushed that insult off.

One of many.

"I can probably handle that," Caesar said. "Someone needs to have eyes on my streets—Capo business never stalls."

Angelo smiled then—thin, and cold. "Someone *has* been, son. Daniele, actually. He's really stepped up in your absence."

Caesar kept his expression blank, but he still heard the underlying threat in his father's words. He heard what the man didn't say.

Daniele could and would replace him.

Easily, likely.

The fucker could *try*.

"But for now, I'm having a dinner tonight with a few of the men from the family, and your brother," Angelo added. "I think you could make the effort to sit at the table, and be some version of *pleasant*. Can't you?"

Caesar started listing names in his head.

Names of men in the family.

Names of their wives.

There was maybe three men whose wives Caesar hadn't gotten to in his special way—it was likely he was going to sit at the table with men who knew *very well* that he'd at one point or another, got a taste of what was between their women's thighs.

He enjoyed that.

Compromising them all in that way.

It was his only control.

He *needed* it.

"Dinner sounds nice; I could eat."

Angelo cocked a brow, obviously hearing the slyness in Caesar's tone.

"Don't pull any shit, *figlio*. You step out of line one more time, and so help me God, I will put you in the grave I should have given you years ago."

"Promises, promises," Caesar called over his shoulder as he left his father behind. "You're always making those, and yet never keeping them."

Death would be a gift.

His father would never give it to him.

Dinner was a fucking *bore*.

Caesar could barely open his mouth without his father glaring in his direction—a silent order for him to sit still, and shut the fuck up. His father hadn't lied, though. Only a handful of men were there to eat and discuss the latest business in the organization, but Caesar was out of the loop in that regard.

Shitty by-product of being gone for so long.

Not that he wanted to talk business.

Caesar was downing his second glass of wine when the high-pitch, nasally voice of his step-mother resounded from the entryway behind him.

"Is the wife not invited to this party of yours, Angelo?" Her laughter felt like nails raking down Caesar's back—a bloody trail of pain and hate he couldn't escape. "I'm offended, *mio bello*."

At the head of the table, Caesar's father hid his displeasure at Martina interrupting his dinner with the men. She should have known her place after two decades of marriage to the man, yet she still kept pushing her boundaries.

Angelo let her.

That was part of the problem.

Well, that and the fact she was almost *always* drunk. And when she wasn't entirely plastered, then she was pretty fucking close to it. Angelo did a good job of hiding his wife's alcoholism, but not from his son. Caesar had gotten a taste of this woman's vile vindictiveness one too many goddamn times.

Martina's hand brushed Caesar's shoulder as she passed him by at the table—her silent hello. She never offered very much more when others were around, and he liked it just fine that way. He did *absolutely everything* he could not to have a conversation alone with the woman, or get stuck in private with her.

She was the woman who replaced his mother.

She was shrill, and horrible.

He hated her.

9

Always had.

He only learned how to hate her more and in different ways over the years, but no one cared to hear about those details.

No one wanted to know.

"Ma," Daniele greeted when Martina bent over his shoulder to kiss her son's cheek.

"My boy."

A pat to his cheek.

Soft, and sweet.

Then, she moved onto her husband, ready to put herself in his path, and in the spotlight for everyone else in the room. So was her way. Typical, and predictable.

Nothing fucking new.

Caesar was still trying to forget the way her hand felt on his shoulder, and how it left a heavy weight behind. He *hated* when she touched him.

It left dirtiness behind.

Caesar was up out of his seat before anyone even knew what was happening, and had tossed his napkin down to the table. He didn't bother to turn and see his step-mother drop in his father's lap, but her giggles were more than enough to send him the hell out of that dining room.

Those feelings her touch invoked still thrummed deep even as he half-jogged down the hallway, and came to the grand entry. They should have left him the moment he was out of the mansion, and calling for a cab. It always went away then, except for this time.

This time, it felt stronger.

It ate at him.

The dirty, awful feelings still lingered long after he reentered the city limits.

Only two things could fix it.

Pain.

Or sex.

He chose the latter when he told the cab driver, "Lucifer's Den—the club downtown. Take me there."

TWO

LIFE AND HAPPINESS were fleeting.

Those were the two details that had taught Aria De Rose the most about being alive in her twenty-six years. Fleeting because anything could happen that took away one's simple happiness, and when a person's joy was gone, their life was effectively over.

Her life had been over for a year.

"De Rose!"

Aria glanced up to find the guard behind the Plexiglas window was gesturing at her. All of the prison guards knew her well enough by face alone to pull the file on her visits to this godforsaken place. A few of them even felt like they knew her well enough to use her first name in greeting as though she cared to greet them back.

Although, she *did* greet them.

Politely, of course.

She had to for no other reason than the man behind bars here—her behavior to those that kept him safe while he was in this hellish place might make all the difference for him. She certainly couldn't afford for him to think something she had done or said to one of the guards made a target on his back.

Standing from her seat, Aria fixed her dress with one hand, and kept a firm grasp on her diamond studded clutch in the other. She might have been visiting a prison, but she sure as hell didn't need to look like it, too.

Her father—a long-standing Camorra boss—wouldn't appreciate seeing her in anything less than her finest, anyway. So was the life of a Camorra woman, and Aria was proudly one of those.

Constantly sheltered.

Revered.

Harshly judged.

More dangerous than a man.

One didn't choose this life—they were either born to it, or it chose them. There was no in between, she had found. And one could either make due with what they were given from the life, or they could struggle and drown trying to get out.

Because there was *no out*.

Aria made small chat with the guard as she went through the visitation process at Curran-Fromhold Correctional Facility. The security checks and paperwork were nothing new now that she had been doing it for a little over a year. Her once, and sometimes twice, weekly visits making her well-known to the guards shortened the time for her whereas it might take someone else far longer to get through the process.

"Enjoy your visit, Aria," the guard said with a smile.

She sat down in the hard, plastic chair he directed her to and nodded back at the man. *"Grazie."*

The guard went back to his post at the entrance door. She was grateful that, yet again, he had opted to seat her at the very far end of the block. A good fifteen chairs with their own private window made of Plexiglas and a telephone separated her, and the guard.

It gave her the illusion of privacy.

A camera was still at her back, though.

That couldn't be helped.

Soon, the man she had come to check in with—as she did every week—came into view as he was shuffled through the metal doors on the other side of the visitation block. Jac De Rose could pull off any look including drab prison gray. His wide smile, and bright green eyes greeted her as he sat down opposite to her on the other side of the Plexiglas window.

Gesturing with his still-cuffed hands to the phone on the wall, Aria picked it up so she could speak to her father. *"Papy."*

Daddy.

Jac's smile softened. "How's my girl?"

Aria tucked the strands of her copper-brown curls behind her ears, and said, "Pretty good, all things considered."

"Things like what?"

Merda.

She still wasn't very good at this whole visiting thing. She was constantly told by those around her to make sure she did everything she could *not* to upset her father during her visits. Any business talk—mafia, always—needed to be good, or *great* things. Certainly not something that would warrant him making a call or two so that he could rage at someone else.

No one wanted the boss upset.

Everyone answered to him.

"Nothing," Aria said with a smile she hoped was enough to distract her father.

Beauty had always served her well even when it came to the man who gave her life. Jac appreciated a pretty face, and the reprieve it could provide in hard times. Aria had learned her beauty was enough to get her just about anything she wanted should she use it the right way. Or … most of the time.

Her father often told her that with her large, expressive green eyes, heart-shaped face, and delicate lips set atop the rest of her dainty features, she looked a great deal like her long-dead mother. That the only thing she had taken from him was her brown hair with the copper tint, and those unruly curls that she had to *hope and pray* every single time she tried to do anything with them.

Aria had seen enough pictures of Carina De Rose to know that was true, but not actual memories given her mother had died when she was a baby after an unfortunate run-in with a rival Camorra clan. Jac killed every single one of them for what they had taken from him—he never remarried after that, either.

"Nothing *at all?*" her father pressed.

He was reaching for something, and clearly, giving her the opportunity to come out and tell him whatever it was before he was willing to admit he already knew. This wasn't an unusual game her father liked to play, and to be fair, she was pretty damned good at it, too.

After all, she was *his* daughter.

Manipulation was her forte.

She racked her brain to come up with whatever it was Jac wanted to know—she kept drawing a blank, though. A lot was going on in different areas for their clan. Business was good, but that wasn't anything new.

Her father's amused chuckle echoed in her ear through the phone before his voice said, "I heard you're having some problems on the streets—you know *he* fills me in when he can, although he didn't have much to tell me this time being he's away. The Accardo family, or so I hear. They have quite a large organization, and not one that tends to intrude on smaller families."

Oh, *that.*

Jac had posed the question as though it was *their* clan having the trouble. Like they had found themselves in a pot of stirred shit by-proxy. She assumed, just from that alone, her father didn't know it was actually *her* who had started this street war with a rival family.

She had her reasons.

None she was willing to share.

"It's nothing I can't handle," Aria replied. "And I am—handling it, I mean."

Jac nodded, but he didn't look entirely convinced. So was the way of a standing-boss, but even more so when she had a pussy between her thighs instead of a cock. It was fine and dandy for her to relay her father's messages, or make an order because he gave it to her to pass along. But anything else, and a Camorra woman had to work ten times as hard as any man to gain the respect, and acknowledgement of those around her.

That was fine.

She didn't mind the work.

"I'll be out soon," her father said. "Six months left, *mia cara*. In the meantime, work on peacefully settling whatever *problema* the Accardo Cosa Nostra has with us. Do *not* entice or incite them more. I don't want to come out of this place to total chaos."

"Whatever you want, Papy."

Jac smiled. "Good. Now, how is Raffe?"

And just like that—with all of *one* question—she wished she could leave.

Except she couldn't.

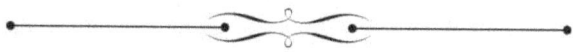

The thing about Camorra was that there was no *real* structure to their organization. There was, of course, what Aria's father liked to refer to as the *cielo coperto*, and the *cielo scoperto*. The covered sky, and the clear sky.

Within their clan, the covered sky was anyone with a direct connection to the top, or a proper position that they were required to handle. Her father, obviously, being the boss even behind bars, and her, acting as the boss while he was away could be put in the *cielo coperto*. She, and her father, were *il Vangelo* of the Camorra—the gospel.

When they spoke, they were heard.

Any man who dealt directly with them—only a handful—were also under the designation of being protected by the covered sky.

The *cielo scoperto* encompassed the larger breadth of their clan, and held less loyalty to the Camorra succeeding as a whole. They were more prone to violence, and at times, were liable to attempt to break off and begin an entirely separate clan of their own.

It was exactly why clans often found themselves in the bloodiest of battles. No clan answered to another, and there was no hierarchy beyond an *us* and *them* situation.

Aria had always thought that given how long her father had managed to control and sustain his Camorra, Jac had been given every opportunity to clean up the ranks. To manage it better, or even, take their horizontal structure into a more pyramid style situation so that fewer problems came up with rival clans.

It meant cleaner streets.

Less spilled blood.

Fewer deaths.

But it was also not the way of Camorra, and the men who only knew the life that they had been taught for decades upon decades were not quite ready to give up the stronghold they had on old traditions.

Shame, really.

Camorra could be *so much more.*

Aria knew it.

She felt it.

Tasted it on her tongue.

It was all right there.

And she could do it.

If only …

For now, business was waiting.

"And what did the boss have to say about this fucking Accardo problem?" Simone asked.

Aria, from the head of the table, barely even turned her head to peer down the way at the man. A favorite of her father's, Simone Bruno, was sometimes like a stand-in son for the boy Jac never had. She figured that was part of the reason why the man was so goddamn mouthy a lot of the time, and tried to use more pull than he actually had.

"He's not willing to bend to the Accardo organization," Aria said, flicking a hand as if to dismiss any other notion that might come up about the topic. "He wants more streets—more territory to control. It's about time we expanded. I see his point."

Simone's jaw tensed, and his wife—Giovanna—reached over to pet him like he was an angry puppy that needed stroked to be calm. It was almost amusing, if it wasn't so fucking sickening, really.

"Did you explain to him that I lost four men in a *month*?" Simone asked.

"You, or *him*?" Aria countered, leaning forward a bit as she tipped her head to the side. "There is only one boss of this clan, Simone. *You* have nothing—it is all his. That's how this works."

The three other men at the table quieted in their conversation as Aria spoke. She didn't need to raise her voice to cut someone down—she'd learned how to be as sharp as a knife without making a scene of herself.

It was a good talent to have.

An emotional woman, a man could handle.

A calm one?

She was *frightening.*

Simone's jaw continued doing that thing it always did whenever he was pissed, and trying to hold it back. Aria wondered how long he would last before he exploded on her. It didn't matter that he knew the rules of Camorra, and that her place above him was rightly done considering their current circumstances.

None of that factored to him.

She was a woman.

A *daughter.*

15

She had her place.

To him, this was not it.

"Fine," Simone snapped, "then did you explain to him about the men that have been killed?"

She chose to ignore the way he phrased the question this time. Poking at that raw nerve of his wouldn't get her anywhere good—at least not tonight.

He was probably going to have to go, though.

Eventually.

"I did," Aria said.

"*And?*"

"Anyone in *cielo scoperto* are easily replaceable, Simone. They are our *batterie*. No one we can't afford to lose, and frankly, we might find less trouble in the future considering how many from that side of our clan seem to step out to form their own organizations. Perhaps work on making those men loyal to *you*, and less loyal to the cash they're making for you, and that might not be such an issue anymore."

"That's not even what the issue is!"

Red-faced, and with fists clenched, Simone raised from his seat at the table. *Her* table, actually, which just irked Aria even more. Disrespect was one thing, but disrespect in her territory was something else altogether.

Oh, yes.

He was certainly going to have to go in due time.

Aria raised a brow, and nothing more, in the face of Simone's sudden rage. He was not the first man to get angry, or to try something with her. He could raise his fist, and she would probably smile at him and dare him to try it.

She didn't frighten *that* easily.

"I want to speak with Jac," Simone demanded.

Growled, was more like it.

Aria smirked a bit, and shook her head once. "No, that won't be possible for a while. You know how this goes while he's in lockup—the less visitation, the better. He doesn't want names and records kept of our coming and going besides his immediate family. *Me*, I mean. If you have something to say, Simone, you are looking at the one woman you get to say it to. Otherwise, sit yourself back down in that chair. I'm starting to think my father has severely neglected some things when it comes to you."

She was acutely aware of the gazes watching her. Of the other men at the table who would report back to whoever they needed to about her behavior, and how she handled this situation. That was fine with her. She *needed* people to know her name. She needed them afraid of the one and only De Rose woman willing to cut them down.

Power came to those who *took* it.

It was never given.

Simone scoffed, although he did sit down. "What exactly has he neglected with me, Aria? Nothing more or less than he neglected with your ignorant—"

"Watch your tongue, or I will cut it out."

He blinked, silenced.

Aria smiled.

Simone's wife was not quite as smart, though. Giovanna's gaze narrowed as it turned on Aria with a burning rage that might shrink a lesser woman.

"Who do you think you are?" Giovanna asked. "You're reaching a bit when you talk to him like that, don't you think? Be careful, Aria. Your father isn't going to be in prison for very much longer."

Didn't this stupid *wife* know?

Getting up from her seat with the slow grace she had been taught was *most* beneficial to a lady who wanted all eyes on her, Aria fingered the rim of the wine glass she'd emptied just before this meeting had begun. The wine bottle was all the way at the other end of the table, so no one seemed to think twice about her grabbing the glass as she moved down the table. All eyes stayed on her, and frankly, they should have *known*.

When it came to her, they always should have known.

Aria had just come to the back of Giovanna's chair when she showed them she had no intention of going for the wine bottle. She smashed the wine glass overtop of the woman's unsuspecting head before she grabbed a fistful of Giovanna's hair, and yanked her head back so wide eyes were staring up at her. Chairs scraped, and warnings murmured along the table, but no one stepped in.

They did know better, then.

Or, they were learning.

Good.

Bending down to murmur in Giovanna's ear, Aria's smile stayed firmly in place when she said, "Check my bloodlines, *cagna*. You'll find exactly who I am."

She was a *De Rose*.

Camorra.

Vicious, violent, and vehement.

And she would bow to no one.

Not again.

It was only the click of a door closing that drew Aria's gaze away from the mirror showcasing her painted-to-perfection features. All her delicate lines had been highlighted and contoured, and her eyes made demure with dark kohl. The red stain on her lips made them appear fuller, and accentuated her small cupid's bow. Heavy, black mascara lifted, lengthened, and thickened her eyelashes enough to frame the green orbs.

She preferred it when her eyes were the first thing a man saw when he stared at her. And then, the man could get lost while he looked at everything else she had to offer, too.

That daze was dangerous.

She played it well.

"Well?" Aria asked.

Nico—the only man who had stayed entirely silent during her meeting with the others—sighed as he stepped closer to her vanity. "They're gone. Not pleased, mind you, but gone."

Aria went back to her reflection, and twisted one stray curl back into place. "I don't care about their happiness, Nico, I care that they *listen*."

"And what if one starts to question you, Aria? What if one decides to find a way to your father despite all the loopholes and barricades you've put up to keep him sheltered from them? What then?"

Oh, that seemed simple enough.

"Then, we kill them."

Nico sighed again.

She almost smiled.

"Don't worry," she said, "we're one step closer."

One step closer to having it all.

To controlling Philly.

To gaining back her *life*.

"Real talk," Nico muttered, "about Jac. What did he have to say?"

Aria met his gaze in the mirror. Nico stood behind her patient, silent, and waiting like he always did. Her most trusted companion, and the one man who had never hurt her. She'd known him since she was just a girl— young enough to still enjoy tales like gold at the end of the rainbow, and when puddle jumping was fun.

She was not young anymore.

Neither was he.

"Peace—my father wants me to make peace."

Nico smirked a bit. "Not going to happen any time soon."

"He doesn't know that, though. Now, what do *you* have for me?" she asked.

"Information on the Accardos."

"I love information."

Nico laughed. "I know."

"Don't keep me in suspense."

She worked on fixing a couple of stray strands of her hair as Nico went in to details about the latest information he had gathered on the family they had been provoking for a while. Tonight would be one step closer to getting *in* on their inner circle.

Really in if it all worked out.

"The latest little spat we had with them worked, it seems," Nico said.

By spat, he meant a drive by shooting of one of their restaurants. Closed, of course. Aria didn't need innocents getting mixed up in all of this. Still, she knew a couple of the Accardo men held regular nightly meetings at the business.

One had died.

Shame.

"Worked, *how?*" she asked.

"Seems Angelo Accardo has finally put someone on the streets to try and handle us—his oldest son, Caesar. He's been back for about a week now."

"Where was he again?"

"I heard New York."

Aria nodded. "So the difficult son is back, then."

Caesar Accardo's antics in his family were well-known ... well, as long as someone had deep enough pockets to pay someone for the information. Seemed the guy liked to cause trouble, and couldn't keep his dick in his pants, for whatever reason.

Aria figured she could use that to her advantage.

"And he is ...?" she trailed off, allowing Nico to fill in the blank she had been hoping for.

"Caesar is at his regular haunts," Nico said, making her grin. "At least in the evenings."

Her plan *was* coming together.

It was beautiful, really.

The two of them quieted as Aria went back to putting the final touches on her look with a black velvet choker around her throat, and diamond studs in her ears. Sexy, and classic, but nothing that might take attention away from her face or her body.

"It's a shame, isn't it?" she asked quietly.

Nico raised one dark eyebrow. "What is?"

"How this has all shaken out for this clan of ours."

He chuckled dryly. "It's really only *you* who has done all of this. It's you who wants to control Philly, and who is determined enough to burn down the city in order to get what you want."

"And you who is willing to help me," she shot back.

Nico nodded once. "We both know why that is, though."

She did.

And it was not because he *loved* her. Oh, sure, he did love her, but like a sister. It was only because of those feelings that Nico noticed what her father hadn't, and was the first to step in and try to help her in any way that he could.

If only it had worked ...

Well, it was working now.

That's what mattered.

"Had it been you that Jac demanded I marry a year and a half ago before he went into prison," Aria said, "I would not have been happy, but I would not be *this*, either."

Nico glanced away. "I shouldn't have said no when he asked."

No, she didn't love him, either. He'd never touched her, and she never thought to try with him, either. It would be like kissing her brother, and that only left her feeling icky. Still, had it been Nico who tied her down, she would have at least been safe.

Instead, it had been—

"Raffe called just before the meeting started," Nico murmured.

That name again.

That feeling in her spine again.

Heavy, hurtful, and too hot.

"What did he want?" she asked.

She didn't let her voice shake.

Didn't let it even *tremble*.

No, she kept it cool, cold, and detached.

That was all Raffaele Ferri deserved. The only thing she had ever been able to keep when her father married her to him was the last name she'd been given at birth. Sure, Raffe had one of his moments when she requested her surname remain unchanged, but her father had rather liked the idea.

What Jac wanted, Jac got.

A lot like Aria.

Even if it took a while.

"He wanted to check in," Nico said.

Aria's throat worked to remove the lump that had formed there. "He's going to be away for two or three more months at the latest. The deal with the Cambria cartel in Italy will not be one that is easy going for him. I made sure of that."

"Careful he doesn't find out how many hands you have in the pot, Aria."

Yes, that would be dangerous.

A danger she could not afford.

"And he said he would be sending Mae over in the morning for breakfast," Nico added when she didn't respond.

Aria did smile at that. "Oh?"

Nico grinned a bit, too. "She'll keep your mind off of things for a bit."

"Mae's good for that."

"She is."

Nico couldn't hide the fondness in his tone as he spoke about Raffe's eighteen-year-old half-sister. The girl looked nothing like her brother with her light brown skin, and wild head of corkscrew curls that flew in every direction. A child born to a mistress of Raffe's now-dead father, as far as Aria knew, although she wasn't privy to a lot about her husband's history. He was making his best effort to scrub the Ferri Camorra clan's history clean, and then turning her father's organization into his own while he had the time.

But Mae ... she was nothing like her brother.

And next to Nico, she was Aria's only friend.

Standing from the vanity bench, she said to Nico, "Help me get dressed. I'll need you to zip this goddamn dress of mine up."

"Are you sure *this* is the route you want to go?" Nico asked behind her.

Aria hesitated when she reached for the shimmering, tight gold number set out on the bed. "Why wouldn't it be? It seems like the easiest way to trap one of them, doesn't it?"

"One pro to how many cons, though?"

He had a point.

Camorra was ... difficult.

Especially for a woman like her.

"Any improper behavior from you noted by *anyone*," Nico said, "and it would ruin you if Jac or Raffe found out, Aria. What you're planning to do is going to absolutely go far beyond *improper*."

Yes, and a good reputation was *everything* to a Camorra woman. It was the only thing allowing her respect in their life, and giving her status. Should she lose that good reputation by doing something improper that might sully her name or family, then she would be nothing.

Worthless.

Unusable.

Dishonored.

Should she find herself in hot water because of her plans, no one would look at Aria and wonder *why* a woman of her name and status had done what she did—they would only care she that she had done it. That would be all that mattered.

"Then, give me another way," Aria murmured. "Tell me another way to do this—to be free of him, and what he does to me. Tell me, Nico, and I will do it."

Nico stayed silent.

Everything about her life—from her every day appearance to even her forced marriage because her father had been facing prison time—was about never breaking that perfect, unsullied image that Camorra demanded from a woman. A dishonored woman would be given nothing, and as it stood, Aria had already been made to give up everything for this person she now was.

She was going to have to take that risk.

Aria was not giving them *more*.

Not of her.

Aria nodded, and peered at him over her shoulder. "Exactly. There is no other way. This is how I get out—this is how I can be free. Now, help me put on my dress, and let me try out my new name with you before I go."

Nico shook his head. "What did you choose to go with?"

"Take a guess."

"Your mother's name?"

Aria shrugged. "I've always loved the name Carina. I think it works."

"You think a lot of things."

She gave him a look.

"Watch it, Nico."

"Yeah, yeah. The prized rose with her thorns."

"My thorns cut like knives. Don't you ever forget it."

"But who sharpened those thorns, Aria?"

Raffe.

Jac.

This life.

"Me," she settled on saying.

It was still true.

THREE

LUCIFER'S DEN WAS a favorite haunt of Caesar's for a number of reasons; most being something people might find salacious or immoral. And that was just fine with him because that's exactly why he frequented the club.

On the outside, Lucifer's Den appeared the same as any other club except for the rooftop parking section for the uber-wealthy that patrons like Caesar were allowed to use by way of a glass elevator that would lift a vehicle up and down. The flat-gray bricks, and simple sign gave nothing away about the goings-on inside the joint.

Certainly not the drugs.

Or the sex.

If a person wanted something, the best place to find it was Lucifer's Den. It was all provided in the plentiful, and Caesar liked to indulge a hell of a lot more than he probably should. But shit, he was going to die someday regardless, and he was not going out with regrets about things he should have done.

He was going to do it all.

Inside the club, once he had come down one of three glass elevators from the roof that led *inside* the club, Caesar was bombarded by the familiar sights on the entrance floor. Red velvet couches, and a bar to the right. Dimmed lighting by low hanging chandeliers, and a DJ set up in his booth where no one could get to him while he worked. A few girls moved over the dance floor in their tiny skirts and sky-high heels with large serving trays filled with either drinks, or empty glasses. The dance floor was full, too.

Caesar might dance.

If he found someone's skirt to hide his hands while he did it …

Passing the main floor, Caesar grabbed a drink from one of the passing waitresses, and she gave him a wink. His face was recognizable, and his tab hadn't been officially closed in this place since it opened three goddamn years ago. Sure, he paid it off, but the owner still kept it open for him to use again and again—he *was* a repeat, after all.

It was the barrel-chested man standing in front of red-velvet upholstered double doors keeping Caesar from getting to the place he wanted to be. Or rather, closer to finding a new pair of thighs to get in between for the better portion of his night.

"Good to see you again, Caesar," the bouncer said.

"And you."

Kevin, he wanted to say?

He wasn't really sure of the man's name.

"I think you alone could make the boss a very rich man with the amount of times you come to this place a week," the guy said, stepping back just enough to open the double doors for him. "Enjoy your evening."

Caesar ticked a finger over his shoulder, and then disappeared into the red stream of light filtering between the crack in the doors.

Hell was a sexy sight—black velvet, red lighting, dark hardwood, and cocaine on a glass table. Caesar passed two girls leaning over in their men's laps to lock onto one another with a kiss, but he had other things on his mind. Cocaine dust powdered one of the girl's noses, and a similar streak of the drug looked like it had been smudged on one of the man's collars.

By the end of the night, he bet *both* of those men were going to be snorting that coke right off those girls' asses. Lucifer's Den was predictable in that way. It always ended with the same thing every single time here.

Another section with couches surrounding the same style of black-glass table had a bowl—pink, blue, purple, and white pills filled it like candy. For the people sitting there with their champagne and painted on smiles, he bet it did taste like candy for them.

Black and red sheer curtains hung low from the ceiling, and dipped down to the floor around each of the seating sections. It allowed someone the illusion of privacy if they wanted to pull the curtains a bit to close out the rest of the club, but it was widely known here that everyone could still see whatever you were doing behind it.

Oh, yeah.

This club was what Caesar's wet dreams were fucking made of.

And sin was always waiting.

He planned to head directly back to his favorite spot in the club—a corner couch section with just enough room for two or three people, should he be interested in that kind of crowd. It gave him the perfect view of the vast majority of the floor, and a good show of whatever was going on around him.

A familiar voice calling out stopped him.

"Caesar, my man!"

His steps faltered as a familiar man straightened from the couple he was talking to a few feet away, and came Caesar's way with his signature grin. The owner of Lucifer's Den was a lot of things, and had his hands in too many pots to count, but he had always been good to Caesar. And he was good enough to let the man know never to fuck with him, either. Sometimes that warning was just enough to keep Caesar from pressing … depending on the man it came from.

"Maverick," Caesar greeted.

The man flashed his white teeth as his hand struck out, and met

Caesar's with a hard smack. Maverick knew Caesar well enough not to draw him into a hug, though. He didn't care for people touching him unless it was to get him off, frankly.

"Place is busy tonight," Caesar noted.

Maverick nodded. "That it is. Shit, didn't I just see you in here two nights ago?"

Yeah.

"Horrible week," Caesar offered.

Really, it was a horrible *life*.

"Well, whatever the fuck it is, you know I never mind seeing your sorry ass in here. You always liven up a party."

Caesar laughed, smirking. "I do try."

"Do you want me to get your regular?"

"Just the drink this time—I'll find my own pussy."

Maverick clapped Caesar on the shoulder with a chuckle. "You got it—can't deny you liked the taste you got of her, though. Pretty sure everybody on the floor heard how much *she* liked it."

"They always do."

"I'll probably see you around tonight, then."

Caesar slanted his gaze in Maverick's direction with a nod. "Yeah, we'll see how it goes."

Maverick went his way, and Caesar continued his trek to the couch and table he considered always reserved for him. He passed a couple of recognizable faces—people in the celebrity and political world that most definitely could *not* afford to be found in a place like Lucifer's Den. He enjoyed snapping a picture of them every once in a while even if photos were entirely off-limits.

What fun was it when he followed the rules?

None.

Caesar wasn't sitting in his spot for more than two minutes before a girl in a tight, black bodycon dress and sky-high red heels came to deliver his drink. She flashed him a sensual smile as her hand came to rest on her hip. His gaze drifted over her to take her in—she was sexy enough, as far as that went, but nothing stirred him to act.

"Anything else I can help you with?" she asked. "Maverick said to make sure you were pleased."

Caesar offered the woman a charming smile. "For now, I am. *Grazie, bella.*"

Her brow lifted at his Italian, and she grinned a bit. Women always did like it when the foreign language came out to play—Caesar never really understood the appeal. He could make a woman come just as well in English as he could in Italian. Who fucking cared what he was actually saying while they were riding his dick?

"Just let me know," the woman all but purred.

He might.

Not tonight.

All it took was a flick of his hand, and the girl was gone. Maverick had trained his staff well, and the girls were used to being either the center of attention when it came to a patron, or dismissed altogether. Caesar usually fell into the latter category here because there was always something a little more interesting that came along to catch his eye.

Like that right there—damn.

The woman sitting on a couch just across from his had entirely passed his view as he scanned the club, and right then, she seemed entirely oblivious to him as well. Caesar liked that because if nothing else, it gave him the time to peruse her.

And damn, was she a sight to see.

The body-hugging gold dress draped over her shoulders dipped low enough in the front to give him a peek at ample, perky tits, and collarbones that made his dick hard. Yeah, he had a thing for those—liked to bite them, really.

A slit in the skirt of the short dress came up to her thigh, and when she crossed her legs, he swore he saw a flash of bright red lace hiding beneath. *God save me.* He would have groaned out loud if he were a lesser man, honestly. Anything red or lace was his weakness, and he wasn't even ashamed to admit it.

Her black fuck-me heels helped to give her long, smooth legs the kind of promise that whispered they would look even better wrapped around his waist or head. Shit, he wasn't fucking picky—she could even have it both ways, if she wanted.

The woman's painted red lips and brown-copper curls framed delicate features, soft lips, and wide green eyes. Her gaze was darkened by smoky makeup he suddenly had every dark urge to smudge and ruin, and he wondered what that shade of lipstick she wore might look like when it was a ring at the base of his dick.

Wow, yeah.

He needed to get laid.

By that female right there.

As though she could *feel* his eyes on her, the woman turned her head from whatever had caught her attention, and her gaze landed directly on Caesar. Those small lips of hers curved in the *most* wicked way as her green orbs took him in from head to toe. He knew what she was seeing—women usually liked what they looked at when it came to Caesar, and he did aim to fucking please.

Black Armani.

Italian leather loafers.

Gold rings on every finger.

A let-me-fuck-you smile.

Sometimes, he could get them with just that smile of his alone.

Unashamed, the woman kept staring. Caesar lifted a single brow, and then pointed a single finger to the drink in her hand. Something red, by the looks of the little bit left in the glass. Probably sweet, but still enough bite to get her buzzed enough not to taste it. Her stiletto red—the same shade as her lips—fingernails tapped a beat against the glass.

"You want another one of those?" he asked.

Even over the thrumming bass from the music, and the noise of the club, he could tell she had heard him just fine by the way her nose crinkled a bit.

"No, thank you."

Caesar stiffened at her voice.

Soft, sure.

But *silken*.

Like the words stroked her lips with each one she spoke, and they probably tasted like sex coming out.

But it wasn't even *that* which made him pause. No, it was the hint of the accent in the background of her words—Italian.

"Care to join me?" he asked.

The woman gave him a second look, and then nodded. It wasn't a blink and a breath in time before she was gracefully standing from her own couch, and crossing to join him on his. He couldn't help but take in the way her trim waist melted into shapely thighs. All that golden skin of hers looked good enough to fucking *eat*.

"You looked lonely," he said to her after she had rested back on his couch. "Couldn't have a beautiful woman being sad on my watch."

The woman shrugged. "My husband flaked."

Oh, Christ.

God was good to him.

He was the worst kind of sinner.

And God still loved him.

At least, for tonight.

"Shame," Caesar murmured, "because I couldn't imagine leaving someone like you alone to fend for herself. Someone might come along and corrupt you."

The woman smiled in that wicked, sinful way of hers all over again. It was enough to make Caesar lean just an inch closer to her—the heady sent of her floral perfume soaking into his lungs with every breath. He didn't miss how her gaze dropped to his mouth, or the way her green eyes darkened just enough to suggest she liked what she was seeing.

"A little late for corrupting me," she whispered.

"Is that so?"

"A bit, yeah."

"Well, if I were an honest man—and I am, a good portion of the time—then I would say you didn't actually look lonely at all, or like you were pissed about your husband."

"Why would I be? Something better is always waiting, right?"

Fucking right.

"Something most definitely is waiting," he agreed.

"Your name?"

"Caesar."

The woman laughed—it was a breathless, yet musical sound. It made a shot of heat gather in his gut, and ricochet right down to his already-thick cock hammering against the zipper of his slacks. He didn't even know how long it was going to take to get this woman's legs spread, but at the moment, he couldn't find it in himself to care, either.

Her tongue peeked out to wet her lips as she murmured, "Like the tyrant?"

"I am far worse than the fucking tyrant."

"How so?" she dared to ask.

Well, if she wanted to know …

"Give me a peek of that pussy of yours, and I'll show you," he countered.

Her gaze widened. "*Here?*"

"What do you think this club is for, *donna?*"

"I—"

Her stare darted over his shoulder, and then toward one of the servers heading to another section to serve.

"Why do you think they're all here?" Caesar continued, not giving her a chance to think or say more. "They come here *for this.* To watch and to hear and to get *off.*"

"You haven't even asked my name," the woman told him.

All the air was gone from her voice again.

He could *hear* how turned on she was.

"Does it really matter?" he asked.

"I might like to hear you say it while you *fuck me.*"

All right, then.

"Give me your name," he demanded.

"Carina."

Caesar nodded. "Okay, *Carina.* Spread your legs, give me a peek, and then I'll show you my favorite place to fuck in this club."

"You have a favorite place?"

"You will too after this."

Her grin was back.

And just like he thought, she spread her thighs, and swept her hand between her legs to move away her skirt. She pushed aside the red lace panties she wore, her pussy was already glistening with wetness, and a pretty pink that made him want a taste. When her gaze lifted to meet his head-on again, and she didn't drop her skirt to hide from him, he was caught like a stupid fucking deer in her bright headlights.

"Do you want me to touch you right now?" he asked.

"What, like a test run?"

Caesar chuckled darkly. "Call it that if you want, but I come with one of those satisfaction guarantees."

"There are very few men who can pull arrogance off, Caesar."

"And I am most definitely one of them."

She didn't even deny it.

"Touch me."

Caesar cocked a brow, and his fingertips skimmed her smooth thigh before edging closer to her pussy. "Ask *nicely*."

Her breath caught, and then shuddered on the exhale when his knuckles grazed the silken lips of her cunt. "And just how do I do that?"

"You don't know?"

"I *asked*, didn't I?"

Oh, a smart mouth.

He liked those.

They were fun to break.

Caesar let two of his fingers slide into Carina's cunt, and marveled at how soft, wet, and fucking *tight* she was. The woman couldn't even hide the way her shoulders relaxed from being filled, or the tremor that started to work its way through her thighs as he stroked her pussy once, and then twice. He could tell by the way her hips grinded against his hands that she wanted something more, but he wasn't there yet.

"You *beg*," he murmured, leaning in close enough to force her to stare at only him. His hand came up to grab her jaw tightly, and hold her in place as his fingers massaged a fleshy spot inside her upper walls that would make her so wet, she'd be a goddamn lake. "You say *please*. You do it repeatedly, and *loudly*. And then when I make you come enough times for *my* liking, you get on your knees, and you ask to finish me off with your mouth. That's how you ask nicely, *mia cara*."

Carina swallowed hard.

Her breaths shuddered.

"Oh, my God," she gasped.

Yeah, Caesar could feel that telltale shake he was looking for, not to mention how tight her pussy was clamping down on his fingers. "That's called your G-spot, and you're going to come so hard from me playing with it that you'll stain this couch with your juices."

A red heat climbed up her throat and cheeks.

Shame, he thought.

Caesar liked that, too.

"Don't even try to fight it," he said, "just ask me nicely, Carina."

She didn't hesitate.

She clearly didn't want to.

"*Please*; oh, my God, please. I want to come."

"Count back from ten for me," he said.

"W-what?"

"*Ten, nine* … keep going."

His fingers worked harder inside her cunt—wet flesh, and a sucking sound that drove him damn crazy. She was going to feel divine when he slipped his cock in between her hot, soaked pussy in just a few minutes.

"Eight, seven, six …" Carina breathed out.

Her shaking was worse.

Her words were followed by a keening noise.

"Five, four, three," she mumbled.

And again, and again, and *again* his fingers drove into that sensitive spot. She was right fucking there, and he knew it.

"Two," she barely managed to get out.

"One," Caesar finished for her before he covered her red-stained lips with his own.

Christ, she tasted like sex and candy on his tongue as he kissed her through the orgasm. He felt her arousal flood his fingers, and like he figured she would, wet the couch, too. There was no hesitation in her kiss, either, only a hungry need that let him know she wasn't going to show anymore shyness with him tonight.

Good.

Pulling his hand from between her thighs, and putting distance between their mouths, he let those two fingers he'd fucked her with tap against her red lips.

"Open up, and taste."

She didn't question.

Didn't even *speak*.

No, those red lips of hers opened, she took his fingers in, and her tongue wrapped around his digits to clean them.

And he found heaven.

Or good God …

Maybe she was hell.

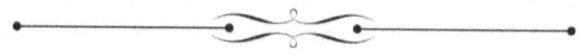

"I thought your favorite place to fuck was *inside* the club?"

"It *is*."

Caesar flashed Carina a dark grin as he reached over and hit the switch on the glass elevator that would force it to stop. Instantly, the floor lurched under their feet, the lights above their head switched to a deep red, and the music that had been pumping through the speakers quieted altogether though they could still hear it from the club.

Carina glanced up, and grabbed onto the railing at the sudden change, and only caught Caesar's gaze when he stalked toward her in the small four-foot by four-foot section of space. Her body relaxed, and that smile of hers was back in a blink.

"Oh," she said simply.

Caesar nodded. "Yeah, *oh*. Look around."

Her head turned to peer out the glass walls of the elevator at the same time Caesar grabbed ahold of her face. He got the first taste of her skin right under her jawline, and the responding sigh he got from her only made him want more.

He licked and sucked at the pulse point on her throat while his firm grip on her face kept her forced against the glass wall. Her skin tasted like heat, sin, and flowers—*roses*, he thought. She smelled and tasted like fucking roses, and it was glorious.

She didn't shy away from his touch—pushing her lower half into his while her hands rubbed the outline of his cock through his trousers.

"I can see *everyone*," she breathed.

Caesar bit down on her collarbone, and then licked the same spot when she hissed. "That's kind of the point, *donna*."

His hands finally dropped from her face to pull the skirt of her dress up. He didn't even need to fuck with her thong because he'd already taken that off downstairs, and shoved it into his back pocket. He had a plan for that.

She was shameless grinding against his hand when he dared to put it back between her thighs, and those soft sounds of hers filled his ears like rushing water. If his fucking cock didn't punch a hole through his zipper, he would be lucky.

"Is this the part where I ask nicely?"

Caesar groaned before he crashed his mouth against hers, and found the lingering taste of her pussy on her lips. "*All the fucking time—always.*"

"And they can all see?"

"If they look up."

"*Jesus.*"

"I love the look of shame on a woman," he murmured into her ear. "Now give me what I want, and you'll get what you want."

The words slipped past her swollen red lips *easily*.

"God, please fuck me."

Fucking yes.

"Turn around, and bend over," he demanded.

When had his voice gone hoarse?

And *why?*

Her breath caught with anticipation even as she turned around, and her gaze caught his over her shoulder. Lowered lashes, a mouth begging to be fucked, and her ass bare under his hands ... what could be better?

Oh, yeah.

Her cunt squeezing him *dry*.

Caesar smacked her ass hard enough to leave a pink imprint of his hand behind, which only earned him one of her deep moans, before he made quick work of shuffling his pants down. The three-pack of condoms he always kept in his pocket came out to play, and soon enough, he had tugged his length out of his boxer-briefs, and encased his dick in latex.

"Widen those legs," he said with a smack of his palm to her inner thighs.

She did.

And *Christ*, she was wet. The sliver of her sex glistened under the red warning light, and he could see her arousal slick on her thighs, too. Nothing got him harder, really.

"Like what you see?"

"Not even a question," he returned.

He fitted his cock between her thighs, and grabbed firmly to her tight ass until his fingertips left pink spots behind on her golden skin. He heard her one sharp inhale of breath before he shoved in with enough force to send her up onto her toes—even in her heels.

"*Oh.*"

"Try again," he grunted, pulling out of her wet, tight cunt to slam right back in again. "Give me the right words, *donna.*"

Oh, those words came.

Jumbled, and fast, and *willing*.

"Please ... harder, *please*."

Caesar started a slow, torturous pace as his hands slipped around her waist. He pulled her hands from the death-grip they hand on the bar, and kept hold of them with one hand. Reaching back, he tugged that thong of hers from his back pocket before bringing it out to play, too. In a couple of quick motions, he had tied her hands together in front of her with her underwear, and then he lifted them against the glass.

"Stay there and let me fuck you like you want," he murmured.

Her body shuddered.

His thrusts came *harder*.

"Y-yes."

Caesar grabbed the back of her neck, and squeezed hard, but she didn't flinch or even tense from the touch. "Yes, *what?*"

She was perfection, really.

She knew, now.

"*Yes, please.*"

"And once I finish with you, what are you to do?" he demanded.

"Ask."

One brutal thrust answered another before he uttered, "Ask, *what?*"

"Ask nicely to finish you."

"With …?"

"My *mouth.*"

"There's my good girl. I bet you'll taste sweeter on my dick. And then I'll see how good you taste after I've been fucking you, too. Remember that."

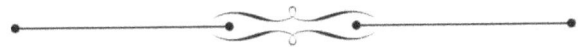

A sore Caesar first thing in the morning was a *happy* Caesar. It always meant good things—either he fought his way into pain, or he fucked his way into it. Either way, he was good with both.

Groaning, he stretched his back against the softness of his bed, and stared up at the ceiling of his penthouse's master bedroom. Living right in the heart of Philly provided him with an automatic alarm—he called it the fucking *city*. The sounds woke him up almost every day, but he couldn't imagine it any other way.

Today, though?

This morning it was a fucking knock echoing through his goddamn place that made him open his eyes. Frustrated, he kicked the comforter off, and only briefly thought to hide his nakedness with a pair of boxer-briefs that he shuffled on as he headed out of his room.

He grabbed a bottle of water from the fridge, and cracked it open as he went for the door, and the persistent fucker knocking behind it.

"Calm the hell down," Caesar barked.

He flung open the front door of his penthouse to see a familiar pair of people waiting. Cain, and his wife, Gina. The only fucker Caesar considered a friend, the one wife of a made man he hadn't fucked—or even tried to, for that matter—and two people he didn't mind waking him up after a night like the one before.

Cain looked him over. "Don't you have fucking *clothes?*"

Caesar looked to Gina. "Why's he fucking talking? Doesn't he know it just sounds like whining in my ear?"

Gina smiled a little. "He does have a point."

"My place, and it's *morning*."

"Eleven, actually," Cain said.

Really?

Well, shit.

Cain gave him a second look. "Fuck, you look rough. Late night?"

"It was good, actually. I'm feeling it this morning."

Neither of the two people waiting in his doorway needed anymore explanation than he just gave them. They knew his habits, and the shit he did. They were quite aware that he spent his evenings looking for a new pussy to bury himself in, and sometimes more than one if he was in that kind of mood.

"Are you going to let us in, or should I take your food somewhere else?" Gina asked, holding up the takeout bag.

Caesar's stomach betrayed him by grumbling. "I guess you can come in."

Gina beamed as she moved past him. "Like there was any other answer."

"Get dressed," Cain told him as he came inside, too.

"Nah, I need a shower first, and I don't think I want to wash her off yet."

Cain arched a brow over his shoulder, asking, "*That* good, huh?"

"Don't be asking about his sex life," Gina shouted from the kitchen. "He'll start, and he'll never shut up."

"She knows me well."

Cain scowled. "Everybody knows you well, asshole."

Caesar tipped his head to the side. "Accurate. That's fair."

Once the three of them were settled into the kitchen, and Gina had plated the spread of brunch foods for them to each have a bit of everything, the husband and wife sat on one side of the island while Caesar sat on the other. He was more comfortable with Cain and Gina than he was with his own family—it helped that he'd known Cain his whole life, and the man had never snubbed Caesar for anything.

Hell, he'd watched these two fall in love in high school.

And maybe that was why ... he never tried to ruin them.

Not that Gina ever gave him a second look.

"I got news for you," Cain said just as Caesar filled his mouth with a bite of ham sandwich. The man knew to talk while Caesar couldn't—smart fucker. "About the De Rose Camorra, since you've been so patient, and all."

Yes, because *Cain* understood Camorra far better than Caesar. Or ... he knew more about them, and the clan as a whole. Any kind of inside information was good for him.

"Speak," Caesar mumbled around his food.

"Gross," Gina grumbled.

He ignored her.

"Strange thing—the boss of the clan, Jac De Rose, has been in lock up for a year and a half. He's got another six months on his sentence before he's out. I've been told that getting in to see him is damn near impossible. Visits are almost always refused."

Caesar finished his bite, and said, "Like someone wants to keep him away while he's ... well, *away*."

"Yeah."

"Who *is* acting as the boss, then?"

Cain shrugged. "Could be any number of people, Caesar. That's the thing about Camorra—there's no real structure like with Cosa Nostra, or practically *any other fucking organization*. They just *are*. There's a boss, and the people he speaks to. Everyone answers to him. There's no boss of my boss kind of thing."

"Wait, *anyone* could be acting boss?"

His friend nodded.

"Even a woman?"

Cain just stared at him. "I said *anyone*."

"Huh. I didn't know that."

He found that fascinating.

Cosa Nostra did not allow women into their ranks, and some syndicates even took issue with working with a female associate of the family. The idea that there were female bosses—of course there were, he wasn't stupid; he simply hadn't *met* one yet—perked his interest in several ways.

Almost none of them innocent.

"What about the other bit I asked for?" he asked.

Cain sighed. "Well, Jac has a daughter—Aria De Rose, she's twenty-six, and married. Exactly your kind of forte, fucker."

"And it could be her, right? Acting as the boss."

"Or her husband," Cain replied. "Or any number of men, but no one is really open to talking *that* much detail about the clan's inner workings."

"But ..."

Cain grumbled under his breath. "There's always a but with you."

"Yeah, but I could probably get to whoever is the acting boss by going through Jac's daughter, right?"

Because that was what he did best.

Manipulate to his gain.

Fuck until he won.

Make pain to ruin.

It all worked for Caesar.

It got him what he wanted.

"I would bet she would be a door to *someone*," Cain agreed.

"She's also married," Gina put in, finally joining their conversation. "In case you didn't hear him say that, Caesar."

Caesar nodded, and picked up his sandwich again. "I know—I heard him. That's what I like best about her, and I don't even know her."

He really was a sick fucker.

His sins were never going to come clean.

"Let's get a bead on her," Caesar said, "watch her for a week, and then move in on her."

Cain passed his frowning wife a look. "Yeah, all right."

FOUR

"MRS. DE ROSE?"

Aria knew what her guard was going to say before she even lifted her head from the book she was flipping through, but she decided to indulge the man, anyway. "Yes, Mario?"

"We need to move—we're being followed."

Again.

Aria did her best not to smile; it would do her no good to have her guard think this was what she wanted and needed to happen. The guard was appointed to her by Raffe, and her husband got all his information from Mario a good portion of the time.

"Fine," Aria said with a sigh.

She handed the vendor back the book, but paid for the magazine she had already put in her purse. The book could wait for another day.

"*Now,* Mrs. De Rose."

Mario was testy today, but really, he'd been like this for a week or so. Ever since he realized someone *was* actually following Aria. And then his irritation ticked up a notch or two when he also figured out said stalker was Caesar Accardo.

It wasn't like the man was making any real effort to hide it was him, either. In fact, that was probably what pissed off her guard the most. The man would be waiting in the most obvious location just to *show* he knew where they were at any given time.

But Aria …

Well, she had been careful.

Careful to keep her face hidden, and to stay out of sight. She never looked at Caesar directly when she knew he was there, and he had only ever seen her from behind. She was not yet ready to show him just who she was, and who he was actually following.

"To the car," the guard demanded.

His hand came to rest on Aria's lower back as if to move her away from the vendor, and push her further down the street. She had all of two rules when it came to her people—do *not* raise your voice, and *never* touch her.

Spinning fast, Aria moved a step away from Mario's touch, and then hit his arm away when he reached for her again. This stupid man didn't know any better, she *swore* it. He didn't like to follow her rules because he was too busy doing what her goddamn husband wanted him to do when it came to her.

Fuck that noise.

"Don't *touch* me," she hissed at him. "I can walk on my own, thank you."

Mario's jaw clenched, but his eyes told her that he wasn't in the mood to argue with her about it right then. "To the car, then."

"Fine."

Aria's large black summer hat tipped just low enough in the front to keep her face hidden from view as she headed back down the street. Today was the day—the last move she was to make on the board before the final show could really begin.

Careful plans had been made.

So very careful.

"*Merda*," Mario cursed.

Aria caught sight of the man glancing over his shoulder, and she peered back in the same direction. Sure enough, Caesar tailed them close enough that she could see the blues of his eyes although he wasn't looking directly at them right in those moments. He was too busy saying something to the tall, dark-haired man walking with him.

Oh, he brought a friend today.

Fun.

Her gaze drifted back to Caesar, though, and she couldn't even help herself but to the appreciative perusal of his dark blue, three-piece suit. He'd gotten a haircut since their encounter a week ago, as the blond strands were significantly shorter than they had been, not that it looked bad.

Far from it.

Nothing about that man looked bad. And hell, she had thought he looked particularly good on his knees as he ate the juices straight from her pussy while the taste of his come still lingered on her mouth.

Jesus.

Wow.

She went to that place *fast*.

Aria quickly turned her head, and stared straight at the sidewalk ahead of her. She had a plan to follow—things to see through. She did not have the time or wherewithal to be getting stuck inside her own head about a man like Caesar. What she had done with him at Lucifer's Den was more than enough to get her killed, and she was going to do her very best to keep from indulging in him again.

Because it would be exactly that, and *only* that when it came right down to it. An indulgent moment for her body, and little else.

She had gotten what she needed and wanted from Caesar—she found her way in, and how to blackmail him to get closer to her goal, but that was all it could be. She certainly didn't have a need for anything else.

Except another fuck, maybe.

Aria ignored her inner voice, and Mario helped when he spoke up suddenly.

"Nico's said he moved over a block—traffic was getting thick, and he couldn't get down here to us quickly enough."

"All right."

Mario jerked his head right, adding, "This alley. It'll give us a shortcut."

Aria silently thanked Nico because he really was just as good at this game as any of them. Oh, sure, Nico moved the vehicle waiting for her, but not because Mario told him to, but because *she* had told him to.

They were halfway down the shadowed alley with the exit on the other side—and Nico's car waiting at the mouth of the far end with *only* the passenger door open—in view when a familiar voice echoed from behind them.

"Care to have a chat?"

Oh, God.

In her four-inch rockstud heels, she shuddered.

It was almost as though all over again, she could feel Caesar next to her on that couch, and despite it being daylight, and in full public view, his tone didn't change. It still sounded the exact same—whether he was approaching the enemy, or stuffing his fingers into her cunt where anyone could see. His voice didn't *change.*

"Keep walking," Mario ordered.

"Aw, no time for us today, Aria De Rose?"

Good.

He had done his research, and he knew her name. Of course, he couldn't possibly know she was also the Carina that had approached him at the club, but still, he had sought her out because he likely thought she was a direct link to the top.

He was right.

She kept moving as Mario had told her to, but chanced a quick peek over her shoulder to see Mario turning to face the oncoming men. That was his job, after all, and it would be far better for him to face whatever might come at him from these men than what her husband would do to him should Raffe find out he left Aria unprotected in some way.

"Crawl back into the hole you came from, Accardo," Mario said.

"Sorry, man, no can do."

"You heard—"

"We want a chat with your boss," Caesar said, and then whistled low. "But damn, I would replace that option for a bite out of that woman's ass any fucking day."

Aria tensed as heat shot through her body. She could practically feel his eyes burning into her ass with the intensity of his stare.

Good God.

The man was *lewd*.

Crass.

Unashamed.

Terrible, really.

And he turned her on like nothing else.

Aria knew what would happen next—any slight against her, or a suggestion of something improper, and Mario needed to correct the man who did it. Not only was that the Camorra way, but it was also *Raffe's* way.

She didn't even flinch when she heard the clack of a handgun being racked back.

"Say that again," Mario urged.

Gangsters were predictable.

One had a gun, the other had a gun.

One pulled a gun, the other pulled a gun.

One threatened, and the other answered.

"Bad move, man," Caesar said.

She had heard enough guns being fired in her lifetime that it wasn't even a blip on her radar. Her footsteps didn't stumble even as she reached the car at the same time she heard Mario's dead body hit the ground with a sickening *thump*.

One fool gone.

Another part of her plan down.

Closer to the goal.

Aria slid into the passenger seat, and peered beyond the rim of her hat still keeping her face hidden. Mario lay dead about twenty feet away—she would have to call someone to come in quickly and grab the body, or just let the officials handle it. She certainly wouldn't be tied to his death in anyway.

Mario didn't really interest her.

It was the man standing with his arms crossed as he loomed above Mario's body that drew in her attention. He didn't looked bothered in the least, and in fact, wore the sexiest smirk she had ever seen on a man.

Arrogant asshole.

Caesar wore the look *well*.

She made sure to lighten her voice with a bit of air as she spoke, although she still saw how Caesar's gaze narrowed like she sounded familiar to him, and made a careful effort to keep her hat in place as to not show her face.

"You're going to have to answer for that, Accardo."

"Oh? Good—I look forward to it, Aria."

He took a step forward, and so did his friend right behind him. Aria closed the passenger door before he could come any closer, and Nico's foot hit the gas to take them further away from the dangerously sinful man, and the problem he had just gotten rid of for them.

"At least Mario won't be reporting back on you, now," Nico murmured from behind the wheel.

Aria nodded, pulled off her hat, and tossed it into the backseat. "Yes, another problem gone."

"Aren't you concerned you're playing with fire there?"

"How so?"

"Too many people start *dying* and Raffe might cut his business in Italy short to come home."

She hid how that suggested affected her in the worst kind of way. Fear, and dread, and heaviness in her blood.

"He thinks we have this whole issue here under control—*and we do.*"

"Except he's going to learn his wife's guard was killed today *with* his wife nearby."

Aria shrugged. "So we lie and say Mario was out on an errand. Crappy circumstances, and nothing more. He won't know the difference."

"He'll replace your guard."

"Offer to be the one to *do it.*"

Raffe liked Nico for a lot of reasons, but most prominently because he believed Nico to be gay on one hand but also because he didn't know that Aria's father had first asked Nico to be her husband before Raffe. Nico wasn't gay, not that it would matter if he was, but all of those things meant he wasn't a threat to Raffe, or his wife.

"Will that do it, do you think?" she asked.

Nico passed her a look. "What?"

"He shot Mario—could that get us the meeting with the boss. He's my guard; I'm the acting boss. That should do it, shouldn't it? It should get me *in.*"

"I'll make a few calls."

Good, good.

Time for the show to start.

The Philly restaurant most famous for its cheesesteaks wouldn't have been Aria's first choice for a meeting with the Accardo crime boss, but that had been Angelo's demand once Nico had finally made contact with the man a few days earlier. He wanted to choose the location, one unrelated to either of their respective organizations other than perhaps by association, and they could arrive first to greet *only* him before his men would enter.

That worked for her.

Except ... Angelo hadn't quite followed the rules.

"Three of his men are inside, and the boss is waiting in the private dining area," Nico said, glancing at Aria in the rearview mirror. "Or, at least three that our men recognized. Unarmed. One of them is Caesar, and his little friend that we had the run-in with a while back."

She heard him, but she was still staring at the missed call on her phone.

Raffe, the caller ID read.

She'd opted to ignore her husband's call if only because she simply couldn't afford the headspace he would put her in should she actually spend two minutes talking to him. She couldn't afford to be off her game at all today.

No doubt, she was going to pay for that choice later. Raffe always made her pay for anything he considered a slight or misstep.

"You all right?"

Aria finally dragged her gaze away from her phone, and met Nico's gaze in the mirror. "Of course, I am."

"So, I have been having a conversation with myself for the last ten minutes for no particular reason, then."

"You don't have to be a bastard about it."

Nico smirked. "Who would I be if not a bastard?"

"My friend."

"Well ... that's fair."

"And I *did* hear you," Aria said, staring at her reflection in the dark tint of the glass as they passed familiar Philadelphia streets. "Three men inside—that we know of, but there could be more. Unarmed as far as they can tell, but that's a toss-up depending on what you consider to be *armed*. Angelo is in the private area. I'm not concerned."

"Not even a little bit?"

"I hate when you do that, you know. Just because you're my friend doesn't mean you can get away with the same shit I'll cut someone else for doing, Nico."

"What did I do?"

His false innocence almost made her smile. "You question me. Don't question me."

"Someday, you're going to be grateful to have a friend who *does* question you, *De Rose Regina*. Someday, it may be that one friend who keeps you from going a little too far when it comes to certain things *because* they make you stop and consider other options."

"This is the only option."

"This time, yes."

Aria fixed one of her stray curls in the reflection of the window, and checked her carefully applied makeup at the same time. A perfect mask of beauty that was sure to be enough to distract any man, or at the very least, soften them to her.

There was only one she really needed to get to today.

"I'm not concerned about the fact he put men in there because we have been watching the restaurant since the day Angelo agreed to the meeting, and told us the location. Nothing has been happening; I've had people on it for twenty-four hour rotations. It'll be perfectly *fine*."

"I certainly hope so."

"Hope is for the weak. Faith is for the *confident*."

Nico said nothing.

Aria didn't need him to.

It was another five minutes of driving before Nico smoothly pulled the car to a stop between two black sedans waiting in front of a modern-looking restaurant. The moment their car pulled in, the doors on the sedans opened and two men Aria had chosen to attend this meeting alongside her and Nico stepped out, and moved to the back passenger door of their vehicle. Nico stepped out, then, and moved back to open her door for her.

A purposeful move on her part.

She only wanted someone from the Accardo side of things to see the De Rose boss when *she* decided it was time. With three tall men flanking her front and sides, she was practically hidden from view entirely.

"The private dining area, yes?" she asked.

Nico glanced back, and offered her a nod.

"Good. And the others are not in there?"

"No."

Even better.

Nico knew that for now, he was to appear as the one running their side of things until she said differently. It was how he posed the meeting to begin with. She was attending—as far as the Accardo boss knew—because *she* was Jac's daughter, and because she had been the one to be approached first.

Simple as that.

And all a lie.

Inside the business, the restaurant bustled with patrons, and activity. Aria didn't bother to pay attention to the décor or the seating arrangements as she wasn't there to eat, or enjoy the place. She couldn't care less what it looked like, or how good their food was.

She did, however, look for the one man she would recognize on the spot. Nico and her other two men were still flanking her, but between their shoulders she was able to get just a peek of Caesar sitting at what appeared to be a small bar. His friend sat beside him. She wasn't sure where the third man Nico had mentioned was.

"Nico, let the others go in ahead of us," Aria said.

Silently, he stepped back at her request. The other men moved forward, and moved to the left where the private dining area was located behind two frosted glass French doors.

It was then that Caesar *looked*.

It was then that he *knew*.

She stared him head-on, and let him take a good fucking look at her. She enjoyed the way his sky-blue eyes widened momentarily, and his jaw fell slack. His rough, handsome features were softened briefly as the realization washed over him, and nothing had quite looked better on him.

Except for maybe when he was fucking her.

That had been quite a sight.

She smiled, and waved two fingers.

A tease, really.

Caesar's strong jaw tightened, and she bet his molars were aching from how fiercely he was clenching his teeth. That surprise in his gaze melted away to show a blazing disbelief mixed heavily with anger.

He kept staring.

She tipped her chin up at him.

A silent, *Try me*.

Caesar didn't disappoint.

"Ah, shit," Nico muttered when Caesar pushed off the barstool.

"Relax," she told her friend. "What's he going to do? This is what I wanted, remember."

"Still trying to figure out *why*, though."

Because he could help her.

Or, she could blackmail him into it.

Either way.

"Let's move," Aria murmured as Caesar came closer.

The two of them headed for the private room where the Cosa Nostra Accardo boss would be waiting for them, but she didn't even reach the entryway—as she expected—before Caesar caught up with her. His warm, calloused palm wrapped around her elbow, and tugged her backwards. Aria didn't even get the chance to catch her footing before Caesar was pulling her upright, and moving them down a dim hallway where bathroom signs flashed overhead.

She breathed, and he spun her around. Her back hit the wall hard before both of Caesar's hands came to land on either side of her head with a hard *smack*.

Aria didn't blink.

Neither did Caesar.

God.

The blues of his eyes were amazing this close.

All sea-deep with flecks of black.

"*What do you want?*"

His words came out through sneer-twisted lips that had kissed and tasted the most intimate places on her body. She was hyper-aware of just how close he was to her. His heady cologne soaked into her lungs with every inhale; a deep, spicy scent that smelled like sex and heaven all at once. He really was a Godly man.

She never denied that.

"Well?" Caesar demanded harshly. "What do you want, *Aria?*"

"Ah, figured that out, did you?"

"Don't mess with me, you crazy woman," he murmured in Italian.

"Your Italian is ... heavenly."

It really was.

Or maybe it was because it was *him.*

"Stop fucking with me," he uttered.

"Oh, yes," she countered, grinning, "I've heard it's usually *you* doing that to other people. I suppose this is a new thing for you, huh?"

A tic showed in his jaw.

She *almost* had him.

"Aria," came a quiet word from Nico at her right.

She didn't even turn her head to look at the man. "It's fine."

"It's *not*. You've been down here for at least a minute. You're supposed to be in the room already. Simone or Jonny could come out to look for you, and you know what they'll see. You're in private with a man— *where you cannot be.*"

Caesar's gaze narrowed at those words.

Aria didn't look away from him, but she had to speak *now*. Get her demands out, and get it over with. Nico had a good point.

"Would your father care to know that you fucked the enemy, Caesar?" she asked, never breaking their gaze. "How would he feel to know while you were put on our tail to clean up our mess, you were actually fraternizing with one of us—and not just *any* one of us, but the acting boss. *Me.*"

Caesar didn't flinch, and even sounded a little too haughty when he replied, "That's not even close to the worst thing my father knows I have done."

And even as he said that, she still found a flash of worry in his gaze. Maybe in all his fuck ups, this man was now walking a very thin line.

"Do you want to test that theory?"

He swallowed.

She smiled.

"We want territory—*more*, you could say. I need it for a bigger purpose, and your family is strong holding it, as they usually do. You're going to help me in that regard."

"You have high hopes and big dreams."

Aria laughed.

Like Nico, this man was wrong, too.

Men usually were.

"Hope is for the weak. I *never* hope."

"*Aria*," Nico hissed.

She didn't need to be told again the risk she was taking, but she had said what she said, and now it was time to move. Before Caesar could think to stop her, she slipped out from beneath his arm, and headed for a waiting Nico.

Aria didn't even look over her shoulder as she came out of the hallway. The two of them walked straight into the private dining area to find the Accardo boss's men had finally arrived—five of them, it seemed.

That made them a bit outnumbered, all things considered.

Angelo Accardo stood in the middle of the room like the formidable man she had expected him to be. Large, a bit too round, and as tall as his son with dark eyes that glared daggers into the man standing beside Aria.

He barely even *looked* at her.

"You're late," Angelo said, his tone colored with irritation. "And I do not like to be made to wait on anyone, let alone a Camorra *boss*."

"My apologies," Aria said sweetly.

It took a beat of time as Angelo's gaze swung in her direction, and then a another second or two as he blinked. "I beg your pardon, girl?"

"I prefer Aria—or De Rose, even. Whichever you prefer."

She bet she was quite a sight in her Versace dress and Valentino heels. Her neck was roped in the diamonds her husband had given her on their wedding night. Right before he bent her over the closest flat surface, and fucked her hard enough to make her bleed—*God*, Raffe had taken great pleasure in doing that to her, and then trying again the next night. She'd swept her unruly curls back into a messy chignon, but left a few loose strands down, and made sure her face was free to be seen and especially beautiful.

She was a woman.

Delicate looking, all things considered.

Distractingly beautiful.

Entirely unassuming.

Nothing that this man expected when it came to a *boss*, and it put her at every possible advantage over him because of it.

"I did not mean to make you wait, Angelo," Aria said, smiling sweetly. "I ..."

The man was speechless.

Unsure.

Wary.

Hesitant.

Everything she wanted.

Aria didn't fidget or move at all as Angelo's gaze drifted over her and took every bit of her in with a slow, confused expression drifting over his old features. "Do you prefer to sit when you do business, or stand? I don't mind either."

That question broke the man from his daze.

"Neither," he snapped. "Not when it comes to a *woman*."

She could feel the change in the room.

The way Angelo's men became uncomfortable.

"You did agree to a meeting," she pointed out, "and with the boss. Until my father is released from his sentence, or my husband returns from business in Italy, that is *me*."

"I was led to believe—"

"That you would be meeting with the boss."

"I talked to a man!" Angelo snapped.

Aria tipped her head in Nico's direction. "I find men are more amicable to other men when details need to be hammered out for these things. I am sure you understand."

"No, actually, I don't."

"Shame, then."

"Yes," Angelo barked, snapping a finger at one of his men, and making a motion with his hand. She knew right then that this meeting was over. "It is a shame. I had hoped to finish this."

"We still can."

He scoffed. "No."

"Then you should know, Angelo, it will only get worse. The streets, and the issues. Your people dying. And oh, sure, mine are too. The difference? Mine are a dime a dozen, and can be easily replaced. It's how Camorra works, and why we are so resilient. Your *Cosa Nostra* cannot say the same, can it? There will be more blood in the streets, Angelo, until you give me what I want. It's a shame you won't even stay long enough to hear what it is."

And he didn't stay.

He couldn't get out of there fast enough.

"And what is our next move?" Jonny asked. "How do we go at them from here?"

"Yes, a plan is needed," Simone agreed.

Nico looked to Aria for direction, but it was the ringing of her phone that stopped her from speaking to the gathered men so that they could discuss the failed meeting with the Accardo boss. She didn't even need to look at the screen to know who was calling her.

She had been waiting for this.

"Raffe," she greeted, not *unkindly*, as she picked up her husband's call.

"Skype, *now*," he snarled.

No one at the table could hear the way he spoke to her, and she didn't give the waiting men any indication how unsettled she felt, either. "Two minutes, okay."

"*One*, Aria, or I will be on a goddamn flight tonight."

"One, then."

She hung up the call, but only after Raffe did. Hanging up on him would do her no good when she did finally get on Skype. Standing from the table, she offered nothing to the confused men but for a quiet, "Excuse me, but I need a few minutes."

Or however long he wants.

It took Aria almost the entire minute just to get to the privacy of her bedroom, and to close the door. The Skype call from her husband was already ringing through. The bastard couldn't even give her the one minute she asked for.

Aria answered the call by hitting the accept button, and sat down on the edge of her bed. She forced her face to remain a blank mask of nothingness even as her husband's angry, scowling face came into view on the video call.

Raffe Ferri was six foot, five inches, and two-hundred-fifty pounds of *anger*. Handsome, sure, with his olive complexion, boyish grin, and dark, wavy hair. He could dazzle a woman with one of his wide, white-toothed smiles, and just as quickly terrify her with a harsh hand. He was demanding, and difficult, and *hateful*.

And he was her husband.

"You ignored my calls today," he said.

Aria nodded. "I was doing business."

"For *what*—what that you couldn't speak to me?"

Behind him, the Four Seasons hotel room looked as though a tornado had ripped through it. Likely him tearing things apart in his rage. It wasn't uncommon, and frankly, she was just grateful that he was on an entirely different continent from her. There was less casualty to her that way.

Small blessings.

"The Accardo family, actually," Aria said. "We are still trying to gain more coverage in our territory. You wanted that."

Raffe's sneer lifted a bit, but not by much. "And how did it go?"

"Pretty well, all things considered."

He *would* have considered today to be a step forward even with the way it ended. She wasn't entirely lying to him.

"I could always cut this deal with the Cambria—"

"We really need that contact, Raffe," Aria said softly, "as our deal with the Mexican cartel fell through, and our supply is low."

Because *she* fucked up the contact with the Mexicans. Not that Raffe knew that. Either way, she was running on a short timeline, and had needed to get him the hell out of Philly at least while her father was still in prison, so she could get this plan of hers to move forward. Sometimes, things just worked.

"I *know* that," her husband muttered darkly.

"Sorry," she whispered.

Raffe softened a bit at her apology. "How are you—missing me?"

"Always."

Lies.

Never was more like it.

"Mmm, I bet. Stand, would you?"

Aria didn't even question him, and stood from the bed. She saw his gaze lift and lower on her in the video, and then he nodded.

"Remove your dress, and whatever is on underneath. Don't fucking dally around like a foolish girl about it, either."

She let out a silent, but shaky, breath. Still, she did as he asked and stripped down from her dress and black lace underwear set. Naked in front of the camera, she came closer when Raffe crooked his finger at her, and then turned like a pretty little doll on a spinning pedestal when he made a circle.

"Move that bit of hair around your face and let me see your neck, so I don't have to break it when I get home," Raffe ordered.

Aria did what he demanded again. She knew what he was looking for. He'd done this time and time again.

Marks from someone else.

Proof of her infidelity.

A reason to *hurt* her.

She had been faithful to this man despite his treatment and abuse of her, and regardless of the fact his mistress had birthed him a baby boy just two months ago. He was a cute baby, and Aria was simply glad the baby wasn't *hers*.

But she had—been faithful, that was, right up until the moment she couldn't be anymore—Caesar. Until the moment her plan had called for something drastic, she had done what Raffe demanded of her.

But he didn't know about Caesar.

Those marks were gone.

The bruises on her ass faded.
His kisses didn't brand.
At least ... not skin deep.
"Still untouched," Raffe murmured. "Good girl."
She suppressed the shiver.
Her attention was on her husband.
Her mind was on her goals—on power and control.
One. Step. Closer.
Rome wasn't built in a day.

FIVE

CAESAR HAD A million and one other things he could be doing; a lot of things he would rather be doing, but here he was watching Angelo pace in his office. The only remotely good thing about the whole shit-show was the fact Daniele had not yet arrived.

But he would.

Soon.

Angelo had been quiet for hours. Never speaking from the moment he left the meeting at the restaurant, and silently stewing in his thoughts. That didn't particularly bode well when it came to his father's moods, but Caesar was unwilling to step in quite yet.

Besides, he had his own shit to work out about all of this. He had been fucking blindsided, too. Like a goddamn deer staring at bright headlights.

Carina was not *Carina.*

He'd spent a week following the woman before he'd killed the man guarding her, and then another week gathering as much information on her as he could before the meeting between their respective organizations. And not *once* in that time had he seen her face, or even managed to get a picture of her. He'd thought it was nothing more than circumstance why he hadn't been able to see her face, but now he knew that wasn't the case.

Aria had tricked him.

No, *manipulated* him.

A part of him respected it and even took a thrill in her effort—the fucked up part of him that found it a habitual need to do the same thing to others. No one ever said he was a saint, after all, and a woman like that with the guts to do what she had deserved some kind of praise. Even if it was the fucked up kind that Caesar tended to use.

The other part of him was pissed. Christ. She hadn't needed to lie to him at all. He would have bent her over and gotten a taste of what was between her thighs regardless of who she was, and probably simply *because* of who she was. That just tended to be his style. He wasn't going to apologize for it.

No, it was her *lies.*

That pissed him off.

That made him feel dirty.

And he didn't like *dirty.*

Not that kind.

Her blackmail still weighed heavily on the back of his mind, and it

51

wasn't letting go. According to her, she wanted territory, and he needed to help his father be amicable to handing it over. That was never going to happen—Angelo didn't hand anything over unless it was pried out of his cold, dead hands.

It went beyond that, though.

Beyond the blackmail.

Why blackmail him at all?

The De Rose Camorra clan had been doing fine all on their own taking over street by street, and block by block. The clashes and run-ins with the Accardo organization seemed like barely a blip on their radar.

They kept on coming.

It was only Angelo finally exploding—at the sight of Daniele strolling through the opened office doors—that drew Caesar from his thoughts. "Where were *you?*"

Daniele's gaze slanted in his father's direction. "Therapy with Alice."

Caesar made a noise under his breath—an oh, Jesus Christ, kind of noise—and ignored the glower his half-brother shot him. "Bet that's going fucking swell, huh?"

His brother opened his mouth to respond, but Angelo beat him to the punch when he snapped at Caesar, "*Chiudi la bocca!*"

Shut your mouth.

Caesar mustered up something that might pass for an apologetic look, and shrugged his shoulders. "Apologies."

Not *his* apologies, though.

Alice had been willing. She barely took anytime to convince at all, and had a great time bent over her husband's side of the bed while Caesar fucked her from behind. She wasn't even his type, really—too thin, and too … whiney, really.

Didn't matter.

It was over, now.

It was done.

"I take it the De Rose meeting didn't go as planned?" Daniele asked, giving Caesar a glare that warned him to shut up.

If the fucker kept that shit up, Caesar was going to figure out another way to knock his arrogant ass down a peg or two. Maybe fucking his wife hadn't been enough.

"You think?" Angelo asked with his blazing eyes attempting to burn a hole into the clock on the far wall. "No, it didn't go fucking *well!* It's a woman running it. A *woman.* Could you imagine a Cosa Nostra boss sitting down to do business with a *woman?* It's abhorrent."

"Why?" Caesar asked. "Because it's that woman putting a major dent into your organization right now, too. I would think that gives her a right to have a seat at the table, and figure out what in the hell you can do to make her knock it off."

Angelo's anger directed its way to Caesar in a flash. "I didn't realize I asked for your goddamn opinion."

Yeah, all right.

Caesar chose to stay quiet while his father went about explaining to Daniele the details of their meeting—none that particularly mattered, really, except the fact their father had gotten flustered and tricked by a woman.

It looked good on no man, and that's what the problem really was where Angelo was concerned. He felt Aria De Rose's little stunt had pushed him down in the eyes of his men, and he had needed to reclaim that lost bit of respect by shunning her and their meeting.

Caesar figured that wasn't going to go well for his father.

"What info do you have on her?" Angelo snapped.

"Me?" Caesar asked.

"*Who else?*"

"You could tone it down a touch," Caesar told his father. "She's not here, and nobody else is here that gives a fuck about the fact you entirely missed it was a woman coming at you from behind."

Daniele blinked.

Angelo's face reddened in his rage.

Caesar shrugged, adding, "She's just a woman. Like every other fucking woman we know except maybe she actually buys her own fur and diamonds. Who gives a fuck about a *woman*? Why do you even care? Had it been a man at that meeting, you would have made nice and fixed the problems, but because she's got a cunt between her legs, you can't do that? Sounds like another one of those *you* problems, you know?"

Angelo spluttered before finally spitting out, "You are *ridiculous.* Unbelievable!"

"All of that and more, yeah."

Daniele sighed, and scrubbed a hand down his face. "I fucking hate saying this—Caesar's got a point. Camorra deals in a different culture and rules from us. You can't expect them to follow Cosa Nostra expectations just because you're coming to the table."

"I did not ask for opinions," Angelo barked, "I asked what Caesar *knew* about that goddamn woman or her clan!"

"I know very little about Camorra," Caesar said. "A lot like you, clearly."

"*Caesar.*"

That was likely his one warning to tone down the attitude, but shit, it was *hard.*

"As far as her," Caesar continued like his father hadn't even spoken at all, "she's been married to Raffaele Ferri—goes by Raffe, I heard—for a year and a half. Married shortly before her father went to prison."

"And where does this *Raffe* come from?" Angelo asked.

"A rival clan that Jac De Rose absorbed into his own after he dismantled them a while back. I don't have all those details."

Angelo went back to scowling at the wall. "Well, where is the *husband?*"

"I was told he's out of the country on business, but it looks like some of this shit started when he was in Philly. I don't think she went ahead on this by herself, if you get my drift. It's not very clear what she wants."

His father's gaze darted back to him in a blink. "Isn't it? She wants territory—the *city*. Power, Caesar. You are not this slow. Catch up to speed."

He didn't think that was entirely the case, all—

"Anyone want a drink?"

Caesar stiffened at his step-mother's voice. He didn't even bother to turn and look at Martina in the doorway. He didn't fucking want to.

"Hey, Ma," Daniele greeted.

He heard the pat of a hand against a cheek before Martina said, "Missed you."

"Darling," Angelo greeted. "And yes, I'll take a drink."

"Caesar, no hello for me today?"

Caesar wouldn't have been able to hide the hatred in his gaze when he glanced at his step-mother even if he tried. "No, not particularly."

"Caesar!"

Angelo's shout fell on deaf ears.

Martina had the gall to look *sad*.

The fucking lying—

"Caesar, greet your mother."

Step-mother, he wanted to correct.

He didn't correct his father.

"Martina," he greeted through a stiff jaw and clenched teeth before he looked back to his father. "Better?"

"What is your problem?"

He could feel Martina's gaze burning into his back, and it almost felt as though she was daring him to speak. He hadn't liked this woman when she came into his life over two decades ago, and he didn't fucking like her now, either. His hatred of her had only grown over time with the help of her, and everyone else around them.

She *earned* it.

She was too close.

Sharing his *space*.

It drove him crazy.

"I will call you when I have something useful on the clan, or the woman," Caesar said.

"Wait just a damn—"

He didn't wait.

He was already gone.

Caesar had been gone for *years*.

It was a shame his father never noticed.

Caesar kept the phone at his ear even as he saw a car he'd been waiting for pull up to a specialty clothing boutique across the road. "The main attraction has arrived."

"Be careful, man."

"Those words don't make any sense."

Cain grumbled under his breath. "Not for *you*, no."

"Then, I don't know why you bother."

"Because for some reason, my wife likes you. And I tend to be favorable to you—friends since kids, and all. Point being, if you make me tell my wife you got your dumbass killed over this stupid shit, then I won't even come to piss on your grave, Caesar."

"I'm not sure if that's supposed to be a bad thing or a—"

"Don't be stupid!"

"This isn't me being stupid," Caesar countered, "this is the least stupid thing I have done."

"Jesus Christ." Cain sighed harshly, and added, "I will meet you after, then?"

"Regular spot, yeah."

"All right. Seriously, be smart."

Right.

Caesar hung up on his friend without a goodbye, and watched as the back passenger door on the black sedan was opened. Aria stepped out of the car in a wine-red dress that looked as though it had been fucking painted on to her body. It made her heart-shaped ass an even better sight. Not to mention the way her golden, smooth legs looked walking in five-inch heels. He found that he liked the fact she had left her hair down in loose, wild curls because it was easier for him to imagine fisting her hair while he pounded into her.

Yeah.

He went there quick, fast, and in a real damn hurry.

Fuck.

He kind of hated this woman. She also turned him on like nothing else. That was probably going to be a problem. Self-control was not a word

Caesar was well acquainted with, frankly, and in fact, he made a game out of giving himself whatever he wanted. Damn the consequences it might bring him, too.

Aria flicked her sunglasses to the side as a man—one Caesar didn't recognize from following her, or from the meeting—spoke to her. She barely acknowledged him at all, and placed her sunglasses on her face as she peered around the street.

Caesar was safely hidden in an alleyway across the street. The shadows kept him hidden from view, but still allowed him free range to watch this woman coming and going from a shop she seemed to visit at least once a week.

Or, that's what he noticed from following her.

Aria shook her head at something the man said, and when he tried to urge her toward the shop, she held up a hand. Damn. Caesar wished he had found a closer spot to hide so that he could have heard their conversation.

It didn't seem to matter.

Aria headed into the shop without another word to her companion who was left looking as though his head was going to explode on the sidewalk. The guy glanced down the street at the sidewalk cop who was checking meters, and zones. The sign in front of the shop showcased a bright, big NO PARKING in red, block letters. Right where the fucker was parked.

Caesar wondered …

He didn't have to think for long—the second the guy got into the black sedan and pulled out onto the street to go look for another place to park, Caesar darted out of the alleyway and headed across the street. He ignored the screech of brakes, and the horn that honked at him.

Who knew how long he had?

He didn't think Angelo would appreciate him killing someone in broad daylight, and in the middle of a clothing store. Considering the way Aria's men seemed to act whenever they were guarding her, it was a very real possibility that Caesar might have to do just that if one of them caught him anywhere near her.

Caesar slipped inside the boutique, and glanced up when the door jingled overtop his head at his entrance. The very second he looked straight ahead again, he found Aria staring at him with wide eyes from the other side of the boutique.

Her mouth popped open.

Caesar grinned.

Shock looked good on her.

Beside Aria, a woman stood holding a lace and satin bralette set for her to look over, but she wasn't paying her any mind, now. In fact, she waved a hand at her as if to shoo her away. That shock was quickly replaced by narrowed eyes, and her lips pressed into a hard, grim line.

Caesar came closer, and Aria moved away from the woman. The two met in the middle of the boutique, although she was careful to keep a good two feet of space between them.

Her gaze darted over his shoulder as though she were looking for someone to come inside. The man who'd driven her, maybe?

All he saw were her nerves.

She was *nervous.*

"What in the hell are you doing here?" she hissed.

"You can look at me when you talk to me," he countered.

Green eyes met his with a blazing fire that threatened to burn him to the ground right where he fucking stood. Damn—this woman was something else.

"You need to leave," Aria said firmly, "*now.*"

"No can do." Caesar waved a finger in the general direction from which she had come. "I liked that set you were looking at, by the way. Don't get the pink, though. Only innocent girls wear pink, and it might make me feel like you're something else the first time I get to fuck you while you wear them."

Aria's mouth fell open briefly before she closed it fast with an audible *snap.* Her jaw stiffened before she squared her shoulders, and said, "*That* won't be happening again."

Caesar didn't know ...

"You sure about that?"

The two stared one another down.

Neither moved an inch.

"You have to *go,*" she finally said, her voice quieting. "Please."

Caesar tipped his head to the side. "It's not a good feeling to have someone blindside you, is it? I quite enjoyed this. I might keep showing up like this if you're going to look like that every time I do it."

"*Caesar.*"

"You sound the same, by the way. When you talk to me, and when I fuck you, I mean. It makes me hard as hell."

Her gaze drifted lower.

Caesar smirked when she could in fact see the length of his erection pressing against his black slacks. Yeah, he wasn't even ashamed.

"What is wrong with you?" Aria asked.

"A lot of things. Right now—*you.*"

"Me?"

"That's what I said, *donna.*"

Aria wet her lips, and did that searching thing again. Like she was waiting for someone to come in and bust up their moment.

"Looking for your guard?"

Her gaze came back to him instantly. "It should be Nico, but he had other things to do."

"Not what I asked."

"*Yes*, I am waiting for him. *No*, you can't be here when he comes in."

"Why not?" he asked, honestly curious. "You can start a war with our family, but you can't have a chat with one of us without a guard to watch you?"

"Exactly that, yes."

"I didn't take you for a frightened woman."

Aria's scowl melted into a condescending smile. "I'm not."

"Then why—"

"*Merda*," she swore.

Caesar followed her gaze to see the black sedan she had come in was now parked across the road, and the man stepped out of the driver's side. He looked both ways, and then waited for a short line of cars to pass before he thought to cross the street.

"I have to *go*," Aria murmured, fear thickening her voice. She tried to push past Caesar, but he grabbed tight to her arm, and swung her back around to face him as he dragged her closer. Maybe that was an asshole move—he didn't tend to manhandle women outside of sex—but she seemed too shocked to do anything. All she gave him was a weak, "Don't do that, Caesar."

"You're not leaving yet."

Her worried gaze darted to the windows. "Please, you don't understand what—"

"I want a meeting. You and me, and no one else."

Surprise stared back at him. "What, *why*?"

"Because I asked for it."

She was afraid the man was going to see him with her, and even though Caesar didn't know why, he was more than willing to use it to get something he wanted from her. He was an asshole that way—never denied it, really.

"It'll have to be on *my* terms," she countered fast, her voice barely a whisper. "A safe meeting *I* set up, not you."

Caesar shrugged. "Fine."

"Now, let me go."

He did, and she moved fast to head for the door. She had just stepped outside of the boutique as the man came to the other side of the road. The two exchanged words, but Aria kept shaking her head, and pointed at the car.

What was she hiding?

Who was this woman?

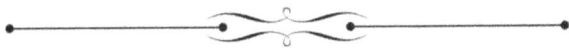

"I swear, it was entirely different women," Caesar said as he cupped the to-go coffee between his palms. "The woman I met today was not the same one I met in the club, or the one who came to the meeting."

Cain nodded, and sipped from his coffee before he replied, "No doubt. Depending on her father or husband's disposition, though, something like that could get her killed."

Caesar stiffened. "Something like *what*?"

"*Anything*, man. Everything she's done—with you, I mean. But beyond that … just today, Caesar. Camorra isn't like our thing, okay. Women may appear like they have more respect and freedom in a clan, but they're fucking heavily controlled in every aspect. It's all about appearance and reputation for them. She probably shouldn't even be wearing fucking lipstick if her husband is out of town, you know what I mean?"

Wait, what?

Caesar blinked a few times as he tried to absorb those words, and still failed to understand. "You're going to have to explain that to me."

"Which part?"

"Most of it."

Cain shrugged, and set his cup down on the table. "A woman is only respected in their culture if she is without shame. And they take it so far as to even say a woman isn't allowed to be in private with a man who isn't of her own blood, or one chosen by her husband."

"Like a guard."

"Yeah, I suspect whoever is watching her at any given time has been handpicked by either her husband or her father."

"More likely the husband, though."

"Considering her father's in jail, yeah."

Caesar hummed under his breath. "So, just being alone with me would be problematic for her?"

"If caught, yes."

The man she'd called Nico—the one who'd warned her while Aria was in the hallway with Caesar—now made more sense to him. Except, he'd been worried *for* her, and not necessarily judging or threatening her for being alone with a strange man.

"I think she has one of them helping her, then," Caesar said.

Cain tipped his head to the side. "I would suspect so, yes. She would have to in order for her to pull of something like the club, right?"

"Why the makeup thing?"

"Ah, yeah." Cain rolled his eyes, saying, "Just goes back to the appearance bit again, you know? She should dress down, not overdo it with her hair, and keep her face clean of makeup. Basically, it makes her look like a grieving woman—she's not available to other men that way."

"And she's supposed to just do that when?"

"If her husband is out of town, or locked up."

"Even for *years*?"

Cain shrugged again. "Guess so."

"What the *fuck*?"

"Hey, people have things to say about Cosa Nostra, too. Like the fact we can't even introduce a man by his name, and instead whether or not he's a friend of ours. We all have our things, Caesar."

"That seems a little drastic, though. And she clearly doesn't follow the rules."

"Or she's being allowed to bend them a bit because of circumstances. She is heading the family right now, isn't she? No one is going to care to listen to a woman who looks like she just rolled out of bed when her appearance is meant to be the first thing presented about herself, and it needs to be perfect."

"Huh."

Cain reached for his cup, and took another sip. "Camorra is a strange and dangerous thing, man. Their entire culture is bred right into their person, and they guard and protect it with everything."

"How do you even know this shit?"

"Worked alongside a captain for a clan a couple of years back when we had an issue on the streets. Nothing big, really. We made friends for a bit."

"And what happened to that?"

Cain smiled bitterly. "What usually does with Camorras. A war sprung up between neighboring clans, and he was taken out in the process."

"Shit."

"Yeah, but see, that's also a part of their life. They *wait* for those moments knowing it's going to happen. That it's all a matter of time. It's why I don't think she's actually scared to go up against your father—Aria De Rose wasn't raised to be easily frightened of death. Not when it comes to her cause."

"But the idea of being caught alone with me terrifies her enough that she's willing to agree to meet up with me again even though that's risky, and she's basically already got what she wanted from me the first time around."

What a fucking juxtaposition *that* was.

Caesar didn't know what to do with it.

"What seems foreign to you right now is probably second nature to her. What I would be more interested in trying to figure out is why a woman like that is going to the lengths she is to deceive her husband—and everyone else in her life—and what she is trying to gain from it."

"Questions, questions."

His friend chuckled. "And not an answer in sight."

Caesar smirked. "I have my ways of getting them."

"Careful—Angelo won't like that."

"You offer that like a deterrent, but …"

"It's more like encouragement," Cain grumbled. "Yeah, I know how you fucking work."

He did.

It was why they were friends.

"Now, when *and* how is she going to set up this meeting?" Caesar asked more of himself than his friend. "That should be interesting."

Cain gave him a look. "Or deadly."

Yes, or that.

He figured it'd be worth it.

SIX

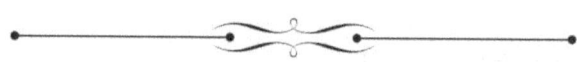

PEPPERMINT SCHNAPPS WAS a favorite drink of Aria's—straight, and not mixed with anything. A cool burn slid down her throat with every sip, and a bite lingered behind with her next breath. She nursed her drink while staring out the window of the hotel she had slipped off to for the evening.

"All's well, then?" she heard Nico ask on his phone call.

Turning to stare at her friend, she caught sight of his quick frown before he put his back to her, and finished up the call. She wasn't too worried about that frown of his—it wasn't because something had gone wrong in her plans, no doubt.

It was because *everything* was going right.

And he worried.

"Well?" Aria asked when Nico came to stand next to the chaise.

"He's on his way."

"Good."

She sipped on the drink again, and reveled in the calm it chased through her bloodstream. Another reason why she loved the drink.

It was calm in a bottle.

"I don't think they'll be long," Nico added after a beat of silence. "Maybe fifteen minutes, or so. Caesar wasn't too far away when they picked him up on the side of the street."

Aria contemplated that statement. "Doesn't he ever drive?"

"Occasionally, it looks like. A red Corvette, actually. Vintage style."

Well, *damn*.

That was a nice car.

Even she could appreciate that.

"Nothing else?" she asked.

Nico shrugged. "Other than the Corvette, no."

"I bet I know why he picked that car."

All its sleek lines, and chrome. A bright, sexy color that would turn heads. An emblem on the front that would make a woman wet at the sight alone.

"Women love pretty cars," she said with a smirk when Nico looked to her for an answer.

"Likely. I take it he's probably always had a driver, or like most Capos, his work is done on the streets with a crew. He's comfortable enough in the city that the streets probably feel like a second home."

"Interesting perspective."

"Yeah, I try," her friend muttered.

Aria sighed at the tension lingering in his voice. "Just get it out."

"It doesn't matter what I tell you, you're going to go through with this meeting anyway. I don't even think you'll need it, but here you are."

"And yet, you want to share your opinion despite knowing it won't make a difference to what I'm going to do. Funny how that works."

"Let's call it force of habit."

"You could do that," she replied, tipping her glass at him, "or you could just say you're worried about me."

"I am. I am extremely worried."

"You shouldn't be, Nico."

She understood why he was, sure, but it really wasn't going to change her resolve in all of this. She had plans to follow through on, and goals she intended to meet no matter the cost. And God knew … God knew she felt it in her fucking *bones* with every move she made—the cost was going to be high.

Maybe the cost to her.

Of course, the cost to others.

And anyone in her way.

What was she to do?

"I just … how far are you willing to go to see this through?" he asked. "How many organizations are you willing to ruin to get what you want, or how many men are you fine with seeing die for this cause?"

She didn't even have to think about it.

Not really.

"As many as it takes."

How else was she to survive this?

Caesar had his phone stuck to his ear when the hotel door was opened to showcase him standing behind it with one of Aria's trusted men—the one other she had besides Nico—close at his side. He barely passed her a second glance where she stood in the middle of the room, and her glowering man didn't faze him a bit, either.

In fact, he ignored them both.

His phone call seemed more important.

"Kind of busy right now, actually," he said to whoever it was.

Aria cocked a brow, but stayed quiet.

Caesar let out a harsh sigh, and glared at the ceiling. "No, I guess you can safely assume I won't be coming to dinner, Angelo. And no, don't bother to apologize to Martina or Daniele for it, either. They honestly don't give a shit."

Ouch.

She bet family dinners at his family's home were absolutely *delightful.* Not.

Aria had done enough research and digging into the personal lives of the Accardo family to know there was tension there. For what reason, she wasn't entirely sure. Oh, sure, she suspected it had a lot to do with Caesar's behavior and tendency to fuck anything he preferred with a hole between its legs, but that only left her with more questions than answers, really.

Like why he would act that way at all.

No man simply woke up one day and decided to make it his goal in life to fuck his way through the organization's wives, and whoever else he felt like. No man was born with that kind of inclination.

It was a learned behavior.

Or … a byproduct of something else.

Honestly, Aria was just surprised Caesar's father had let him go on as long as he did. Cosa Nostra had its own set of rules and expectations, and she bet Caesar had pushed every line he could, and snapped a few altogether along the way.

How was he still alive?

Questions for another day.

"I'm offending you?" Caesar asked, grinning a little bit. "That kind of sounds like another one of those *you* problems, Angelo."

Angelo's loud, angry reply echoed through the speaker enough that Aria could actually hear the hum of his words. She couldn't make out exactly *what* he was saying, but it was enough to tell her that he wasn't pleased.

She was just about done with this show.

Done with the game Caesar was playing.

"Shut off the phone," she told him quietly.

For the first time since he had entered the hotel room, his gaze drifted to her, and lingered for a moment before drifting up and down her body. His unashamed perusal of her, and the way his stare lingered at the junction between her thighs, and the swell of her breasts under the tight, shimmering fabric of the dress was enough to heat her blood.

Men looked, sure.

They never really *appreciated.*

Aria had only been with a couple of men before her husband—and he took great enjoyment in making it miserable for her—and then, Caesar. All of her sexual encounters had been for the purpose of furthering her family's agenda should the need arise, although she had always been careful not to be caught, or to blackmail a man to the point she had him crippled under her control. Other than a boyfriend when she was a sixteen-year-old girl, there had never been a sexual relationship that she went in to because she thought she would actually enjoy it or *wanted* it, for that matter.

It had not been worth the risk to her life for a taste of dick just because she felt the urge to lay down with a man—being caught would have shamed her family, and ruined her reputation. So, before Caesar, sex had simply been something she used to her own advantage, or a need she fulfilled for her husband. Not for her own enjoyment, and even Caesar hadn't been meant to be anything but something she *used.*

Except it didn't work that way.

The club had happened—one single moment with a man who without knowing he had done so, taught her that she was as much of a sexual human being as the next woman even if she did well to ignore it, and it did feel damn good. He'd made her *want* to get on her knees for him, and taste him on her tongue. Something she had only been forced to do before. He also taught her that sex was dirty, addictive, and it simply took the right person for it to make a goddamn difference.

So, maybe it made her hot to see him stare because she knew *why* he did. Maybe it messed her up a little to think he wanted to do it again because she wasn't even sure if she could refuse. She didn't know if her new weakness would allow her to.

And that was *bad.*

"Hang up the phone," she repeated when Caesar kept staring. This time, her tone came out sharp, and authoritative. She wasn't fucking around anymore—he'd wanted this meeting, and so they were going to have it. "*Now.*"

Angelo's voice kept humming on, too.

Raging on, really.

Caesar gave her a cocky smile as he pulled the phone away from his ear, and ended the call without a word to his father that he was going to do so. "Happy?"

She didn't even get to reply.

The phone started ringing again.

"Turn it off," she demanded.

Caesar laughed darkly. "You don't know much about the rules of made men, do you? Never shun a boss, sweetheart."

"I'm far from sweet. Shut your phone off."

"I don't know—I thought the taste of your pussy was awfully sweet, actually."

Jesus Christ.

She felt the heat trying to climb up her throat and into her cheeks, but she took a quick breath, and urged the emotions down. Glancing at the waiting men behind Caesar, she gave the two a nod.

"Close the door, and wait outside."

Nico nodded, and followed the other man out without needing to be told again. She was grateful that he was at least letting his concerns about this meeting and what might follow to remain unheard for the moment.

She couldn't afford to deal with Caesar, and Nico at the same time. One drove her crazy with urges she wasn't ready to handle, and the other one made her crazy with his constant worries taking over every fucking conversation.

"Oh, no guards?" Caesar asked. "But what if you need them?"

His grin showed off arrogance, and amusement all rolled into one. A sexy sight if she had ever seen one. Today, he was dressed in a flat black three-piece suit, and had a vest and tie to match. Were suits all he ever wore? Did he even own a pair of jeans?

"Why would I need my guards?"

Caesar shrugged. "I suppose because I might hurt you."

"You could try."

His grin melted into a smirk in an instant.

Sex *walking*.

"How do you do that?" he asked, arching one brow high.

"Do what?"

"Flip back and forth between different women depending on your situation—the one who tricked me in a club, and looked like sin had been poured into a dress, and the one who ran scared at the idea of being seen with me in a store. Oh, and let's not forget the woman who walks into a meeting with a Cosa Nostra boss, and threatens him. I just … find it very fascinating."

"Is that what you call lust?"

Caesar's tongue peeked out to touch the upper corner of his lip in his smile. "No, actually. I call that *interest*. See, if lust was all it was, I'd have been satisfied with the taste of you that I already got. I wouldn't be thinking about more, or wondering which surface would be best in this room to spread you open, and bury my face into your cunt."

Holy mother of—

"But I don't think a good fuck is why you had me brought here, and that really wasn't what I asked for, either," he finished.

Aria blinked. "You are something else."

He nodded. "I've been told that a few times, yes."

It was … disconcerting.

Strange.

Curious.

She didn't like it.

And yet, she did like it, too.

I am a mess.

66

She needed to get him off of this conversation, and fast. Him talking about spreading her open did nothing but make her hot, and wet between her thighs. Neither of which was something she could afford to focus on right now.

"Why does your father hate you so much—besides the obvious reasons, I mean?" Aria questioned.

Caesar didn't look the slightest put off by her question, and it didn't really seem to take him by surprise. His ready answer did kind of take her off guard, though. "I'm not sure he does hate me, actually."

"Really? I don't know many fathers who yell at their sons like yours was just doing when they love them."

His broad shoulders lifted uncaringly. "It's only because he doesn't hate me that he hasn't killed me yet. The better question is what haven't I done to make him hate me the way I hate him, and why the fuck hasn't it worked yet."

Aria blinked, stunned.

So, *that* was it?

He hated his father?

Why?

"But back to the other thing. Do I get a peek at what's under your dress tonight, or no? 'Cause, I am a curious little shit, and—"

"Stop playing games, Caesar."

He barked out a laugh. "Me? You think it's *me* playing games between us? I'm straightforward, Aria. I don't need to play games. I can't help if shit affects you, and you can't hide it. You're the one who manipulated and tried to blackmail me. And *then* had me picked up on the side of the street to bring me to a hotel room for a meeting I am sure you could have given me a heads up on in some way. You make demands, you direct the conversation, and you question me about *my* personal business. So, really, who is playing games between us?"

She stayed silent.

He apparently didn't care.

Aria stiffened into a stone-still statue as Caesar suddenly moved closer to her with the slow grace of a predator. She couldn't possibly step away from him—that might make him think she was afraid. She couldn't tell him to back off—it would look like she was uncomfortable.

It meant *weakness.*

So, no.

She stayed still with her hard gaze and sly smile firmly in place even as Caesar came close enough to her that she could see those black flakes in the blue of his eyes again. Close enough that the warmth of his body heated the space between them.

Too close, maybe.

"And if you ever think to try that manipulative shit with me again," he told her, his head dipping low enough that his lips almost grazed hers when he spoke, "then you'll get the pleasure of learning why people like to say I use sex as a weapon, *mia cara*."

"Threats will get you nowhere with me, Caesar, except for a grave."

Her voice didn't shake.

Her tone never wavered.

And yet, she still lacked air. Her words still felt *hot*.

Fuck this man for putting her on edge.

No man did that.

"Try me," Caesar urged, his lips quirking up in that sexy way again. "I know how damaging it would be for you should someone find out about us, and what you did with me. You think I haven't done my homework, like you did with yours? I *have*."

Again with the threats.

"The better question is, *would you?*" she asked. "I don't think you would, actually. I'm just a woman, and what have I really done to hurt you?"

"I fucked my half-brother's wife because I think he's an arrogant little shit that needed to be kicked down from his goddamn high horse. They do couple's counseling three times a week with a priest who tells him he can't divorce her because it'll go against God's will. They have to sit at a dinner table with me at least twice a month, but sometimes more. My father barely punished me for it because he's still holding onto that idea of me being his favorite even though it kills him inside knowing I won't ever be what he wants me to be."

Caesar sneered at the sight of Aria's widening gaze, adding, "So, yeah, tell me again how I won't fucking ruin you because you're *just a woman*, and you haven't hurt me. I don't need you to make something hurt for me to justify being a fucking asshole—I just am. I don't ever justify anything I do. That would mean I actually give a shit."

She tried to speak.

Tried to find *something* to say.

"I …"

Caesar nodded, and took one step back. "And don't forget it, either."

She refused to let this man knock her off balance for too long, though. She wouldn't be a De Rose if she wasn't resilient, and able to quickly bounce back from anything that was thrown her damn way.

If she couldn't appeal to his empathetic nature—if he even had the capability to feel empathy for someone else—then she would try a different direction. Whatever it took to get this done, then she would do it.

"Perhaps, I could help you, then," she suggested.

Caesar tipped his head back, and stared down at her unaffected.

"There's nothing you have or could do that I need or want, actually. There's nothing you can give me."

"Maybe not *directly*. I need you to step back and let me do whatever it is I have to do, and *will* do to get control of this city. Including your family—your father. It's what needs to happen, or … in the effort to gaining control, I will get what I want in another way. You could get something you want out of that, couldn't you?"

"To what, kill my father?"

Aria smiled at lilt in his tone. "Is that what you need and want, Caesar? For your father to be out of the picture for good?"

He said nothing.

His eyes gave away nothing.

He was cold all over.

"Give me what I want," Aria said, "and maybe in a roundabout way, you will be able to get what you want, too."

"I still don't know what that is—what you want, I mean."

"Isn't it obvious? *Power.*"

Because the power to control and manipulate would give her everything else. She only needed to get there first, and she was running out of time to do it.

Caesar came close again—no warning, just all in her space and coloring her vision with him entirely. His head bent down, and hers tipped upward. She wouldn't be able to move a millimeter without kissing him, but she held back.

"I don't think that's all it is, though," he murmured, "and that's where I start to get concerned. You can't trust someone who doesn't give you all the details."

"I—"

The click of the door unlatching before it was opened sent Aria stepping back from Caesar quickly even though she knew it couldn't be anyone that might catch her doing something wrong. And it wasn't.

Nico stood in the doorway, and his gaze only drifted to her when he said, "Raffe is going to call in ten—he's on his way back to the hotel from another meet with the smugglers."

Aria nodded. "Okay, *grazie*, Nico."

She looked back to Caesar once the door was closed, and swore he hadn't once stopped staring at her through the entire exchange. She hadn't given anything away—she couldn't have, not about her husband, or how he made her feel the worst kind of dread and shame all at once.

And yet, he looked at her like he knew something …

"You're going to have to leave now," she said. "I'm sure you'll find a way home, Caesar. Have a good night."

"I need to find a way to get control of him, or have him work to my benefit," Aria said, voicing the thoughts that had been troubling her for well over an hour.

Nico glanced at the phone resting on her lap that was now turned off. "Raffe?"

"No. I have him handled."

Her friend lifted a brow.

Aria rolled her eyes.

"Well, I have him as handled as I can for now," she corrected. "There's not much I can do on his side of things until he's back in the country."

And even then ... none of the things she had planned for her husband would be possible if she didn't get everything else under control first.

"Ah, you mean Caesar," Nico murmured.

Aria shrugged, and tipped her glass of schnapps up for another drink—her third glass, and she was starting to feel it. Thankfully, Raffe hadn't noticed on the phone call or she wouldn't have heard the end of it, and probably would have still been talking to the bastard.

"He needs to be controlled," she said again. "I need to know that he's going to do what *I* need or want for him to do, even if he doesn't realize that's what he's doing. I can't have him holding the threat of something over my head like that. It's a game I am not willing to play."

"You can't afford to."

"I don't need the memo."

Nico gave her a look.

She returned it with one of her own.

"You shouldn't play with fire where Caesar is concerned," Nico said. "I don't think he's the kind of man who responds nicely to that sort of thing."

To say the least.

"He's dangerous for me," Aria admitted, "and not in the obvious way, either. Not in the way that might harm my standing, or any of that. I'm not worried about that. I can handle him there."

It took Nico a second.

And then *two.*

"You ... like him?"

Aria sighed. "I don't know what I think about him, frankly."

"You should probably get that figured out."

Yeah, probably.

"I have to get control of him," she repeated for a third time.

"You keep saying that."

"Because I don't think you'll like how I'm going to do it."

It was time to turn the tables on Caesar, and to let him have a taste of his own medicine, even if it was only to benefit *her*.

Sex is my weapon.

His words still lingered.

She was going to use them.

SEVEN

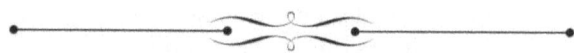

CAESAR UNLOCKED THE door to his penthouse, and balanced the phone between his shoulder and ear at the same time.

"You can't still be thinking about it," Cain said.

"Thinking—considering. It's all the same, isn't it?"

"But *why?*"

"Maybe there's something there," Caesar offered, saying nothing more. The less Cain knew, the better it would be for him, anyway. He didn't like to involve his friend in his schemes when they got to be too dangerous. It was his way of caring, if it were possible. "I don't think she's—"

Caesar stepped into his place, dropped the keys into a waiting crystal bowl next to the door, and quieted instantly. It wasn't the faint hum of Cain in his ear interrupting him with more concerns, or even the fact that the hallway light was turned on when he knew he had shut it off before he left that day. None of that made him hesitate.

"Hey, you okay?" Cain asked. "You went quiet."

Was he okay?

That distinct floral scent that seemed to be a favorite of Aria's lingered in the penthouse hallway. It was faint, sure, but un-fucking-mistakable. All at once, it made his blood boil, his dick hard, and his confusion shoot up.

That woman made him a *mess.*

"Caesar," Cain said again.

"Yeah, I'm good," he replied, snapping out of the daze for a second. "I will call you back, all right?"

"What? We're having a conversation here."

"Yeah, yeah. Go fuck your wife and blow off some steam."

"*Hey.*"

"Later."

Caesar ended the call, and dropped the phone into the pocket of the blazer he then shrugged off. He also pulled the gun out that he kept hidden in the inner pocket, but left it hanging limp at his side as he walked deeper into his place.

Apparently, it wasn't just the hallway light that someone had turned on, but also the living room. It was there that he found her—sitting on the chaise that rested in front of the tall floor-to-ceiling windows overlooking a busy downtown Philly.

Aria passed him a fleeting glance over her shoulder at his entrance, but little else. She went back to staring out the window as though she had better things to do. "This is a great view."

Caesar kept a tight hold on his gun—he wasn't quite ready to lift it or let it go just yet. "How did you get in here?"

"I flirted with the security guard, and told him you were expecting me. A gift from a friend, I said. He fell for it hook, line, and sinker."

The money he paid for good security in this goddamn shithole, and this is what they do? Well, that fucking idiot was going to have to *go*.

Caesar didn't say that out loud.

"I suppose they probably see enough women coming in and out of your place that it wouldn't be such a stretch for one to be sent to you as a surprise," she added.

"Wrong."

Her shoulders tensed, but she didn't turn around. "Pardon?"

"Women don't come here. I don't bring them here, either. Ever."

Which was exactly why the security should know better.

Aria reached for a glass of water sitting on the small table next to the chaise, and picked it up for a drink. The sight made Caesar's throat tighten—she had gone further than his hallway and living room if she had gotten herself a drink.

"Did you search my place?" he asked.

"What would I find?"

Caesar arched a brow. "Pretty damn sure that's not what I asked."

"Yes, but it is what *I* asked."

"You're insufferable, *donna*. It's only the fact that I like the look of your face, and the shape of your ass that I haven't thrown you out already."

Aria shrugged dainty shoulders. "Is that why, or is it something else?"

"What else would there be?"

She set the glass aside again, and stood from the chaise. It gave Caesar the perfect view of that ass—he hadn't been lying when he said he liked the shape of it—covered by a tight, short red dress with a slit in the thigh that would make any man's mouth water. She bent down to snatch the clutch she'd left sitting on the chaise, and he got a peek of matching red lace beneath the dress.

Goddamn.

Caesar didn't even realize Aria had turned to look at him because he was too busy taking in the red patent leather peep-toe pumps she wore, and the smoothness of her golden calves. She cleared her throat, and his gaze jumped up to meet hers. He didn't even attempt to look ashamed at being caught staring.

"What were you saying?" he asked.

Aria smiled a little. "Distracted, Caesar?"

"I don't know what you expect from a man like me when you wear a dress like that and bend over in front of me. What, do you want me to *not* look?"

"I like it when you look, actually."

He stiffened a bit—in more places than one. It was only then that he decided to toss the gun to a nearby couch. Not that he didn't think she was up to something because he did think exactly that. But really, he was more interested in finding out what it was, and he didn't think he could do that with a weapon in his hand.

Aria hadn't even given it a second glance, anyway.

"I was saying," she drawled, ignoring his question altogether, "that maybe there's another reason—other than the fact you want to fuck me— why you haven't thrown me out yet."

"Try me."

"Maybe you'd like to finish our conversation from last week."

It wasn't even a question.

And she was right—to an extent.

Caesar thought that staying quiet and letting Aria speak might be the better option because this woman let more things slip when someone else wasn't talking. He should have tried to use that to his advantage for now, and see what he could get from her, but he wasn't very good at that whole self-control thing. It only took a mention of their hotel meeting to make his blood boil.

"You know," he said before he could stop himself, "I haven't forgotten how you threatened me."

Aria nodded. "Good—you shouldn't."

"That's not a good thing to do to a man like me. It pisses me off. And when I get pissed off, bad things tend to happen."

"That's kind of the point."

What?

Her quick-witted yet still flippant replies only irritated him more. Like this was some kind of game for her, and she was enjoying getting under his skin. She didn't try to make sense, or clarify, either.

Hell ...

It also kind of turned him on. Caesar decided right then and there—he was broken. He was some kind of fucked up man that just ... was altogether *broken*.

Ruined.

There was no other explanation.

"I went to see my father today," Aria said, changing direction in their conversation just like that with everything still left hanging. "He's a good place to go when I need to clear my head, or get a different perspective. He reminded me—sitting in his prison uniform and behind Plexiglas—that everything and *anything* is fair game when it comes to getting what I want."

The mention of her father made Caesar take notice—the man was in lockup for what, he didn't know, and for how long, he didn't care. It was the first time she had mentioned him to Caesar, however, although he didn't know why that irked him so much.

It shouldn't matter at all.

He didn't miss the fondness in her tone, or the way her painted-red lips curved softly at the edges in happiness. He didn't get those kinds of feelings at all when he thought about his own father—hatred and bitterness, sure. Not happiness or love, though.

It was … strange to him.

Foreign, even.

Aria had come closer to Caesar at an antagonizing slow speed until she came to a stop right in front of him. It had given him the chance to take all of her in again, but now he was only staring at her face, and those bright green eyes of hers meeting his blue gaze.

She was fire, he thought.

But he felt like ice.

"Have you thought about what I said?" she asked. "About stepping back, and letting me do my business … or even *helping* me? I let you have a bit of time to think everything over, and now here I am to get an answer. Do you have one for me?"

"I don't have all the details, so no."

"Shame. I *hate* waiting on a man."

She came subtly closer again—enough that he could see the way her dark, long lashes curved high, and he could count the diamonds in the cluster studs she'd put in her earlobes. It was distracting and disconcerting.

Aria smirked. "Does this feel familiar, Caesar? You seem to like crowding my fucking space, and setting me off balance. That's your game, isn't it? That's how you get what you want from women, or it's how you mess them up enough to find your *in?*"

Caesar laughed bitterly. "What, did you take a few days to recoup from our meeting, and decide you wanted a second go at it? Now it's your turn to try and fuck with me? That's not how this is going to work, Aria."

"Isn't it?"

Her simple, soft-spoken question was punctuated by a sexy grin before she tried to slip past him to leave. Caesar acted out of the sudden dark urge that pummeled its way through his insides, and nothing else when he reached out and grabbed hold of Aria's elbow. Swinging her back around to face him again with a sharp word on his tongue, he nearly missed her open palmed slap coming his way.

Almost.

"Don't you dare—"

He caught her wrist with his free hand, and her blazing gaze with his own. It silenced whatever retort was about to come out of her pretty mouth, but he didn't really care. Her show of anger had his own irritation soaring high.

"I told you not to play games with me," he murmured. "Didn't I?"

She never blinked—never *flinched*. "You think this is a game, Caesar?"

"I think—"

"I don't *care* what you think," she snapped. "Now let me go."

"I don't think so."

His response was clearly not what she wanted. Aria moved fast, then, dropping her clutch to the floor and using her free hand to swing at him again. Both of his hands were tied up in holding her some way and he didn't get the chance to catch her in time.

Not before her hand connected with his face, anyway.

Crack.

The force of her slap sent his head snapping to the side as a sting radiated over his cheek. He swore he could taste a bit of blood blooming in his mouth, too.

Fuck this woman.

Damn her.

He found himself *laughing*. Because she challenged him. Because she wasn't afraid. Because she didn't care at all, and she actually dared to fucking *hit him*.

Caesar righted himself but there was no way he could hide the rage flashing across his features, not to mention the bulge of his hardening cock trying to hammer its way out of his fucking slacks. Aria's heavy breaths made her shoulders and chest heave up and down with every one, and her lips had flattened in an angry, grim line.

"I don't get deterred by an emotional woman, or a violent one," he told her. "it just turns me on. I take it as a challenge."

Aria blinked, and glanced down at his crotch before her gaze jumped back up again. "I—"

"And I don't think you came here because you wanted me to fucking *talk*, either."

"You have no idea what I want."

"Don't I? I bet all you want right now is for me to find the closest flat surface, and fuck the defiance right out of you."

She hesitated.

Her eyes blazed *yes*. Her trembling shoulders and clenched fists all said *yes*.

Her words came out saying, "Let me go right—"

Stubborn woman.

Caesar shut Aria up by yanking her into him, and slamming his mouth down on hers. It took all of one bruising kiss, and her lips parted for his. He couldn't find a single part of himself that wanted to be easy, and so he wasn't. All teeth, and lips, and tongue—tasting her again, and drawing blood from her bottom lip when he bit down hard, and making her whine when he threaded his fingers into her hair and pulled.

She hit him again for that.

"Fuck," he hissed, rearing back from the second slap's sting and pressing his fingertips to his hot cheek. "Now you get my hands on your throat for that one."

Aria didn't back up at his threat.

Didn't raise her hands again.

Didn't look *scared*.

"Good," she murmured.

Damn him straight to hell.

This woman would kill him.

"You're a fucking asshole," she told him.

And it got her hot.

Clearly.

Caesar laughed, and stepped forward. Aria still didn't back down. "And I bet your sweet, tight pussy is weeping for a taste of me, too. *Admit it.*"

She didn't say anything.

Instead, she let her hand slide between her thighs under the skirt of that teasing dress, and then brought it back out again to flash wet fingers. "Want a taste?"

His chest ached.

His throat tightened.

"Yes," he said.

"Too fucking bad."

She punctuated her words by slipping those fingers between her own lips, and sucking them clean. Caesar's lust spiked higher, and so did his *anger*. Aria didn't have the time to react before he jolted forward, grabbed her throat in his hand, and stuck his other one right up her dress.

She sucked in a hard, ragged breath and grinned when he squeezed her delicate neck, and fisted her damp panties at the gusset. She wasn't going to keep anything from him like it was some kind of game—there was no push and pull here. He was *taking*, and she was giving it.

Simple as that.

It took one hard pull, and he ripped the lace before pulling the ruined panties from her body.

That had to hurt.

Sting, at least.

She only laughed.

A dark, bitter laugh that urged him on, and promised sin, relief, and sex was fucking close. She didn't look afraid of him at all.

"Do it," she said as his fingers danced higher between her thighs again. "Don't you want a taste of *gold*, Caesar? How many times have you gone back for seconds when it comes to a woman?"

"Shut up."

She grinned.

He sneered.

God, she was wet. Warm and soft and sleek as hell on his fingertips when they slid between her thighs. Slick arousal coated his fingertips, and her whole body shuddered when he stroked her pussy, and then let two fingers stretch her open. Inside, she was impossibly softer—silken, even. Wetter, too. And so much fucking hotter.

She clearly wanted more of his touches if the way she was grinding her cunt into his hand was any indication, but he *refused*. He wasn't giving her anything just yet—not something she wanted, anyway.

He was too pissed for that.

She was going to know it.

"*Plea*—"

"Don't think so," Caesar said before her begging could start. Oh, he'd love to hear it. Would have her screaming it soon enough, sure. Not right then. "You owe me a taste, you crazy woman."

Aria sucked in a sharp breath when Caesar's hand tightened on her throat again, and his fingers left her pussy. It took a second for him to flip her around, and bend her over the back of the couch. He kept a firm hold on the back of her neck, and refused to let her up even as he bunched her skirt up around her hips.

Beautiful ass.

Pink pussy.

Wet thighs.

Damn.

He bent down and bit her right ass cheek, but didn't even give her the chance to respond to that action before he'd buried his face between her thighs from behind.

Fuck.

She tasted better when she was angry. Hotter, if it were possible. Tarter, too. Her loud shout and the push of her ass backing into his face had him humming in approval. She couldn't do very much—couldn't move very fucking much, either.

And that was fine with him.

He took his time tunneling his tongue into her clenching cunt, and then sucking on her sensitive spots. He teased with little nips, but refused to give her anymore.

Even when her words came out jumbled, high, and *needy*. Even when her desperation came out so strongly he thought she might cry for it.

No, he wasn't giving her that.

She hadn't *earned* it.

"Fuck you," he heard her say. "*Please* ..." And then a new one, "*I fucking hate you.*"

Shit.

He hated him, too.

And just when her body finally started to shake with the promise of her orgasm, he pulled back altogether, and kept it away from her again. Caesar grabbed Aria by her hips, and flipped her around so that her ass was resting on the arm of the couch, her legs were spread wide open, and her body sprawled across the cushions. Those wild curls of hers flew over the couch, and her wide, angry eyes sought his.

Caesar wasted no time shuffling his pants down, freeing his cock from their confines, and rolling latex down his length. He fisted his cock as he reached out to stroke his thumb between Aria's slick, hot folds. Her legs trembled, but she stayed spread open for him.

Good girl.

"What happens now?" he asked.

She glared.

He grinned.

He bet she liked the sight of him like this—his mouth still wet from her pussy. It was all for her, anyway. She'd done this to them both.

"Well?" he demanded harshly.

Aria swallowed hard. "Now you're going to fuck me."

"*And?*"

"Choke me."

Almost there.

"What else, *mia cara?*"

The tension in her shoulders softened momentarily as she whispered, "When you say I've had enough, I'll ask to finish you." Her gaze jumped up to meet his when she added, "*Nicely.*"

Caesar nodded. "Anything else?"

"And I'll like it."

Of course, she would. Women liked to act as though they had to be treated a certain way during sex, but they all came the same and wailed the same when he was fucking them how *he* liked. He enjoyed stripping a woman of their crazy, nonsensical notions about pride and dignity. Sex was the easiest place to lose all of that trash.

"Why do you sound so surprised when you say you'll *like* it? Has every man treated you like a delicate flower? Has one even made you come before me?"

Aria's jaw stiffened. "Shut up, and fuck me."

He figured he got his answers with that.

And he didn't really mind.

Aria stiffened, and her back arched when Caesar's hand struck out and wrapped tight around her throat again. He fitted himself between her thighs, and in one hard thrust, found his own personal heaven.

And *hell*.

Her high, keening whine when he filled her was the most addictive sound. Her body tensed all over when he pulled out, and slammed right back in again. "Hit my arm if you want me to stop. Got it?"

He got a nod.

That was good enough for him.

"Jesus Christ," she breathed, grinding her body against his for more. "Oh, my God."

"You've got no self-control like this."

And he liked it.

A lot.

"A pretty little slut under me," he added.

Aria's head tilted back with his next thrust, and her cry came out airless and broken. Caesar had both of his hands wrapped around the delicate line of her throat then, and he started to squeeze. Easy at first—just enough for her to feel it, and to take away her air a bit at a time. With every thrust, he squeezed a bit harder until her noises came out choked, and her eyes flew wide to find his.

She was so close to coming.

Shaking all over.

Sweat-slicked skin.

Pink from losing her air.

Mussed hair.

Smudged makeup.

Beautiful, really.

He found a wildness staring back at him—a desperate need to come or breathe or *do* something. Yet, she didn't tap his arm. She didn't want him to stop.

"Do you want to come?"

He got another nod.

"Would you beg for it?"

Please, her eyes blazed.

He released one hand from her throat, and slipped it up under her ass. All it took was his thumb sliding into the tight ring of her ass, and his fingers curving tight around her throat, and she was *screaming*.

His name never sounded better.

Caesar waited until she stopped shaking. He gave her that much time at least. And then he pulled from her wet cunt, and tugged the condom off before discarding it in a small bin under the coffee table. Moving around the arm of the couch, he already had his cock in hand, and waiting for her.

"Ask," he demanded, "and then I'll see what else I can do for you."

She was already reaching for him.

Ready.

Wanting.

"May I finish you, please?"

Perfect, really.

Even if he hated her.

It took all of two days.

Two single days for Caesar to know he *fucked up.*

Or rather, Aria had fucked him over.

Yeah, that was better.

Across the room, his father raged on. Angelo in all his anger never stuttered or stumbled over a single word he threw at his oldest son like daggers. Thing was—Caesar was Kevlar to this, now. It didn't hurt him a bit.

"I thought you *had learned,*" his father snarled. "I thought you were finally getting it."

That was another one of those Angelo problems, but Caesar didn't think his father would like him pointing it out.

Thankfully, the office door was closed, but he was sure whoever was waiting outside was getting a damn good earful.

It wouldn't be the first time.

"I told you to *fix the issue,*" Angelo roared, "not *fuck* it!"

"For what it's worth," Caesar murmured, "she was a good fuck."

Twice.

Well, more than twice. But two separate occasions, so he counted it like that.

Angelo's molars crunched when he clenched his jaw. "I have overlooked a lot of shit, but I can't pretend like you didn't do this. We are in the midst of a war with this woman and her clan, and you *slept* with her. You're fraternizing with her. You're betraying *us.* Was that always the next step for you, *figlio?* To betray me?"

Caesar didn't answer. He didn't figure his father wanted one, really.

Spread out on the desk were a good fifteen or so pictures. Images Caesar hadn't expected to be thrown in his face when he arrived at his father's office after being called in with little to no explanation.

Photos that showed Aria.

Walking into his building.

And leaving looking like he'd fucked her for half the night—which he *had*.

Those were the innocent ones.

There were others, too. Photos looking in his windows—Aria on her back, and her knees. Naked, and so was he—mostly. Someone would have needed to be on the roof, or even in an apartment, of the building next to his to get those photos.

His anger simmered hot and dangerous.

She'd set him up.

She'd done it *purposely*.

He was the one who used sex as a weapon, and she had turned the tables on him. It was disconcerting, and it pissed him the fuck off like nothing else. He didn't know what to deal with first. His father. The woman that did this to him. Or the fact that a part of him was just as turned on as he was angry because *Christ*, that woman had balls on her. She had some kind of nerve, and he respected her as much as he hated her.

It was as amusing as it was *infuriating*.

"This is it, Caesar," Angelo said, his anger dissipating as he stared blankly from behind the desk. His father waved at the photographs. "I can't keep protecting you like I have, and excusing you. *This is it*. We won't be allowing this information to get out, but especially not to our men or the Camorra clan. I can't have people thinking someone on *my* side, and inside my organization is playing both sides. No more, though. I won't be doing anymore for you. This is it, son."

"Okay," he replied dully.

Angelo had been saying this for years.

This shouldn't have been a surprise.

"Vecoli—Tony Vecoli."

Caesar blinked. "Canadian Cosa Nostra boss. What about him?"

Angelo sighed, and glanced down before he pulled out a file from his desk and tossed it to the top. "All the details are in there if you want to look. But the short version is this. He's got a girl—a year younger than you that he needs to marry off, and get her out of his hair. He's also quite aware of the circumstances you've put me in here, and we agreed. You'd do better being *away*. And so, that's where you're going to go and stay. Indefinitely. You will not be welcomed back to Philly, and you will no longer be under my protection or control. Step out of line there like you have here, and the next time I see you will be when you're resting in a casket."

Uh.

"No," Caesar said.

"I didn't pose this like it was negotiable because it *isn't*. This deal has been in the works since before the New York one. I always have a backup plan, son. You should know this."

Wait, what?

"Haven't you figured it out that I won't fucking marry *anyone?*" Caesar snapped.

His father didn't even flinch. "You will, or you will die. How many times have you broken your oath to Cosa Nostra? How many made men have you dishonored? How many times have you shamed your family?"

And how many times did someone do the same thing to Caesar for *years?*

"Don't you understand?" his father asked.

"That your way of correcting what you see as an issue is to send me away?"

Angelo shook his head. "It's because *I love you* that I do this," his father said, gesturing at the Vecoli file, "instead of killing you. I am still trying to help you, son."

Caesar scoffed.

"What?" Angelo barked.

"It's amusing, that's all."

"What is?"

Caesar shrugged. "That you love me while I can barely stand to be near you."

Angelo waited a beat in time.

And then two.

"Get out," his father murmured.

Caesar didn't need to be told again. He did make a phone call as he was leaving, though. Aria had started a whole different war, now, and she was going to have to answer for it.

"Yeah, *hello?*"

Cain sounded like he had been sleeping.

Oh, well.

"Jac De Rose—Aria's father. Pull up everything and anything about him, the prison, and whatever else you can for me. I'm going to need it."

She'd slipped up, too.

She let him find the place where she cared—her *weakness.*

And now he would take it away.

"Shit …" Cain grunted on the other end of the call before he asked, "Why the fuck do you want info on a man who is in prison?"

"Because she loves him." *Clearly.* He'd heard it in her voice when she spoke about him. "Let's see how well she does when he's gone."

"What's your usual success rate?"

The man with the sniper rifle carefully balanced and angled on the edge of the rooftop three-quarters of a mile away from the prison's main yard didn't even look away from the scope he was adjusting. "Pretty good."

"Actual numbers would be great, Hudson."

It was only his name coming from Caesar's mouth that finally made the sniper glance away from his work. "How much are you paying me for this again?"

"A quarter of a million."

"If you keep talking, that rate is going to increase."

Well, then.

"Someone's touchy," Caesar muttered.

"I took this job as a favor to a friend, and nothing more."

Yeah, Cain.

He made a mental note to ask his friend how he had come across an assassin like Hudson, and where exactly the man came from in the first goddamn place. It took three days for Cain to get someone in to work with Caesar who his father wouldn't know or be able to touch—Angelo was still trying to get his son out of the city, after all, so he had enough shit on his plate without this being added to it.

But now he was curious about the man on the roof, and how he had dropped everything to get here with very little notice. He wasn't willing to pay more for this kill, though, so he shut up like he had been told.

"*And,*" Hudson added, a now-lit cigarette dancing from his lips as his strong features roughened and dark hair fell into his eyes, "I don't usually have a tag along when I do a job—so pipe the fuck down, Italian."

Caesar's brow lifted.

He had a serious issue with taking everything as a challenge.

"Who do you work for?" he asked.

Hudson sighed. "An organization."

"Oh, you don't do this alone?"

The man went back to his scope. "Seriously going to fucking delete Cain's number from my phone after this."

"Cain is good shit—answer my question."

"I have someone that oversees my jobs—call him a handler, or a boss. Or whatever the fuck you want, I don't care."

"How did you get into this?"

Hudson didn't answer, but instead, tipped his chin up just enough that his gaze narrowed *over* the line of the scope. "About six-foot-three, a little pudgy in the middle, dark brown hair, and usually sticks to the south side of the prison yard with three heavily tattooed Latinos?"

Caesar glanced in the direction of the prison yard. "That's the info I got."

And that Aria visited her father twice a week—never failed.

"Well, he matches the picture I was given. I'm confident in saying it's him."

"Take the shot," Caesar said.

Hudson tilted his head to the side in acknowledgment, before tipping his head back down to glance in the scope and asking around his cigarette, "Why do you want this guy dead, anyway?"

"To hurt someone."

"It's not ... business or something?"

"Not particularly. I need to prove a point."

And this seemed like the best way to do it.

It would really drive it home for Aria.

Caesar was not fucking around.

"That seems petty." Hudson stubbed the cigarette, slipped it in his pocket, and went still, saying, "But hey, it's your fucking money."

He waited a second—then, *two*.

The shot came out loud, quick, and hopefully precise. Hudson lifted his head from the rifle, and his lips moved silently. Counting, Caesar thought. Or that's what it looked like.

One, two, three, four, five ...

Finally, the man looked back in his scope. "Target hit, and down. Clean shot through the back of the head. Now, move your stupid ass and get off this roof. We have to go."

EIGHT

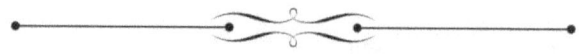

MAE'S LAUGHTER FILLED up the table full of people, and Aria couldn't help but smile. Her young sister-in-law was rarely as happy and carefree as she currently was in her joy—usually Raffe's presence was more than enough to keep his eighteen-year-old sister quiet and meek.

It bothered Aria like nothing else, but she supposed she understood, too. Her husband had a tendency to keep all the women in his life submissive, and pretty—unmoving dolls on a shelf that he occasionally liked to take down and play with, or show off. It all depended on the day and his need, frankly.

"And it all went well?" Aria asked.

Mae nodded two seats down—with all eyes on her, she didn't seem the slightest bit bothered. Her light brown skin was flushed with a pink from her happiness, and her corkscrew curls bobbed in her excitement.

"It did, surprisingly," Mae said. "We didn't think we could pull it off—somehow, we did. The mural went up, and we were out of there."

Aria grinned. "Quite a statement."

"That's what they wanted."

"Raffe won't like that," came a quiet, nasally voice down the way.

Aria rolled her eyes, and then cut her gaze to the bitch that had thought to speak out of turn at her dinner table. Giovanna Bruno—the wife of a man who regularly tested every bit of patience Aria had—surveyed her nails like she hadn't spoken at all. Hadn't the last time she sat at Aria's table and got a wine glass broken over her head been a good enough lesson to shut the hell up?

Apparently not.

"Doesn't he think art is a waste of time, Mae?" Giovanna continued. "Not sure he'd appreciate you joining a protest to do a popup mural for them."

Mae quieted at the statement, and all her happiness bled away. All of eighteen, and people already had to take away this girl's joy like they had any business doing it. Aria had all she could do not to get up out of her seat—she forced herself not to.

Tonight was supposed to be a good dinner. *Peaceful.* Just because she wanted to give Mae a moment in the spotlight. So few Camorra women had their moments when they were constantly stifled, or a man was pushing her out of the way to have it shined on him.

Assholes.

"I don't remember asking you what Raffe would think," Aria said calmly from the head of the table. "I asked *Mae* how it went."

Giovanna smiled sardonically. "Yes, well—"

"Raffe is neither your husband, nor your brother. But he is *ours*. I think we can handle him, Vanna."

The older woman—although only older than Aria by a couple of years—narrowed her eyes down the table, but didn't seem to have anything else to say. Or maybe she was remembering the pieces of glass a doctor removed from her scalp with tweezers because of her last run-in with Aria.

Either way, her silence was best.

For Giovanna.

For Aria.

For anyone in their direct vicinity.

Mae shot Aria a small smile—her silent appreciation and thanks. Aria returned it with a subtle nod, and then reached for her wine glass to empty what was left of it. For the remainder of the dinner, Aria mostly stayed quiet and watched her young sister-in-law engage with members of their clan that Aria considered close enough to be allowed in her home.

These dinners were commonplace, and needed. Long after the food was done, and the guests who were not part of business—like Mae—were gone, then Aria would sit down with the men and a few women, and discuss whatever was needed for the clan. Business, an upcoming arrangement, or even the next attack on the Accardo Cosa Nostra.

Whatever was needed.

It was the ringing of the house phone that quieted the conversation at the table in a flash. Aria stood, waving to her guests for them to continue their conversation, before she stepped out of the dining room to grab the cordless phone in the kitchen.

It only took her one look at the number on the screen to know who was calling ... and probably *why*, too.

She took one breath.

One moment.

One second to steel herself for what she had been waiting for.

And then she picked up the phone.

"Hello?" Aria asked.

"Mrs. De Rose, this is Warden Kyle Stanford from Curran-Fromhold Correctional Facility. We have some ... uh, well ... are you sitting, Mrs.?"

Aria blinked at the clock on the wall, and watched the secondhand tick down as an entire thirty seconds passed before she answered the man. "I don't need to sit."

"I think perhaps you should, Ma'am."

"I think you should tell me what happened to my father."

It took the man a beat in time.

And then *two*.

"How do you know it's about your father?"

"He's the only person in that facility you would call me about," Aria said dryly.

"Ah, yes. Sorry. It's been a crazy couple of hours here."

Aria glanced over her shoulder, and listened for the guests at her table. None of them had any idea that everything was about to change in their lives again. Another uproar was coming their way fast. Another upset to put them all off balance.

All because of *her*.

Because she manipulated.

Because she needed to.

Aria brought herself back to the conversation with a quiet, "Treat it like a Band-Aid—rip it off fast, please."

The man on the other end of the line cleared his throat, and said, "All right. Your father was having his usual yard time this evening after his dinner, and was shot through the back of his head by a long-range sniper shot. From what we can tell, anyway. Attempts were made to revive him, but ..."

The man trailed off.

Aria nodded to herself.

"They were unsuccessful," she murmured.

"Unfortunately. I am *very* sorry. You should know the officials are involved, and are on their way to you right now."

Of course, they were.

Aria expected no different. The officials would be there in record time, no doubt, to question her about everything and anything they could while going through her home. While the Warden of the prison thought to treat Aria with kindness and respect on the phone, as though she were a victim, the officials most certainly would not be as nice.

Her father was a criminal to them, even if he was a dead one. And she was nothing more than his daughter which meant she was the same kind of scum on the bottom of their shoes.

None of that mattered much to her.

Caesar worked *fast*, though.

She was most surprised about that, really. It had only taken him a few days from the moment she had the photos of them delivered to his father for him to decide to strike back—as she figured he would do, he struck back against her where he thought it would hurt her the most with killing her father. The only opening Aria had given him to see a bit of care she afforded another person *was* her father, after all.

She had news for him.

He was just a puppet.

He moved at her will.

"Thank you for informing me, and on a timely manner," Aria said to the man on the phone.

"I understand this is upsetting, and I didn't want you to hear it through the officials when they showed up at your home. Seems you're a well-known face in my prison, and many of the guards have only nice things to say about you."

Sure.

Because she padded their pockets.

Her father had needed protection, after all, and she had to use what she had to get it to him while he served out his sentence. The thing was— Jac De Rose didn't realize the person he needed protection from the most was the woman he had handed off to a man he should have known would only hurt her time and time again.

Business, he'd said.

Can't dishonor your name, he'd explained.

Keep your reputation intact, he'd demanded.

Yes, well, look at him now.

Six feet under was not a warm place to rest.

Aria said a final goodbye to the prison warden, and hung up the phone. She took another minute to gather her thoughts, and steel her emotions. Everything *was* about to change—in more ways than one, and not just for the people at the table.

For her, life was going to get a little more difficult.

Oh, well.

Win some, lose some.

Aria moved back to the dining room, and stood in the entryway separating the kitchen from the space for the amount of time it took for someone else to notice she hadn't come back in yet. Slowly, one by one, each person at the table quieted as they looked to her for some sort of explanation about her suddenly reserved demeanor.

She took one more breath.

One more second.

"My father was killed today," she said to the room, "someone will need to inform my husband, and ask that he come home. I don't think I should do it."

More like … she didn't *want* to.

The words were no sooner out of her mouth and the room erupted.

Chaos.

Anger.

Disbelief.

Confusion.

She watched it all with a knowing eye, and a detached heart.

Rome wasn't built in a day.
One step closer.

Aria stared at the altar of St. Augustine's Church and watched as the flowers that had surrounded her father's casket were carted away. She never particularly understood the need for flowers at a funeral—no one ever did anything with them but stare at the useless things. It was just another reminder for the grieving about what they had lost when all those flowers they were left to care for started to die one after another in their home.

She loved flowers.

Roses, specifically.

Not for funerals.

The spot where her father's casket had rested was now empty, and the church was mostly quiet. She'd done her part, collected the body when it was released a couple of days after the shooting, and had her father's funeral within a week. She didn't see the point in waiting—even after someone pointed out Raffe would not be home in time to attend.

Shame.

The funeral had been pretty standard—all things considered. Camorra men were typical in the way they lived their life by a code, and that code always demanded they pay the heaviest price should it be necessary, and that they do it happily. That price was death, and so, they planned accordingly.

Aria barely needed to do a thing.

Jac's wishes for a funeral were clear.

"Just about ready to leave when you are," came a voice to Aria's right.

Nico stood waiting in his sharp, three-piece black suit. Even the shirt, tie, and vest underneath were a flat black. She, too, had worn an appropriate knee-length, black dress with a modest neckline, no slit in the skirt, and a hat with a partial veil to keep her face hidden. She didn't need people seeing her dry eyes, and wondering.

"He's sent a car, then?" she asked, sighing.

"He thought you should be home by now."

"I *should.*"

But she had wanted as much time as she could get.

That time was now up, it seemed.

"Do you think I could get away with taking a walk?" she asked. "Or is he already in a rage?"

"I think he's willing to let you stretch the rules a little," Nico returned with a shrug, "you know, all things considered. Your father *did* get buried today. Who wouldn't need a moment?"

A woman like her.

One who was unfeeling.

One that did not care.

Still, Aria took the chance she had, and ran with it. "I think I'll say one more goodbye, then."

Nico nodded. "I will be waiting at the gate for you."

"*Grazie*, Nico."

Aria waited until her friend had drifted back down the aisle of the church before she stood from the pew, and fixed her hat before smoothing her hands over her skirt. She used the east exit of the church that had a pathway leading out to the graveyard. Having already navigated these paths once today as the funeral procession took her father's casket to his final resting spot, it didn't take her long to get back to the gravesite.

Aria stood at the edge of the grave, and peered down. At the bottom of the hole, her father's casket waited to be covered by the mound of dirt still hidden with a tarp to keep it from getting too wet by the drizzling skies. Only a small handful of dirt had been tossed down on the casket by the priest earlier—custom, and nothing more. The black glossy wood still stood out prominently and maybe even with a warning.

She heard it.

This could be you soon.

She didn't heed it.

Gray clouds hung overhead.

It was appropriate.

Even if her father had betrayed her, she still loved him.

Or, a piece of her did.

Strange how that worked.

Bending down, Aria dragged her fingers through the dirt at the edge of the grave. She tossed it inside, and watched it spatter the top of the black casket. The cold detachment she had been feeling in her heart lifted just enough to let her experience the heaviness left behind.

It didn't matter.

She'd made her choices.

"Until we meet again, *Papy*, and then, I hope you've forgiven me," Aria murmured.

Standing straight again, Aria brushed her hands together to rid them of any lingering dirt. She peered up at the gray skies, and let out a little sigh. This was it—time to put her mask back on, and get back to the plan. She had wasted enough time.

Turning to move back down the path and meet up with Nico at the graveyard's gate, she almost stumbled over her knee-high leather boots at the man who was currently leaning against a ten-foot statue of an angel cradling a child in her arms. His intense blue gaze all but nailed her to the spot, and when his lips quirked up in a half-smirk, Aria sucked in a sharp breath.

Still, she straightened her shoulders, and refused to let him see her shock at him showing up at her father's *grave*. And on the day of his funeral, no less.

"Caesar," Aria greeted as she came closer.

He didn't push away from the statue, and his arms stayed loosely folded over his broad chest. In a tailored suit, with his black shoes shining against the pathway, he looked entirely cool, confident, and calm.

"You don't look terribly sad," Caesar noted as his gaze drifted over her features, and then traveled down her body to linger even longer. *Jesus*. This man was something else. "I'm not sure whether to be happy about that, or not. I was hoping for …"

Aria quirked a brow high. "What, for me to be a sobbing mess over my father's grave because you *took him* from me? Would that have pleased you, Caesar?"

Fast as a blink, his gaze cut back up to hers.

That smirk of his deepened.

"Maybe," he offered simply.

There was something about this man's voice that needled at Aria's insides. In good and bad ways. She tried her hardest to ignore it, but it was becoming all the more difficult with each and every encounter they had.

"Well, surprise," Aria deadpanned, "I am not the woman who weeps over a man."

Ever.

Caesar slanted his head to the side, and grinned a bit. "No, I didn't really expect you to be, honestly. I thought I should show my face, and let you know, though. I couldn't have you thinking I was hiding away after all of …" He gestured at her father's grave up the pathway, saying, "… all of this, now could I?"

"That is your modus operandi, isn't it? You like the glory of it all—you have to let someone know it was *you* who hurt or took from them."

"Point is," he returned easily, "you should know now, *donna*. Don't ever fuck with me because I will answer back each time that you do. This time, it was your father. Next time, it'll be someone else I know you care for. I won't be a game for you to play and win—I am no one's pawn. Remember it."

Aria couldn't help herself.

She laughed even as she passed Caesar by.

"Who do you think *really* killed my father, Caesar?"

She didn't give him a chance to answer.

She didn't *care*.

"Has he been drinking?" Aria asked as she walked the path leading up to her home.

Nico, keeping a respectable distance behind her, made a noise under his breath. "I couldn't get a clear answer on that one, and I didn't want to press lest someone get suspicious on why I was asking."

Well, *damn*.

"I'm sure—"

"It's fine," she said quickly.

She didn't want Nico to worry, or concern himself with what might happen once she opened the front door to her home. It would do neither of them any good at the end of the day. He did his best to look out for her from afar, and that was all she could really ask for. Anything else, and he might be the next target.

Straightening her spine and shoulders, Aria kept her head high and gaze straight as she opened the door to her home. She could smell him the moment she walked inside—a strong, masculine musk that he preferred. One that could damn near make her sick to her stomach every time she got a whiff of the cologne.

It reminded her of a heavy, sweaty body pushing her smaller frame over a footboard, and forcing her legs apart. It reminded her of delicate lace being torn away from her body time and time again when all she wanted to say was *no*.

"Aria—*angelo bellissima*."

Aria did her best not to stiffen at Raffe's voice drifting from down the hall. She found him standing in the shadows between the enclave of the kitchen and the light in the hallway. Tall, large, and formidable, he was not the kind of man a woman wanted to meet in an empty alleyway in the dark.

And yet, she had been forced to meet him in the dark for a year and a half.

"Raffe," she replied kindly.

Somehow.

Aria found it easy to keep her attention off her husband as she removed her coat, and shoes. Hanging the items up on the coat hanger with her purse as well, she turned only to find Raffe had moved silently down the hall to stand in front of her.

Nico had not come inside.

The house was *empty*.

It was just … them.

She peered up at her husband—he towered over her by inches.

"I'm sorry I didn't get back in time for the funeral," he said.

Aria nodded. "You couldn't help the delay."

And frankly, she was grateful for it.

The less time with him, the better.

Raffe's dark eyes drifted over her features with the slow grace of a predator taking in his prey before he pounced. His hand came up to cup her cheek, and his thumb stroked her skin with a softness she knew was a lie.

"I will handle the Italians for what they did," he murmured.

"I have no doubt."

"You will need to step back, now, you know. I'm home—let the boss handle this little problem. I am sure I will get it done in no time at all, and we will have the territory we want to show for it. Hell, maybe even more."

He posed those words like all her efforts had been in vain. As though she hadn't gotten anywhere, or gained any ground on the Accardo organization. And maybe she hadn't—not in a way that Raffe would see as good, anyhow.

That hadn't been the point.

She put something *else* in motion.

That's what she needed.

"I'm sure you've been enjoying playing the little queen, though," Raffe murmured, his hand drifting from her cheek to rest on the side of her throat. Still soft to the touch, though, so she forced herself not to stiffen. "You have enjoyed it, haven't you?"

"I tend to be good at it," she replied.

"You do; that's fair, my sweet girl. But you *will* step back now."

Aria nodded. "Of course."

To *him*, anyway.

Then, Raffe's hand tightened roughly around Aria's throat, and she instinctively sucked in a breath at the harsh action. His fingers dug into her neck, and her airways constricted.

"Now, do you care to explain to me why Giovanna has been to visit several times, but you were nowhere to be found? Or why there's rumors that you were leaving the house late at night without the proper people knowing?"

Shit.

Sometimes, things were just too good to be true.

"Nico took me to the movies," she lied, "and I had business, also. I always had someone with me."

Raffe's gaze narrowed, and he tilted his head back to search her face for any lie. "Giovanna says—"

"Giovanna doesn't like being punished for stepping out of line against me, Raffe."

And the bitch would *die* for this.

Aria guaranteed it.

Raffe's hold loosened. "Maybe so."

"There's no maybe about it. She's a petty cunt who enjoys the misfortune of others, but especially when she is the cause of it. She doesn't even try to hide it, Raffe."

"Yes, well, at least the woman is warmer than you when she's told to please a man."

Aria blinked.

He was *fucking* Giovanna?

"Does Simone know you're—"

"Mind your business," her husband snapped. Then, he twisted her around, grabbed the back of her neck, and pushed her down the hallway. "Meet me at the foot of our bed. Be naked by the time I get there."

Aria said nothing.

She simply went.

NINE

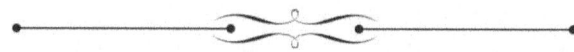

CAESAR SLIPPED HIS hand into the pocket of his slacks, and silenced the phone that wouldn't stop vibrating with one call after another. He didn't even bother to check who the caller was, but no doubt, it was his father asking if he had made his flight.

To Canada, that was.

Caesar glanced down the familiar city street of Philadelphia, and grinned.

Nope.

He sure hadn't.

And he wouldn't.

As long as he could avoid Angelo for a while, then he wasn't too worried about whatever his father might have to say or try to do about Caesar refusing to follow through on his orders. Besides, for the moment, Caesar had other things to do.

Better things to do.

He couldn't do them in Canada.

Angelo wasn't going to understand that his son was practically obsessed with knowing and understanding every little detail he could about Aria De Rose—only so that he could use it against her, of course. She thought to use Caesar like a pawn in her game, whatever it was that she was playing, and he had news for her.

It wasn't happening.

The woman was smart, though.

Keen, really.

Deceptive.

Manipulative.

Quick as hell.

Any other time, and he might have appreciated the cunningness that was Aria, but not so much when it was his ass on the line.

Who do you think really killed my father?

Caesar hadn't been able to forget those words since she told them to him three days earlier in a graveyard. It had been with those words that his decision was cemented—he wouldn't be leaving Philly, and his business with this woman was far from fucking finished.

He had killed her father. He had put it into motion, and paid the hefty goddamn price for the job. He had done all of that.

But now he was left wondering … *why?*

Nothing with Aria was what it seemed to be—her surface was not even close to being similar to what was inside. He had figured out she was quick to direct people to the things she wanted them to see, or know about her, for that matter. And she made a very careful effort to hide her real motives, and actions.

Caesar had gone after her father because *she* mentioned him; she had made sure to bring the man into her conversation with him, and plant the seed. Like a fucking weed Caesar hadn't even known it was there, it grew, and he chose to use it against her.

But had it really been against *her?*

Or had it been *for* her?

A part of him was amazed, and another part of him was infuriated. *And all for a fucking woman.*

Across the street from Caesar's position, a black Mercedes pulled up along the side of the road. The windows—tinted a dark black—kept the passengers from his view. That was fine as he didn't need to see who was inside to know who it was.

After all, these people were creatures of habit.

Or so he was coming to learn.

First, the car stayed idling in a *No Parking Zone* for a good two minutes before the driver's door opened. It wasn't the first sight Caesar had gotten of Aria's husband, Raffaele Ferri; he'd been tailing the two ever since the man arrived back in the country. The bull of a man was nearly as tall as he was wide with dark hair he liked to keep slicked back with some kind of gel or oil.

Raffe—as Caesar had been told the man liked to be called—had eyes that never stopped darting from one thing to the next as though something might jump out at him. In three days, Caesar had seen the man intimidate the men who worked for him, stay permanently close to his wife's side whenever they were out, and make his daily rounds around the city.

That was how Caesar knew where they would be today.

Yeah.

Creatures of habit.

Raffe was quick to move around the front of the Mercedes, and when he came up to the passenger side, he waved his finger in a circle at the window. A silent order for the person in the passenger seat to roll it down.

She did.

Aria, that was.

Even in the shadows of the car, Caesar had a perfect view of Aria sitting in the passenger seat with her hair down in loose curls, and a scarf fixed around her throat. That was probably the first time he'd ever seen her wear anything other than a necklace or choker.

Not that it mattered.

Her gaze drifted to her husband as Raffe leaned down to speak to her, but it was the shake of her head at whatever he said that made the man stiffen. She shrugged, and then gestured at him before nodding at the restaurant they were parked in front of.

One Raffe regularly visited.

It took another minute or two of the husband and wife talking before Raffe stood up straight, and nodded once. Then, he slapped a hand against the hood of the car before he darted back around the front of the car. Three seconds later, and the man disappeared inside the entrance doors of the business.

No doubt, Raffe would be busy inside the restaurant for a good twenty minutes or more. Caesar didn't know what kind of business the man had here, but he always left with a doggy bag of food in one hand, and a thick manila envelope in the other. Dinner *and* cash ... fascinating.

Except Caesar didn't care.

At all.

Now's my chance.

Caesar hadn't gotten one of those in days—a chance, that was. Not one to approach Aria, anyway. Her husband rarely left her side, and now that he was back in the country, it seemed the woman couldn't even leave her house without the man next to her.

The graveyard had been a spur of the moment decision, and looking back, maybe a bad one at that. Then again, Caesar had never had much respect for the dead, or their grieving family. He didn't care for rules that dictated his behavior or what was expected of him. In fact, he was known to do exactly the opposite of everything he was told to do just because he fucking could. And so, he had gone just to see ...

Lucky him that she had been alone.

That he could get her alone.

Kind of like now.

Caesar pushed out from under the enclave entrance to a small café, and into the bright sunlight of the day. Across the street from the business, it had kept him hidden well enough from view, and allowed him the chance to wait.

Plus have a drink of coffee.

Win-win.

Caesar dropped his to-go cup in a trash bin just before he stepped out onto the quiet street, and shoved his hands in his pockets. His aviator sunglasses kept his gaze hidden from view as he came closer to the vehicle Aria was waiting inside.

Her gaze drifted to the side, and caught him coming her way just as she had started to roll up the window—it was a little hot out, he supposed. The sight of her eyes widening almost made him smile.

Fuck.

She always looked good when he surprised her.

"Question," Caesar said as he came up to the side of the car. "If you wouldn't mind answering, that is."

Aria's surprise quickly melted into anger as she glanced between him at her window, and the restaurant. "What do you *want?*"

"Oh, we can't talk now?"

"I don't—"

"You didn't really expect to leave me at the cemetery with that little nugget about killing your father, and then think I *wouldn't* want to know more, did you?"

She turned her head, and kept her eyes on the stretch of road and walkway in her windshield. Even with Caesar now leaning against the car, she all out refused to even look at him. Any other time, and he might have been fucking offended.

Today, he just found it amusing.

"Leave," Aria murmured. "It's the only warning I can give you."

"Can't do that, actually. Sorry."

She sighed, and glanced down at her lap. "What do you want?"

Caesar reached inside the window, and fingered the small golden tassel on the end of the scarf wrapped around her pretty neck. "This is new—I think I like your throat naked more, though."

As quickly as he had touched her, Aria was quick to slap his hand away. Her gaze burned when it turned on him again—hateful and bitter in a blink.

"*Don't.*"

Caesar put his hands up in mock surrender. "My apologies. I can't touch you now that your husband is back in town, or what?"

All that fight and fire seemed to drain out of the woman in a *breath.* With nothing more than a simple question from him, and she reverted back to the pretty little doll staring out the window. A doll with no expression, no emotion, and probably no fucking brain.

It irked him.

Pissed him off.

This was not the woman who had tricked him—the woman who had made his dick as hard as steel just as easily as she had irritated him. And at the same goddamn time, too. No, this wasn't that woman, and he had no intention of dealing with this fucking *shell* of her, either.

This was not what he wanted at all.

He wanted to fuck with her.

Like she had fucked with him.

Fine.

Then, he would try for something a little more pointed if this wasn't getting a reaction out of her.

"That question I asked about," Caesar said.

"You really need to go," she deadpanned.

"Nah, I'm good." Caesar kneeled down a bit to rest his arms along the window ledge of the door, and stared straight at Aria even though she refused to look at him. "That question—was it for him, your husband, I mean?"

"Was *what* for him?"

"Killing your father. I didn't forget what you told me, after all. So, if I am to assume you manipulated me in to doing that for whatever reason—since apparently nothing I do is because I actually chose to do it when it comes to you—then *why?* I figured … it must have been for him. It's Raffe, right?"

She stiffened at her husband's name.

Maybe she didn't like Caesar saying it.

So, he did it again.

"Yeah, Raffe, they told me," he murmured. "And now that your father is out of the picture, I bet it's your husband that'll be heading your little clan."

Heat colored her cheeks with a light red.

Anger flashed in her eyes.

Still, she stayed quiet, and unmoving.

"Was that it—all your work was to move your husband along in your business while you had the chance?"

He got nothing in response.

Not even a blink of those long, dark lashes.

Goddammit.

"I wonder," Caesar drawled, going for broke, "how he would feel then to know that you did *everything* you possibly could for his cause—including getting on your back for me, and spreading those legs of yours as wide as you could? Would he care that I know what your pussy tastes like, or how you sound when you're screaming my name? *Would he*, Aria? Do you care to find out?"

Her throat constricted beneath that silk scarf at the same time her eyes closed. A tic showed in her cheek, but just as quickly, she relaxed and opened her eyes again. Only this time, she wasn't staring out the window.

No, she was looking at *him.*

Caesar didn't see the anger or fear he had hoped to find looking back in her gaze, but there was a threat. A silent promise of violence coming his way, and *fast*, if he continued to stay in her path.

Hurricane Aria.

Beautiful.

Enthralling.

Dangerous.

It was fitting.

Finally, something.

He had gotten something from her.

Caesar flashed her one of his grins. "You know, it's better he learns now what kind of woman you are—that *all* women are exactly the same when it comes right down to it. They'll do whatever they want to get what they want. They don't give a fuck who they harm in the process. You're not any different. You'll still get on your knees or spread your legs for a man the same way the next one will."

He couldn't hide the heat in his words.

The *hate.*

Not even his pain.

Not pain because of her, no, but pain nonetheless. Pain he refused to indulge because it all too often left him in a terrible and desperate place. A place that led him to bad and rash decisions, and left him with a deep need to hurt others just to get rid of his own ache; to get rid of his own *shame.*

No one could possibly understand.

But he was right.

"All women do this," he told her, "just in different ways."

Aria was silent for a long stretch before she finally spoke again. "That's it, isn't it?"

"Excuse me?"

"*Women*," she clarified. "For you, that's what it is. You hate women. Why do you hate them so much, Caesar? What woman hurt you this badly that this is the first place your mind goes when you feel slighted by a female—to a place where you have to hurt her, and humiliate her with something like sex?"

Caesar chuckled dryly, and stood straight. "What, do you think you don't *deserve* what I am doing to you?"

"Oh, Caesar ..." Aria shook her head, and gave him a pitying look. "You're not doing anything to me that I didn't already expect. I did ask for you to step back—to help me that way so that we could both get what he wanted. Remember, I tried to *warn* you."

Wait, what?

Caesar opened his mouth to ask just that, but the man stepping out of the restaurant earlier than he should have kept him quiet. Raffe's gaze narrowed in on Caesar standing beside the car the second he stepped into the light.

The rage in the man's eyes should have been a clue to leave.

The mask of calm Raffe kept firmly in place was a *lie.*

"He has people watch me all the time," Aria murmured, her gaze never drifting from the windshield. "Why do you think I wouldn't even *look* at you? I can't entertain even the idea of impropriety. I warned you."

Again with that shit.

He didn't hear warnings.

He only heard challenges.

A smaller man—with no pride and a hell of lot less ego—might have taken a step back from the car, or even made an effort to put more distance between themselves and the man coming their way, but Caesar wasn't that guy. Arrogant to a fault, even if it was the very thing that might kill him one day.

He couldn't help it.

He was who he was.

"Caesar, right?" Raffe asked, dark eyes narrowing into vicious slits. "Yeah, Angelo Accardo's oldest fucking prick. I haven't gotten the chance to speak with your father since I got back in the city, but today seems like a good damn place to start—a lesson, if you will. I think you're all due one. Especially where my fucking territory is concerned."

"This isn't your territory," Caesar returned. "These streets are no man's land."

And it was well known.

Raffe laughed darkly. "I'm not talking about the streets, *cafone*. Step away from my *wife* before I use your head and the cement to make a piece of conceptual art for my goddamn living room."

Damn.

Caesar always did appreciate a good threat.

Even if it was on his life.

Aria still hadn't moved. Her gaze never drifted away from the window.

Raffe came closer; Caesar refused to move.

The two men came toe-to-toe next to the car, and Raffe reached in to cup Aria's cheek with a large palm that all but swallowed half of the side of her face whole. Caesar didn't miss the way her eye twitched, or how her flinch came and went all in a blink.

But he had seen it.

And he wondered …

"I'm sure you know the baseball analogy," Raffe said, drawing Caesar's attention away. "This is strike one for breaking my rules—now your family loses something for it."

Caesar smirked even in the face of the man's rage. "Is that a threat? My father doesn't take kindly to threats."

"You—"

"But me?" Caesar asked. "Well, I fucking love them."

Raffe nodded, and his white teeth flashed in a half-sneer. "Good to know. Unfortunately, you haven't had to deal with me yet in this business as my wife has been handling it. So, it's a good time to learn, isn't it? Don't ever approach my wife again. And do let your father know what comes next could have been avoided, and should he want to prevent it from happening again, then I am willing to negotiate for what I want."

"*Call from Cain,*" said the robotic voice over the speakers of Caesar's 1969 Corvette. The Bluetooth and stereo system was just about the only thing that *wasn't* vintage on the car.

"Answer," Caesar said.

Cain's voice came over the speakers not a second later. "We've got a fucking problem, man."

"If it's that my father is calling you because I won't pick up his calls, then I really don't consider that a fucking problem, Cain."

"What—*no.*"

Caesar's attention was firmly on the road, and on the fact that he was nearly home. Another block, and he could get inside his place, shut out the world, and figure out his next move against Aria ... or her fucking husband.

Yes, that sounded—

"Alice is dead," Cain said.

Caesar saw black smoke coloring the sky at the same time his friend said three words he never really expected to hear. He was stuck between trying to figure out a response for his friend, and realizing that smoke in the sky was coming from ... shit, *his* penthouse apartment at the top of the apartment building.

He could already see it from a block away.

He knew it was gone.

He just ... *knew.*

"Delivered flowers ... doorstep ... your brother was upstairs when it went off ... not hurt ... she's dead."

Yeah, yeah, yeah.

Cain droned on.

Caesar drove slower until he was forced to pull his Corvette to a stop behind a barricade set up by a team of several firetrucks. Probably trying to contain the blaze.

He probably should have been sad about his half-brother's wife, but he hadn't felt anything for that woman since the moment she jerked him off under the table at a family dinner, and then let him up her skirt. That was just how it worked for him, really. He couldn't change it.

Hey, at least Daniele survived.

"The boss got a call right after—Raffe Ferri claiming the bomb on

Daniele and Alice," Cain added.

Caesar nodded, figuring that's what it was.

Shit.

The man didn't waste time.

He gave a threat; he followed through.

Interesting …

"Caesar, did you hear anything I just said?" his friend asked.

"He doesn't fuck around, huh?"

"*What?*"

"Raffe—he threatened the Accardos today when I had a run-in with him. Said we were going to lose something."

Caesar's whole life—his only safe place in the world—was burning down right before his eyes, and he felt cold all over.

"You're going to need to get to your father's place, Caesar."

"I guess Canada is a bust for now."

"Why are you—"

"Gonna call that a win," Caesar added in a murmur.

Silver linings.

Even if his home was burning.

"Are you okay?"

No.

No, he wasn't okay at all.

Far from it.

He just had to figure out what he was going to do about it.

TEN

"SMILE."

Raffe's order raked like hot coals over Aria's nerve endings, but she did as he told her. He gave her a little nod from the driver's seat as he navigated the car into a parking spot close to the front door of a restaurant *she* preferred.

At least, he had given her that today.

"*Bene*," Raffe murmured in praise, his hand snaking across the middle of the vehicle to curve tightly around her thigh under Aria's skirt. "It's about time you stop pouting—you need to do this, and you know why."

She hoped Raffe didn't feel her shiver.

Or see the fire in her eyes.

It was getting harder to hide it.

"Better business, I know," she said.

"Yes, and after those tricks I pulled on the Accardo family last week, we cannot afford for any of our clan to be fighting when we have to be focusing on the bigger picture. Even the *women* of our clan."

"Have they called yet? The Accardos, I mean."

Aria was out of the loop more often than not now that her husband was back in the picture. Raffe, like he *always* did, stepped in, took control, and managed every little detail down to the very last thing someone might think of. He didn't care to fill Aria in on things he didn't think were important for her to know.

Especially now that she wasn't handling it all.

It irked her.

How could she plan when she didn't know what she was fucking planning for? How could she work her angles when she didn't know when the corners were coming? How could she keep her secrets from Raffe when—

Raffe arched a brow. "Not yet."

Aria let out a tiny breath.

To her husband, it might have sounded like frustration. To her, it was an exhale of relief because *yes*, she was still one step ahead of Raffe.

At least, for now.

He still didn't know the things she had done to get them where they currently were with the Accardos, and if she could help it, he would never know until it was too fucking late. She had been banking on the fact that Angelo Accardo wouldn't want his own people to know his son had been messing with the enemy, too.

But all that guesswork was just that—a *guess*.

"Are you dallying now?" Raffe asked sharply.

Aria passed him a look, and then the restaurant, too. "I thought we were talking, actually."

"Well, now we're done. Go to your lunch, and make nice like I know you can. Be *pleasant*."

Yes.

Be pleasant to a woman who had challenged Aria at every turn, spoke out against her, and was very possibly fucking her husband. Although, she really didn't give a shit about that last one at all. She had no care or concern for her husband in the grand scheme of things. Certainly not enough to try and stake claim over him because of petty jealousy.

The bitch could *have him*.

Aria nodded, and reached for the passenger door handle. It was Raffe's voice that made her hesitate just a moment longer.

"And remember, Nico is watching—he'll report back. I'll be three blocks over checking on some business."

Yes, Nico …

She smiled slyly.

Raffe didn't see it because she was already getting out of the car, and closing the door behind her. He revved the engine—another warning to Aria—as she rounded the front of the Mercedes, and headed for the restaurant's entrance. He didn't even pull away and drive off until she was safely inside the place.

Aria hadn't even gotten a glimpse of Nico, but it didn't matter. He was *watching*.

She checked her watch—quarter after twelve, it read. Fifteen more minutes. Nico would do his job. It just wouldn't be for Raffe.

Aria might not have been in the game to her husband, but she was sure as hell still playing what angles she could to make sure the plans she had worked so hard for went down how *she* wanted and needed them to.

She did a quick survey of the restaurant, and the small bar. Her guest was nowhere to be seen as she stepped up to the podium to speak with the woman tapping on a tablet.

"Mrs. De Rose," she greeted, never glancing up. "Private room today?"

"As usual."

"Follow me, then. Your husband won't be joining you?"

"Not today."

Unfortunately.

"But I will have another guest," Aria added.

This whole thing might have gotten rid of him, too, but Raffe had other things to do. He didn't like to go along with whatever Aria asked of him. But she damn well better do everything he asked of her.

Funny how that worked.

Aria kept a close watch on the time even as she was led into the private area, she seated herself to the right side of the table just offset from the large windows, and her wine glass was filled halfway with a pink Rosé. No schnapps today. She needed to be fully alert, and ready to fucking move when the time called for it.

She only grew more irritated the longer her guest made her wait. Whether they showed up or not, the show was still going to go down at twelve-thirty sharp.

"Drinking this early in the day, Aria?"

And there she is.

Aria tilted her head just enough to get Giovanna Bruno in her sights, and smiled coldly. "I think this whole lunch calls for a drink, doesn't it?"

"You can't even pretend to like me, can you?"

Even as the woman spoke, she moved across the private dining room, and sat down opposite to Aria on the other side of the table. In full view of the windows overlooking the busy main street in front of the restaurant.

Exactly where she needed to be.

"Why would I pretend anything?" Aria asked.

Giovanna—in her tight red dress, full makeup, and perfectly coiffed black hair—seemed almost *smug*. And Aria wouldn't be surprised if the woman felt like this whole day and lunch between them was some kind of battle won for her.

A lunch Raffe ordered.

Peace he wanted.

Apologies from Aria.

Giovanna's respect intact.

It was never going to happen.

"Why would I pretend to give a shit about the woman who acts against me?" Aria asked quietly. "Or who fucks my husband, and thinks I don't know about it?"

Giovanna's face turned a molten red at Aria's statement, but she was more interested in checking the time on her watch.

12:29 PM.

Almost.

Aria glanced up. "Oh, and don't try to deny it. I really don't care. I do wish that if he was busy fucking someone else, he would leave me the hell alone. But we don't always get what we want, do we?"

"I—"

"Is he softer-handed to you in bed than he is to me?" Aria laughed, and tugged the scarf away from her neck that had become a permanent fixture in her life again since Raffe's return. Giovanna's gaze drifted to the dotting of bruises along the side of Aria's neck—all in different shades of healing. Fingerprints imbedded into her skin where Raffe liked to grab and squeeze for any number of reasons. He was not careful. He didn't stop when he was told to. She didn't want *him* touching her at all—certainly not like this. "For your sake, I hope he was."

Giovanna's gaze snapped back to Aria at that remark. "Was—that implies it won't happen again."

It was a familiar black sedan slowing a bit down the street outside of the restaurant that caught Aria's gaze, and her attention momentarily. Just as fast—because the show was about to start, and she couldn't afford to make a mistake—her attention went back to Giovanna.

"Because it won't. You'll be dead. You should have known better. Anyone who gets in my way *dies*."

Giovanna opened her mouth to speak. Aria dropped to the floor as soon as the bullets started flying. It was chaos—utter pandemonium from the glass breaking to the gunfire, and even the people screaming who were safe and secure in the main restaurant area.

They didn't know they were safe, though.

Only one person was meant to die today.

It was a lot to take in, and Aria's only job was really just to stay low to the floor, and keep herself safe until the bullets stopped coming.

She got to hear the bitch next to her take her last breath, though.

Nico was a damn good shot—even with an Uzi.

That made it worth it.

"*Get out!*"

Raffe's roar sent the two nurses in Aria's hospital room scattering like little mice that had been caught in the sights of a cat. It would almost be amusing if it wasn't for the fact his attention was now on her.

In three long strides, he was in front of her. Hands on her face, and clouding her vision. She had gotten two blissful hours of being away from this man while she was transported to a hospital and then checked over by the doctor in the emergency room. And all that went to shit when Raffe walked in through the doors.

"What happened?" he asked.

His grip on her face tightened a bit, and she winced. A bit of glass from the shattering windows had left scrapes on her right cheek, and a small cut on the back of her left hand. Nothing that was terrible, but it didn't feel good when he was pushing on it.

"Be easy," she returned.

Raffe loosened up. "Sorry. I was worried about you, *bambola*."

She had all she could do not to cringe when he called her a *doll*.

"They didn't say who died," he continued, "and I didn't know ..."

He sounded genuinely hurt—*scared*, even. It was such a bright contrast to the way he treated her. Apparently, it was only okay to hurt her as long as it was him who did it. And of course, he could justify it.

Ah.

So, he could be easy.

He could be sweet.

Aria no longer cared.

"I'm fine," she said.

That had been the point, after all.

She would like to get back into her dress—even if it was bloodstained—and get home to take a shower. As much as she had wanted Giovanna dead, she didn't feel like using spatters of the woman's blood on her face and arms as a facial mask, or anything of the sort. Having blood on her hands was only good in the proverbial sense.

"Barely," Raffe grumbled, shooting a dark look over his shoulder.

In the corner, Nico stayed quiet and unmoving. He watched the exchange with a cold eye, but never stepped in or spoke up.

As was his job.

Raffe didn't want to hear the man speak—he only wanted him to follow orders when he was given them. Nothing more, and nothing less.

"And where were *you*?" Raffe asked Nico.

"Inside."

Lies.

He'd been behind the trigger.

"As you told me to be," Nico returned.

"I didn't see your car when I pulled up."

"Because I parked it around back."

Raffe's gaze narrowed, and Aria knew she needed to figure out a way to divert his attention back to her, and *fast*. "Had she been hurt, it would have been your head."

"She is *fine*, Raffe. She is smart and quick. She knows what to do in a bad situation which was exactly what she did."

Yes, *that*.

She gave Nico a subtle nod, but he didn't return it. He couldn't with Raffe's gaze currently nailing him to the wall, and looking for any sign of a lie.

"I guess there's a reason why the Accardo family didn't call for that meeting," Aria said.

That did it.

Raffe's attention was back on her. Over his shoulder, she saw Nico relax a slight bit. Not a lot, but it was enough for him to roll his eyes, and take a quick breath.

"Because they had their own plan to answer me back," Raffe murmured, his thumbs roving over her cheeks with a soft touch. Oh, it felt nice, sure. Had he been a kinder man, she might have enjoyed his attention and affection. Except she didn't, and he was nothing more than a lie wrapped in a pretty package. "I would say the diplomatic way to resolve this has now passed after today."

It had passed a long time ago.

Aria made sure of that.

She wanted *war*.

She wanted Raffe to die.

And it couldn't be by her hand.

"You'll have to go for a bit," he told her with a nod. "Head out of the city to be safe, and settle in somewhere else where they can't find you. Let me handle what I need to for this to be over. Understood?"

She didn't want to be away.

She needed to be here.

Aria didn't get a choice; besides, being away meant not being under Raffe's control all the damn time, and that gave her another opportunity.

And when opportunity knocks ...

"Where do you want me to go?" she asked.

Raffe smiled. "Nico knows where."

Of course, he did.

The highway was dark, and the sedan was quiet. Nico focused on the road ahead of him while Aria stayed lost in her thoughts. It had been like this for a good hour, but she knew her companion was just about ready to spill his thoughts in a vomit of words.

He was predictable like that.

Aria prepped for it.

They drove another fifteen minutes before Nico finally spoke for the first time since they had left the house with a bag of Aria's things in hand.

"You were lucky today," he murmured.

"We had the whole thing planned out to a—"

"No, I mean with *Raffe*. We both know he isn't a stupid man, Aria. You pull too many tricks on him, and he will start to notice. When do you think he's going to notice or figure out that it's actually you who has been rising tensions between our clan and the Accardos? And when he does figure that out, it's one step away from him figuring out *why*."

"You know," she mused, "that might not be such a bad thing. Him figuring out the why, I mean. A part of me wants him to know it's because of me that he'll die. It would be even better if that was the last thing on his mind before his heart stopped beating."

She took great joy in that thought.

The idea made her *gleeful*.

"You are playing with fire," Nico muttered heavily.

"This is my only way to be rid of him—he won't let me go unless he kills me. I will finally be rid of him. He was forced on me, and I was given to him like a pretty little gift. All I did—my whole life was to be exactly what my father wanted of me, and furthering his cause. I did everything he wanted!"

"I know," Nico said quietly.

"And look at what he did to me. *Look*. He gave me to a man who raped me on my wedding night, and who hurts me all the time. And *what of you*, Nico?" she snapped, glaring at him from the passenger seat. "What, you want me to back off or be safe because he might find out? It doesn't *matter*. I have come too far and done too much to back off now. This is my *one chance*."

Nico quieted, and his gaze drifted to her.

Pity stared back.

Empathy.

"Don't look at me like that," she mumbled, turning her gaze to the passenger window. "You know I hate it when you pity me like that, Nico."

"I wasn't pitying you."

"It sure looked like it."

"I was thinking … I don't think you would be the Aria De Rose you are now without the things that have been done to you. Would you give her up if you could choose something—someone other than Raffe?"

She didn't even have to think about it.

"No."

She was who she was.

And she would *win*.

"You know," Aria said, peering back at Nico, "you never did tell me why Raffe thinks you're gay."

And why he trusted him enough that Raffe assumed Nico would never even consider touching Aria in a less than innocent way.

Nico shrugged. "He saw me kissing a man once in a club."

Her brow shot up. "*What?*"

Her friend laughed. "My tastes vary. I never said I was gay—never said

I was straight, either. It all depends on my mood."

Huh.

"And you … never thought to correct his assumption?"

"Why would I?" Nico asked. "It's none of his fucking business, and it worked well for you in the end, didn't it?"

"I suppose."

The two quieted for a while longer.

It was him who broke the silence.

"He's got you a room at a hotel in New Jersey—under a different name, of course."

Aria nodded. "And is my shadow still following me?"

Caesar, she meant.

He hadn't stopped tailing her in *weeks.*

She was banking on him still being close behind.

"As far as I know," Nico said, "or he's got someone doing it for him. They do have a funeral to handle tomorrow, you know. I believe he will be there given it was his sister-in-law killed by Raffe's bomb."

Aria nodded to herself. "Good, good."

She suspected—and hoped, despite always saying hope was for the weak—that Caesar Accardo would not let her get out of his sights for too long. He didn't give a shit what his father was doing, or what her husband was planning. He only cared about figuring out *Aria's* plans, and working against them.

That meant, he would need to be wherever the hell she was. He would not let her leave the city without soon following behind.

"You left a trail for him to find, didn't you?" Aria asked.

Nico sighed. "I did, but I still think that might be a bad choice. Caesar is unpredictable—you can't plan for every single one of his moves, but especially when they are against you."

"And yet, even when he moves against me, he still seems to work for me, doesn't he?"

Nico didn't reply to that statement. "You need to be careful with that—"

"I need to use what I have, and Caesar Accardo is one of those things."

She couldn't possibly lose.

Not now.

ELEVEN

A CHAOTIC ACCARDO home was one Caesar knew well, and could handle. A tense one was even more familiar to him, especially if the cause of said tension was *him*. A sad Accardo home, however ... one silenced with sadness and grief was not one he cared to be inside, or anywhere near, for that matter.

It reminded him far too much of being four years young again, and watching person after person file into his childhood home dressed in all black. He'd been a small child—even for his age—and people towered over him with their apologies, red-rimmed eyes, and sad faces. Some had bent down to give him a hug, and apologize for the woman who rested in a shiny white casket in the middle of the living room.

His mother, that was.

Caesar had never understood why his father allowed the viewing of his mother's body to be in their home—he'd never cared to ask, either. All he knew was that here he was over two decades later, and he still couldn't walk into that living room without seeing the pale alabaster face of his mother resting in white silk.

His father had never told him before that day or the years that followed how his mother died. Or why she had to wear a purple dress in her casket with sleeves that covered her wrists. He'd heard enough that day, and those words had stuck with him over the years, for him to know exactly why.

Shame she lost the baby, some had said.

Couldn't get over it, someone else whispered.

The worst kind of sin.

Slit her wrists.

Angelo had found Caesar's mother in what would have been the baby's nursery. Although, apparently, his mother hadn't quite got far enough along in her second pregnancy to even know the gender of the child. None of that had made a difference, as the apparent depression she fell into after losing the baby had hung on despite everything she had around her. Despite her marriage, her four-year-old son, and even her life full of wealth.

None of it helped.

None of it brought her back, either.

That was the thing about loss, though.

It didn't matter how small.

Or how insignificant.

Loss was still loss.

The loss of Caesar's mother had been small in the grand scheme of his life—at least, to the appearance of others. A death that happened when he was young, and when most people believed he probably wouldn't remember a lot about his mother.

How wrong they were ...

He remembered her smile; how she smelled first thing in the morning when he crawled into bed beside her. He remembered the sound of her voice when she read him books; how much she enjoyed singing in the shower. He couldn't possibly forget that she liked wearing white the most, even when she wasn't supposed to.

And he never forgot how she loved him.

Or rather ... how she was supposed to love him.

Then, she left him.

It was mere months after his mother's suicide when a new woman walked into his house, and filled the empty spot next to his father's side. *Months* ... and then years of confusion and shame followed.

Caesar did his best to avoid funerals—*all* funerals, really—but especially ones where his father invited people into his home after for dinner or whatever the case may be. It always threw him back to his mother's viewing, and then as a byproduct because it was fucking unavoidable ... *that death* had been the one catalyst ... he then had to think about what happened after, too.

So, no, he didn't want to be here.

He didn't want to fucking remember at all.

And yet, here he was.

It was almost over, though.

Small blessings.

Caesar tipped his glass of cognac up, and took a sip. At least, if he had a drink in his hand or his mouth was full of liquor, he was less likely to be approached by someone and need to talk. He had been told by his father to be polite, and respectful.

Today wasn't about him.

His half-brother needed to say goodbye.

Right.

In the corner of the living room, Daniele sat in a chair while he nursed his fifth glass of whiskey. He barely moved, and if he did, it was only to ask someone to get him another drink. For all the hell Caesar had put his half-brother through, and despite how much he thought the man despised his wife after everything that happened ... clearly he had been mistaken.

Daniele was *grieving*.

He hurt.

Maybe it was the mother thing for Caesar again—or just all the fucking terrible reminders keeping his shoulders heavy and his mind dark— but he actually felt bad for his half-brother. He felt some kind of empathy for a man he had only wanted to hurt time and time again before today, and he wasn't quite sure what to do with it.

Beside his half-brother, his step-mother had perched on the arm of the chair and comforted her son with a hand rubbing his back as she said things too low for anyone else in the room to hear. It was only the sight of Martina that really ebbed away whatever care he did muster up for Daniele.

Fuck.

A constantly drunk mother comforting her grieving, drunk son.

How fucking *sweet.*

Caesar hated that woman—being in her presence was more than enough to bring up every tangible emotion that he fought daily to suppress for two fucking decades. All his anger, confusion, and *shame.* All the ways he knew how to kill a person and how easily he could do it to her flooded his thoughts, and taunted him.

Because he *could.*

He could ... he could.

Jesus Christ.

He could do it.

She would deserve it.

And yet, the closer he got to her ... the nearer she was to him, the more disgusting he felt. The worse his mind became, and the faster his heart beat. An anxious, hard beat that flooded his veins with a torrent of *pain.* An ache so deep—so fucking embedded into his very being—that it was never coming out now.

He'd lived with it—and *her*—for far too long.

There was just no way around it.

The departing guests at the mansion gave Caesar the chance to step out, and say goodbye to a couple. At least, it got him out of his step-mother's direct vicinity. The more distance he put between himself and her, the better he felt.

It was only when the final guests drifted from the Accardo mansion did Caesar's father finally come and find him sitting on the back deck staring up at the stars. He didn't even bother to greet his father, or acknowledge Angelo's presence for that matter.

Caesar wasn't really needed here today. He certainly hadn't been wanted.

His presence had likely only been a painful reminder for his half-brother about the ways his wife had betrayed him—and with his own blood, no less. Still, to keep the peace and the Accardo reputation intact for their people, Angelo demanded Caesar be there, dressed appropriately for the funeral, and to keep his fucking mouth shut.

Well, I kept up my end of the bargain.

So far.

"We need to talk," Angelo said as he settled his hefty form into the wicker chair beside Caesar's.

"If it's about Canada, save your breath."

Because he *was not* going.

"It is, actually. You might want to shut up, and listen to what I have to say. It could be ... beneficial, *figlio*."

Caesar highly doubted that. "Unless it's to call off the arrangement you have for the marriage, then—"

"It is, yes."

He eyed his father from the side, but Angelo was otherwise distracted by staring up at the inky sky. It was one of the good things about the estate being outside the limits of the city and away from all the pollution and lights—one could actually see the stars.

"Go on," Caesar urged.

"Oh, now you want to talk?"

"Can we not play games? I did what you wanted today—played along more than enough. I won't be doing any of that after this moment, though. Especially not when it comes to Canada, or that bullshit arrangement you came up with."

Angelo's lips flattened into a grim line, and his gaze drifted from the sky to Caesar's face. "You know that everything I do is *for* your best interests because I love—"

"Let's not and say that we did."

"*Impossible.*"

Caesar chuckled. "And yet, you've never asked me why."

Not why he hated his father.

Not why he was the way he was.

Not why he did the things he did.

None of it.

No one ever cared to ask.

She did, his mind whispered.

Aria De Rose.

She had asked.

She had looked him right in the eyes and *asked*. Like she had any right to do so. Like she knew there was something the rest of the world didn't know. Like she could see it, and all his effort to hide it was for nothing.

Why do you hate women?

Such a simple question.

It owned a far more complex answer.

It wasn't just women he hated—he simply found it easier to hate them than men, usually. But typically, he hated everyone. No one was special.

That was all.

Angelo sighed, and leaned back into the chair. A false appearance of relaxation if there ever was one; Angelo rarely relaxed around his oldest son. He was always prepping for Caesar's next fuck up in one way or another.

"You have access to the De Rose whore, don't you?" Angelo asked.

Caesar's brow lifted. "I'm sorry?"

"Raffaele Ferri's wife—*Aria*, yes? The one you were fucking. I assume he doesn't know about that—or if he does, it was something they had planned."

"I don't think he knew, no," Caesar said.

He still wasn't sure *why*, though. Or what Aria's reasoning for that had been other than to blackmail Caesar. Surely, she was causing enough damage between their respective organizations without adding him to the mix, too.

Apparently not.

"Regardless," his father said with a wave of his hand, "do you have access to the woman, or not?"

"You told me to stay—"

"You're not answering my questions, Caesar."

He cleared his throat. "I *could* get access to her, if I needed to, yes."

Aria was out of the city—had been since yesterday. Some shooting had caused her husband to send her away for protection. Shame the foolish Camorra boss didn't realize his wife had already signed and sealed her death warrant when she fucked with Caesar. There was no way in hell he was going to allow that woman out of his sights for too long.

She might plan something.

Caesar needed to know what it was.

"I want the Ferri man to answer for what he did to Alice … and Daniele," Angelo murmured. "I am tired of trying to play the diplomat here."

When have you ever been a diplomat?

Caesar kept his thoughts to himself.

Angelo wouldn't appreciate them.

"I think starting with the man's wife will really drive a point home," his father continued, "and since you seem to have some … knowledge about her, and a way to get to her, I figured it might be best to put this in your hands. One thing for you to do—*surely* you can do it, Caesar. Without fucking up, I might add."

Caesar heard his father's words.

He didn't trust them, though.

"And what does giving me this job have anything to do with Canada and the new arrangement?"

"I will nullify it," Angelo answered. "No marriage—your latest misdeeds will be entirely forgiven. We will hit the proverbial restart button, and start fresh, so to speak."

Like he needed forgiveness.

His father just assumed he *wanted* it.

"You're to kill her, and then we can draw in her husband," Angelo said, shrugging his broad shoulders. "You know how I feel about killing women … either way, you can do this, and then I will give you what you want, too. How does that sound?"

Hell, he'd do it even if dissolving the marriage thing wasn't on the table.

Caesar owed Aria after everything …

"I will need a couple of days," he told his father.

Angelo nodded. "Under—"

The bitter, drunken laughter coming from the French doors leading out to the back deck stopped Angelo from saying more. Caesar was surprised to find Daniele had actually moved from his spot in the chair where he'd stayed for most of the day, not to mention, that he'd moved just to come spy on them.

"You're going to *forgive* him?" Daniele spat out, half-stumbling out the doors, yet managing to right himself at the last second before he fell on his face. He pointed his glass—full again with whiskey—at Caesar, and didn't seem to notice he spilled a quarter of it in the jerky action. "After everything he's done to us—to *you*—you're going to pretend again like it didn't even happen?"

"Daniele—"

Angelo's words were again cut off by Daniele's laughter.

"You're still trying to *protect* him, Dad. You're still fucking saving his worthless ass. And he doesn't even give a single *fuck* about you or the rest of us!"

Well, his half-brother was right about that.

Daniele's drunken gaze fell on Caesar as he mumbled, "I guess maybe he does give a shit about you, Dad. Your wife is the only one he hasn't fucked, right?"

Caesar stiffened—liquor loosened lips, and sunk fucking ships.

In more ways than one …

His brother shook his head, and then turned before he stumbled back into the house. The deck was silent, and the problem was gone. Yet, Caesar still couldn't relax, and his father hadn't said a word. In fact, Angelo didn't react at all.

He was cold.

Even as he looked back to Caesar.

It made him look at his father again.

Considering *again* …

"Seems you have something to handle now with the De Rose woman," his father said.

That was it.

Nothing else.

Did Angelo know?

Could he?

Not possible, Caesar told himself.

It just wasn't possible.

"And I think it best you stay away from your brother until he's … beyond this stage in his grief," Angelo added before he pushed out of the chair.

Huh.

A bit—or a lot—of money went a long way.

A few thousand dollars into the pocket of an eighteen-year-old who Caesar trusted to do what he was told and keep his mouth shut while he did it, and it didn't matter that he was unable to follow Aria around and keep tabs on her whereabouts. He had someone else to do it for him.

"Guy didn't even really try to hide where they were going," Cason said as he chewed on his ever-present toothpick. "I don't know how you're going to get into her room, or—"

Caesar pulled a roll of bills out of his jacket pocket, and handed it over to the kid—the rest of his payment for doing relatively decent and providing information, too. "That's for me to figure out. Is that where she is right now?"

"Dinner in the dining room with the guy—Nico?"

"His name isn't important."

"Yeah, well, there. They have different rooms."

Good to know.

"Get back to Philly, huh?"

Cason nodded. "Got it."

The kid stepped out of Caesar's rental, and disappeared into his beat up Toyota. There was no way in hell Nico—considering he seemed to be the fool constantly tasked with watching Aria—didn't notice that piece of shit following him to a whole new state.

But hell, who was Caesar to say anything?

Maybe he just wasn't a good bodyguard.

Caesar checked his mirrors to make sure no one was watching him from anywhere, and then stepped out of the vehicle. He headed for entrance of the five-star hotel that Aria's husband had holed her into—for protection, likely.

At the front desk, Caesar smirked at the sight of a pretty, young receptionist behind the desk. Like taking candy from a damn baby. He strolled up to the desk wearing his usual fuck-me smile that women fell for every single time.

Never failed.

And it wouldn't this time.

The receptionist smiled at him—Courtney, her tag read.

Okay, Courtney. Let's see what you can do for me.

"How can I help you today?" she asked after her welcome-to-this-shithole greeting.

Caesar stuffed his hands in his pockets, and leaned against the desk a bit. "Well, it *might* go against policy, but ... see, I sent my wife away for the weekend. Three kids, and she never stops, you know?"

The woman nodded like she understood—the chick was way too fucking young to have any kids, but a good looking man was smiling and talking to her. No woman would ignore that. Caesar banked on it a lot of the time.

"Anyway, I meant to surprise her with me being here. Thing is, she checked in under a different name. I don't want to—"

"Oh, you don't want to ruin the surprise."

Caesar shrugged. "You got it. Think you could help me out?"

Another long stare.

Another smile from him.

All he had to do was describe Aria, and the woman practically threw the fucking spare room card at his face with a giggle. Caesar wasted no time—lest Aria come out of the dining room and run into him—getting up to the fourth floor, and inside Aria's hotel room.

A room fit for a queen, really.

Caesar didn't take time to look around, or familiarize him with the space. He just took in the laptop sitting on the desk by the wall, and the dress that had been thrown over the foot of the bed. He didn't have time to do much else because the murmurings coming from just outside the hotel door told him dinner was over, and the woman of the hour was back.

He slipped into the shadows of the darkened bathroom, and stayed out of sight.

"It'll be fine, Nico," he heard Aria assure.

"Let me come in—he's less likely to—"

"He said me. He gave me three minutes. That's more than Raffe usually gives me. Just ... go back down and enjoy your dinner. You know how he is."

What was happening?

Caesar stayed in his hiding spot.

"Come on," Nico muttered.

"I will call you after," Aria replied. "I don't have time for this. It's worse when I make him wait."

The door closed, and then a lock clicked, too. Caesar got his first sight of Aria as she moved across the room quickly, and tossed her purse aside to a chaise. He didn't know what he was expecting, but it wasn't for her to go to the laptop.

Except it chimed with a Skype call.

Aria kept her arms down at her sides as the Skype call picked up.

"Cutting it close," he heard a familiar voice say.

Raffe.

Her husband.

"I was several floors down, and enjoying dinner with Nico," Aria said softly. "I told you that when you called."

"Mmm, and so did he. Point remains the same—I speak, you *move.*"

"I know, Raffe. Here I am."

Caesar's brow dipped.

Why did she sound so ... *meek?*

Weak and quiet.

Dead and flat.

That was not the woman who used words against others like they were weapons to wield power. That was not the woman who had all the passion in the world when she was on her knees and wanted to beg for a man.

That was not Aria.

Except it was.

He was looking at her.

Caesar wasn't sure what made him step out of the shadows of the bathroom, but he thought his father might enjoy knowing Raffe had—at the very least—seen or heard his wife be killed by the Accardos. Angelo's whole thing seemed to be to make a point of it, after all.

Across the room, Aria's gaze drifted from the screen at the moment Caesar stepped out of the bathroom. Her eyes widened a bit, but just as fast, her attention was back on the screen and her mask of nothingness was firmly back in place.

"Something interesting in there?" Raffe asked.

"The lightbulb in the bathroom keeps flickering. It's distracting."

To make her point, Aria glanced Caesar's way again—this time, though, surprise was *not* what stared back at him. A fear lingered there—thick and heavy. Like she was pleading with him through her green eyes to stay put, and *shut up.*

It struck him.

Silenced him.

Shocked him.

What in the fuck was happening?

"For the money I pay for that room, they better jump from the damn floor to fix the bulb," Raffe grumbled. "Now, stop wasting time. Undress."

Aria blinked. "Raffe, you know I've been here with Nico, and—"

"And he sleeps in a separate room. *Undress.*"

Aria's head tilted a bit to the side; not to look at Caesar, but simply to stare blankly at the wall as she undid the buttons at the front of her dress, and began the work of removing her clothes. It wasn't very long before she was standing naked.

Well, except for her heels and the scarf around her throat.

"Turn," her husband demanded. "Show me what I want to see, *donna.*"

Aria let out a quiet breath, but did as she was told. She turned when her husband demanded it, and came closer to the screen when she was told to. She did it all like a little doll on a turntable being forced to move, and not because she wanted to. Her husband took his time looking her over, or as much as he could through the screen.

You look untouched, he said.

Good girl, he praised her.

Caesar swore with every word, Aria's jaw tightened more, but her eyes remained *dead*. Entirely cold, and unseeing. Unfeeling, even. It was … baffling.

This was not what he expected …

Not what he thought.

"Remove the scarf," he heard Raffe order.

For the first time since the lightbulb mention, Aria's gaze lifted past the screen to find Caesar's prone form on the other side of the room. She didn't give Raffe the chance to order her again to remove the item; instead she reached up and tugged the silk away from her throat with slightly shaking fingers before she dropped it to the floor.

Caesar froze.

He blinked.

Bruises dotted her throat—varying in shades of yellow, blue, and brown. Her golden skin marred with fingerprints all over the delicate column of skin and muscle. Like she was regularly grabbed around her throat, and with some force to leave marks like those behind.

Caesar had held her throat.

Choked her, even.

But not—

"You can't keep wearing scarves," Raffe muttered. "Someone is going to notice."

"They already do, Raffe. You could always try listening when I say—"

"Who are you?"

Aria straightened in her heels, seemingly unbothered by the scene happening or the fact she was entirely naked but for her red heels. "Aria De Rose."

"You'll change that last name one day—mark my words."

"Daddy let me keep it for a reason."

"And now he's *gone*. Point is—who do you belong to?"

Aria's heart had to be racing; Caesar could see her pulse in her throat from all the way across the room. Rage, he thought, not her nerves. It had to be rage because that deadness in her eyes was gone, and had been replaced by something else entirely.

And oh, he knew that look well.

He knew those feelings *too well*.

Hatred.

She stared at the screen with utter hatred.

Caesar got it, then. He really fucking got it.

"Who?" Raffe asked again.

"You, Raffe. I belong to you."

"Exactly. You do not get to tell me no. You do not get to refuse your husband, Aria. Not your body, or anything else I want. And if you want to keep me from adding more marks on that throat of yours, you'll learn to listen and *like it*."

This hadn't been about his family, or the streets of their city. This hadn't been about Caesar, or hurting him. It hadn't been about a father she wanted killed, or a woman too greedy for her own good, and desiring more power.

This was about this woman.

This woman right here—manipulated, and abused. With a husband who used her, and one she probably couldn't escape.

Caesar knew, then.

None of this had been what he thought it was.

She was not who he thought she was.

"And don't you ever fucking forget it," Raffe snapped.

The laptop chimed with the ending of the call. It took Aria a second, and then one hard, shaky breath before she reached over, grabbed the screen, and slammed it shut. She bent slightly over the laptop and desk as her shoulders hunched.

Caesar didn't move.

Couldn't move.

When she looked up at Caesar again, tears had streaked glistening lines down her reddened cheeks.

Humiliation.

Shame.

Sadness.

It all stared back at him, then.

God.

He knew that well, too.

"Have you come to kill me, then?" Aria asked in a whisper. "Because right now, I might even ask you to do it."

No ... not anymore.

TWELVE

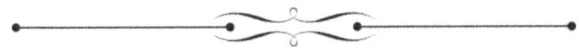

ARIA REFUSED TO look up again—would not allow someone else to see her shame and degradation one more time. Wasn't it bad enough that she was standing there naked for Caesar to see after everything? She had done so well to hide this part of her marriage; she kept Raffe's treatment of her hidden so no one would ever know.

Then, no one would ever think she was weak.

Or incapable.

Broken.

It was the one thing she could control in her marriage—her *reputation*. And it was lost.

"Fix your face," Caesar murmured.

Aria kept her head tilted down. "I beg your pardon?"

"Clean your face—wipe off the tears. Do whatever you have to do, but *fix* it. You don't want me to see it."

A laugh burst from her lips.

Bitter and sad.

She finally tipped her head up and glared at him from across the room. "I knew you would come—I was fucking *betting* on it."

Caesar arched one brow high. "I figured that."

"What?"

He gestured a finger between the two of them, saying, "This … all of it. And us, maybe. The whole thing you're doing—the war you're trying to start. All of the manipulation and games. Every step you've taken. For yourself. Against me. *Around* me. None of it was what I thought it was. It couldn't be when it was actually just for you, right?"

Aria's heartbeat pulsed hard in her throat. "I don't know what you're—"

Caesar came closer, then. Suddenly closing over half the distance between them in a blink, but stopping in the middle of the room with a gaze that burned her on contact. It was his eyes that dared her to deny—urged her to *lie*. He was angry and disbelieving, and if he were another man, she might consider him to be too close to her.

Except he wasn't another man.

He wasn't *Raffe*.

Caesar was him.

And she had yet to be scared of him.

"Don't," he uttered. "Just … fuck, don't lie right now."

Aria straightened, and for once when she was naked in front of this man, his gaze never wandered from her face. He didn't leer at her body like he had all the times before, or even make one of his crude comments that irked her as much as it made her hot.

Maybe that was why she had the deepest urge to reach for her dress, and cover her nakedness. She held back, but only because he was talking again. She found it was usually better for her if she listened when Caesar talked.

He let things slip.

Right now, the slip wasn't in his words. It was in his gaze—confused, and hurt. It was in his posture—ridged, and defensive. It was in his tone—low, and deep.

She could see it; feel it.

He *cared*.

Aria didn't know what to do with that, or how to handle it. If he was angry at her, or if he was trying to hurt her, then that was an entirely different story. That was something she could work with, and something she could most certainly use where Caesar was concerned. She could handle him when he was promising violence, or fucking her ... or *anything else but this right here*.

What even was this?

And why did her heart hurt because of it?

"This is not how this is supposed to go," she mumbled with a shake of her head.

Caesar's brow furrowed, and he came one single step closer. "How *what* is supposed to go?"

Christ.

Didn't he know?

She waved her hands between them, knowing damn well she probably looked crazy, but not giving a single fuck about it. "*This*! You can't *care*, Caesar—you don't get to care! You get to be angry, and ... unpredictable. I know how to fight back against that. I know how to—"

"Use it," he interrupted softly.

Aria stiffened all over, but stayed quiet.

Caesar nodded like he didn't need her to say a thing. "Oh, yeah, I do know now. That's what you use, girl. Sure, you make it seem like the person is doing it because it'll help them by hurting you, but that's never what it is, is it? Your *father*, for one. Tell me different."

She refused to look at him.

Caesar only sighed.

She heard his next step, though. Another move that yet again, brought him closer to her. A part of her wanted him to get the hell out of her room, and then maybe she could salvage her pride; fix her fucking plans. Another part of her found it strangely easy to be around this man, and wanted to keep him near.

God.

What was wrong with her?

"I can't …"

"What?" Caesar asked.

"I can't *like* you," Aria said under her breath. "It messes with *everything*. Don't make me like you, Caesar."

His laughter came out like raw honey.

Dark, rich, and all too sweet.

"That's amusing," he countered, "considering everyone around me seems to think I'm rather easy to hate."

"You are."

And he wasn't at the same time.

"Aria," he murmured, "would you look at me?"

She did, but the same thing stared back at her. A man who both confused and infuriated her. A man she had been able to trust in—because he would continue to do the same thing over and over again without even knowing he would help her in doing so. A man who turned her on as much as he drove her crazy.

A man who cared.

He shouldn't *care*.

There was a hell of a lot less than half a room of space between them now, but he quickly closed it. She couldn't breathe nearly as well when all she could smell was his distinct scent, or see only his gaze locked on hers and nothing else. His hand came up, and his palm curved around the side of her throat, and part of her jaw.

She would have flinched.

Except he wasn't Raffe.

"You could have asked me not to touch your throat," he said gently.

"I would have—"

"I like it when you do that. I don't like it when he does it."

Caesar nodded subtly. "You don't love him at all, do you?"

"I was given to him. I never chose him. There was no choice. I gave my father everything, and was all the things he wanted me to be. And yet, this is what he did to me in the end. This was who he gave me to."

"Why not just kill your husband, then?" Caesar asked. "You can't say you're *incapable*. I have seen you at work. You are more than able to get that done."

Aria smiled a bit. "It would be easy, actually. I have a knife in my nightstand. I think about killing him every night he sleeps beside me."

"Then why—"

"They'll know. The clan, I mean. My people. They'll challenge me after. Kill me, at the most. Shame me, at the least. I need my position to be unchallenged."

Caesar laughed, and glanced up at the ceiling like he expected it to crash down on them. "You're doing all of this—*this* ... production of a war just to kill one man? It's not even about the streets or the power at all, is it?"

"It is—it's the high I keep chasing. Power, I mean. The more power I have in the end, the less likely I am to be challenged. It gets me so fucking high. It's the heroin that's either going to save me, or it'll kill me. Either way, I'm going to be free of him, and I'll take it."

His gaze came back to her—blue and stormy in a blink.

It was shocking, really.

"He doesn't know what he has in you, does he? He doesn't know at all."

Aria stilled. "I don't—"

"He doesn't know what you'll do. Or what you're willing to do. What you *can* and have done. He doesn't know how smart you are, or how cunning you can be. He just ... doesn't know at all."

"He doesn't have to know, Caesar," Aria replied. "He only wants to be able to say that I'm his—I just need to be his *thing*."

"What a waste of a woman."

Aria found herself smiling again.

Caesar blew out a slow breath. "He's so fucking *stupid*."

"Most men tend to be when a beautiful woman is in front of them."

"That's fair." Caesar still hadn't let go of her, but he loosened his hold, and scrubbed his other hand down his jaw. "I came here to do something, but uh ... I don't think I can now."

"And what was that?"

Although, she thought she knew.

Caesar shook his head once. "Not important."

"All right. Then, would you stay for a bit?"

His gaze cut back to her in an instant. "You don't have to pretend like this is anything more than what it is with us—you use me, and I was stupid enough to let you."

Aria shrugged. "Maybe it is more; I tend to be good at multitasking, *il mio tiranno*."

His gaze darkened, and that smirk of his deepened.

"Your *tyrant*, huh?"

"Fits, doesn't it? I think so. You were named well."

He laughed again.

Aria grinned.

Yeah, he wasn't going anywhere. She was going to hate herself for it, but she wanted him to stay. To make her *feel*. To let her be alive. To give her that escape.

He did that.

He barely had to try.

It was everything else that made her feel dead.

Funny how that worked.

Warm sunlight woke Aria first, and then the buzzing of her phone second. She stiffened all over as the hard body pressed against hers shifted, but relaxed when his voice filtered through her sleep-dazed senses.

"You should tell Nico you're alive," Caesar muttered, tone thick with sleep. "Otherwise, he's going to wake me up again, and then I'll have to kill him."

Aria would have laughed.

Except he sounded serious.

Even as Aria rolled over on the bed to put more distance between them, Caesar's hand still grazed her spine. His fingertips making a soft path from her lower back all the way up to her shoulders. Her skin prickled with heat and need while her mind flashed back to the night before.

The phone buzzed again.

"Goddammit, Nico."

Finally, Aria snatched the phone off the bed stand, and checked the messages. No missed calls or texts from Raffe—not surprising as he rarely rolled his ass out of bed before nine, and it was only six. Nico, on the other hand, had been messaging and calling since five.

"He's worried about you," Caesar said.

Even through the thickness of his sleep, she could hear *something* there. A hint of heat in his tone that he might have been able to hide had he been properly awake.

"Nico is a friend," Aria said.

"A *good* friend?"

She smiled, and glanced over her shoulder at him. Unsurprisingly, she found his stormy blue eyes looking back at her from the mountain of white blankets and pillows. A question lingered there in his gaze, but nothing more.

"A friend," Aria repeated. "People do have those. Don't you?"

"Not with women."

"Right."

She sent off a quick text to Nico, and told him not to bother her again. Putting the phone back on the nightstand, she attempted to keep some of that distance between them. At least for the moment. It was made more difficult by the slight ache between her thighs that reminded Aria it was much nicer to have Caesar *very fucking close.*

He was good at that.

To say the least …

"Does your husband rape you?" Caesar asked.

It came out so cold.

Not indifferent, but just … flat.

Aria answered the same way. "Often."

"I don't understand, then."

She glanced over at him. "Understand what?"

"How you can be with me when someone's hurt you like that. I get why you would want to—sex is just another weapon to use, right? Sex is the best way to manipulate or cause someone pain in a simple way. That I get. But … that's not what this is, or last night."

No, it wasn't.

"It was before with you," she said stretching a bit. "I manipulated you with sex."

"You can't really fake liking it the way you do with me, though, can you?"

Aria laughed softly. "I didn't say I didn't like it, Caesar. I do—quite a bit."

"That's my point. *How?* I just … sex isn't *sex* for me," Caesar admitted quietly, staring blankly at the ceiling. "There's always had to be something underlying to it, maybe. Or maybe it's just women that make me feel like that. They've always got something up their sleeve, and I would much rather hurt them first before they get to me. Or shit …"

"Prove all women are the same?" Aria asked.

His gaze cut to her.

Silence thickened the air in the room.

"It's not hard to figure out that's what you do, Caesar," she told him, shrugging her naked shoulders. "Sex is your weapon. You said it, not me. It's the *why* that makes me curious."

"Because that's what I was taught."

Aria frowned. "What?"

"I was taught very young by someone who had no business putting their hands on me that sex was just another weapon to hurt people. It's all I've ever known. It's easy. Maybe it gets me off in some ways, and maybe I just want to ruin people like I was because making things dirty like me is what feels good. Like the shame I can't wash off, well they can't get me off, either."

"Does it?"

"What?"

"Feel good," she clarified.

Caesar sighed. "This is why I don't talk in bed unless it's to tell someone to shut the fuck up and swallow my dick."

Aria glanced over at him. "Tell me."

"I don't know if it feels good—I say it does."

"But?"

"Don't shrink my head, Aria. Suck my dick. Climb on for a ride. Let me fuck your ass while I gag you, or tie you up. *Anything else*. But not this. Everything else is easy, and this is all the things I never want to talk about."

Point taken.

"I'm sorry."

The words were barely out of Aria's mouth before Caesar had rolled on top of her. Every dark, fractured, confusing part of him clouded her vision, and took up all of her space. Her ability to take in a proper breath was gone with the first kiss he slammed down on her mouth—a bruising, violent kiss that left her lips tingling and swollen. But damn her if she didn't *love* it. It was his fingers curving around her throat that made her wet between her legs, though.

Well, that and his already hard cock grinding against her bare pussy.

"Don't *ever* apologize to me," he muttered against her lips.

"*Ever?*"

"I don't deserve it."

His other hand snaked between their bodies, then, and Aria couldn't help herself when she felt his knuckles graze against her sex. She widened her legs for him—just like the whore her husband liked to claim her to be. She opened for another man, and she took every single inch of his cock in.

And she did it with a smile and a *moan*.

Because fuck, he felt good.

And damn, he filled her so well.

Christ, he made her *ache*.

"Shit, you need to relax," Caesar grunted. "So fucking *tight*."

"You don't know what it *feels* like."

"Tell me, then."

Soft, warm lips drifted over her trembling mouth, and cheekbones. Tender, and sweet, and entirely *hot*.

"*Fuck*, tell me," he demanded when she couldn't form words.

His order was punctuated by a hard jerk of his hips that had his cock hitting her inner walls in just the right spot to make her clench, and soak him even more with her juices. Aria let out another one of those broken moans.

"I'm so full," she breathed, "and it's not nearly enough. You make me want *more*. And then I want to breathe, but I want you to squeeze so I can't, too."

He did just that.

Long, strong fingers gripping tight to her delicate throat, and making her breath hitch.

"Keep going," he murmured along the seam of her lips.

"I'm hot—all over. I just want ..."

"More."

"More," she echoed.

Jesus.

He pulled out fast, then, and dove right back in. It started a brutal pace between them that could only end with an ache between her thighs, and sweat slicked down her skin. She needed it, though. Needed to have *this*. She never got this, now.

Never would again.

His hand at her throat kept her pinned to the bed, and under his weight. A heavy, substantial weight that she couldn't escape, and didn't want to. His other hand between her thighs used the slickness of her sex to ease the sensation of his fingertips dragging harsh circles over her throbbing clit.

One.

And then two.

Three.

Four.

"Don't even fucking ask me for it—just *take* it."

She knew what he meant.

Her orgasm.

He always wanted her to beg.

To be *sweet*.

To ask him.

She couldn't have done any of those things even if she tried. It came on too quickly, and far too fierce. Not something she could control, or hold back. It was there all at once like a wave crashing into the sand with violent intent, and taking parts of her away with it when the tide went back out.

And *fuck* ... it was wonderful.

Caesar had her flipped over before the orgasm was even done, and was shoving his cock back into her clenching cunt before she realized he was gone. His arm wrapped around her middle, and pinned her arms against her body. He fucked her like that, too, with his mouth against the back of her throat, and his face buried into the mess of her hair.

Dark, hot words whispered along her skin.

Take it.

Fuck it like you want it.

And *breathe and scream for me.*

She was a mess by then. Arms and legs she couldn't control—nerves that felt on fire. She thought he fucked a lot like he just *was*. Uncontrollable, and unpredictable. A little too wild for his own good, and always with the intent to get what he wanted in the end.

She came again.

And then a *third* time.

Aria expected him to pull out, and paint her back with his come. Or to turn her over, and get her to finish him off like he had before. He didn't— bare, and deep, and *hard* ... he filled her full, and she felt every fucking drop.

She didn't care; despite every effort her husband had tried to use to get her pregnant, she had the means and the ability to keep exactly that from happening. For as long as she wanted or needed.

"Jesus Christ," Caesar uttered through shuddering breaths.

It edged along her skin.

Sharp like a razor.

Soft like a kiss.

Still hard inside her, and with shaky hands holding her down against the bed, Caesar said, "I have to kill you to get what I want—it's the deal I made."

Aria stared at the bright sunlight filtering in through the window. "And what is it you want?"

"Not to be tossed away—not to be married to someone else."

"Is that all?" she asked.

"I don't think I want to keep being broken."

Her emotions tipped.

Her heart *raced*.

Nothing made sense anymore.

Nothing seemed simple or easy.

Not with this man.

Not like he was.

"Are you going to do it, then?" she asked. "Kill me to get what you want, I mean."

"I'm trying to figure out another way."

Yes.

She could tell.

Because this was dangerous, now.

It was always dangerous when hearts got involved.

"How long is he going to make you hide out here?" he asked.

Aria smiled. "Until someone finds me, I suppose. You should probably hurry up and do that, Caesar."

THIRTEEN

CAIN WAS ALREADY waiting in the Four Seasons hotel room that Caesar had been calling home ever since Raffe had his penthouse—and half of the rest of the building—burnt to the ground.

"Well?" Cain asked.

Caesar tossed his wrinkled blazer over the back of the couch, and glanced at his phone. An incoming text from his father wanting an update on the *situation*, as Angelo kept calling it. It amused Caesar to no end that his father could so easily order the death of a woman, and yet refused to actually call it what it was. Her *murder*.

Except that hadn't happened.

And he had to figure out something else.

"Well, what?" Caesar asked.

"Is it done—the job?"

Cain glanced up from the sheets he had spread out on the small kitchenette table. Caesar made an iffy noise in the back of his throat, and shrugged. Cain had been the only person Caesar let in on his little deal with his father—Aria's life for his freedom. Cain figured it was a good trade all things considered.

Caesar did, too.

Not so much now.

"Not really," he said.

"Jesus Christ. You fucked her *again*."

"Hey."

"*What?*" Cain grumbled.

"I mean, the least you could do is give me some dignity and *pose* it as a question. You don't have to just assume right of the bat that I—"

"You fucked her again, Caesar. I know you did."

Fine.

"In the midst of other shit, I may have done that, too," Caesar offered.

"You can't even control it, can you?"

"I *can*. I just choose not to."

Yeah.

That.

That was a good way to put it.

"And," Caesar added, drawling out the words with a leer, "if you had gotten a taste of that woman, you would go back for more, too."

"I have a wife."

"Yeah, shame that is."

"*Watch it, asshole.*"

Shit.

Yeah.

"Sorry," Caesar said, stuffing his hands in his pocket. "I know you love Gina—force of habit."

And it was exactly that. A force of habit. He didn't know if he could change the urge to mock or ruin every good relationship he saw growing around him. Like a need to prove those things were as fragile and useless as glass in the face of the oncoming storm that was Caesar Accardo. Sure, he didn't mess *in* Cain's marriage, but that didn't mean he was always quiet.

Plus, he did like Gina.

That helped.

Cain straightened a bit, and cleared his throat. "You know, you've never said that before."

Caesar cocked a brow. "Said what?"

"That I love my wife—*love*, Caesar. The actual word. Like it's a thing you believe exists."

"It doesn't—"

"It does, and you just said it does. At least, you said it in regards to the way I love *my* wife. That you see it there, and you know it's there. You've never done that before. No, what you do is make snide comments or some other kind of shit. But not actually *that*."

Caesar blinked.

Cain kept staring.

"Don't make this into something," he told his friend. "It was a slip of the tongue. And it won't happen again."

Cain gave him one big nod, as if silently saying, *Sure, man, sure.*

"What are you doing, anyway?" Caesar asked, hoping he could get his friend onto another topic of conversation. Maybe then this weird thing he was now thinking about would get the fuck out of his head fast, quick, and in a hurry. He didn't need to be bothering himself with things like *love*, and whether or not it was something that actually existed to him. Love ruined things—love was a vulnerability, and something he would much rather destroy. Not something he actually wanted. "What are these?"

He approached the table, and picked up one of the sheets of paper Cain had set out on the table in front of him. They looked like ... condos, and penthouses. Or rather, details for different places in the city. Ones for sale.

"You need a place to live; you can't keep staying here," Cain muttered. "Or, that's what Gina told me this morning. She said if I didn't kick your ass into gear to find a new place, then you would never do it. And she is tired of you showing up every night for supper because you don't like the restaurant here."

"The chef is an asshole," Caesar returned.

"Whatever—point is, pick one."

"Maybe later."

Finding a new place was the last thing on his mind at the moment. He had far too many other things to do, and this was at the very bottom of the list.

Dropping the paper back to the table, he turned to his friend and said, "I couldn't do it—kill her, I mean."

Cain flattened his palms against the table, and let out a sigh. "Why not?"

"A lot of reasons."

Not of them were particularly important, and Caesar also didn't think they were any of his friend's business. Nonetheless, he wasn't giving out details even if Cain did try to push for them. Thankfully, Cain didn't ask.

No, Cain went in a different direction.

Always the rule-follower.

The *good* made man between them.

"Your father isn't going to like that," Cain muttered. "And that means you've negated the deal—so the marriage will be back on the table."

Like it was ever off.

And when had he ever given a single *fuck* what Angelo wanted or thought?

Caesar made a dismissive grunt. "I'll give him what he wants. She was a *detail* to him. That's it, and that's all. Just something else for him to add to the pot, and nothing more. She's not actually important to Angelo's plans other than removing her from the equation to piss off her husband. He can still do that without killing her at the same time. She doesn't need to die."

Cain cleared his throat, and glanced over at Caesar. "And what, she isn't just a detail to you? You *don't* want to get rid of her?"

"Don't do that."

"Caesar—"

"Don't even try to do that."

"Now—"

"This isn't *something*, Cain. And don't try to make something out of fucking nothing."

Cain glared at the ceiling. "You're impossible."

"Yeah, well …"

It was all he could say, and he'd offered it rather lamely. Caesar had never claimed to be anything but exactly what he was.

"How many times have you slept with that woman now?" Cain asked.

"A few times."

Are we counting the encounters, or the number of times one of us has come?

Because those were two very different numbers, and one was a great deal higher than the other. Soon to be a hell of a lot more the second he got a chance. He was done pretending in that aspect—he liked fucking Aria, and he was going to keep doing it as long as she wanted him to.

Caesar didn't see the issue.

"You do realize when you go back more than once, you can't keep calling it nothing, right?" Cain asked.

"Just ... fuck off."

Cain laughed. "I'm just saying."

"Fuck off, and find me two guys Angelo won't care about if they die."

That quieted his friend.

"Why would they die?"

Caesar grinned. "Aria is predictable. That's why."

And it was time to put some of his plans in motion.

"What are we standing here for?" Angelo asked.

More like *grumbled*.

"Something fun," Caesar said. "Wait for it."

He checked the screen of his phone again to see the men he had tasked with snatching Aria from her safe hotel were at the bottom of the driveway, and currently waiting to be granted access to the Accardo estate by security. *Almost.*

"Fun for me is not standing around," Angelo said with a sigh.

"You could indulge me a little."

Angelo gave his son a side-eye. "In case you missed the goddamn memo, I indulge you far too often. It's every reason why you are the way you are."

"That's not the reason," Caesar returned, "but you can keep thinking that way, if it's easier on your conscience."

His father opened his mouth to speak, but quickly shut it. Really, it was a smart move on Angelo's part, but Caesar opted not to point it out. Frankly, he had probably stretched his father's good graces just about as far as he could for the evening.

"Where's Martina?" Caesar asked.

Her name came out a little twisted—dark and bitter with his tone. He hated the taste it left behind on his tongue, too.

Still, he had to be sure ...

Angelo gave him another look; surprised, likely, that he'd asked about his step-mother. Caesar *never* did that, if he could help it. Most times, he made every fucking attempt to act as if the woman didn't even exist. It didn't escape Angelo's notice, but the man rarely said anything. And *only* if Martina mentioned it.

She was like a weed.

Growing where she shouldn't.

Impossible to be rid of.

A fucking *pest*.

"Out with friends," Angelo settled on saying.

"For how long?"

"Until someone brings her home, I imagine."

His father offered the words dryly—unaffected, even. Like the fact his wife was probably out at some bar or club plastered and making another one of her scenes wasn't even the smallest blip on his problematic radar.

It disgusted Caesar.

And amused him.

"Well, good," Caesar said.

"Why is that *good?*"

"I wouldn't want her walking in on this. I don't think she'd do well standing up against this one."

"What—"

Caesar's phone dinged with an incoming message before his father could ask more. He checked the message to find the men had parked the van, and were coming up to the front door. He sent back a confirmative text for them to come right in, and not to bother with knocking as they were already waiting.

"So, fair warning," Caesar said to Angelo, "I didn't *exactly* do what you wanted. I think you'll have more fun with this option, though."

"Didn't do what I—*what?*"

Caesar tipped his head toward the door as it started to open. A woman entered first—Aria—although with her head covered by a black hood, and her arms pinned behind her back by the hands of one of the men leading her inside, it was nearly impossible to tell it was her. Except *he* could tell.

A body like hers ...

All that anger and tension ...

Her rose perfume ...

How could he not know her?

Caesar knew the moment his father realized exactly who was being delivered to his home hooded and captured like a prize—when Aria *spoke*.

Or rather ... cursed.

"*Vaffanculo! Vattela a pigliare in culo, merda!*"

Angelo's gaze widened as he cleared his throat. "Those are quite the words for a *lady*."

"I don't think she cares if you think of her as a lady," Caesar mused.

"This is not what I asked for, *figlio*. She should be dead, not standing in my home!"

"Yes, well—"

"Remove her hood, and let her go," Angelo ordered the men, not even giving Caesar a chance to speak.

That's a mistake.

Caesar didn't tell his father that.

He actually thought Angelo might see the show Aria could put on, and appreciate it. Or rather, maybe think he could use it to his advantage. Angelo was always looking for the next thing he could use to advance his business, after all.

The taller of the two men yanked the hood off Aria's head while the stockier, dark-haired man let go of her arms. Her wild curls flew in every direction as her blazing glaze searched the room—painted-red lips pulled back in a challenging sneer, and fists clenched down at her side.

Goddamn, was she ever a *sight*.

Caesar liked it.

Too much.

Aria took a second—one to find who was in the room.

Then, *two*—to fix her dress.

And then she acted.

Spinning fast, her hand slipped between her legs and the men never saw her coming. Caesar only caught sight of the barest glint of metal before she struck out at the stockier of the two men. She sliced the small knife across his face, leaving a nasty, bleeding gash behind. At the same time, she reached for the jacket of the other man.

Her hand came back with his gun.

She didn't blink.

Didn't hesitate.

Racked, aimed, and *fired*.

A single shot right to the face sent the man flying backwards.

Caesar heard the cock of his father's gun in the next second, and so did Aria if the stiffening of her shoulders was any indication. The man who had been sliced across his face was holding the injury with one hand while thick blood poured between his fingertips. Caesar could still see the man's rage as clear as day as he stepped toward Aria.

Angelo spoke first.

"Don't touch her," his father uttered. "And you ... turn around, *donna*, and drop the gun carefully to the floor."

Aria's shoulders heaved, and her back tensed. Still, she did as she had been told. Turning slowly, she put the weapon to the floor as her fiery green eyes landed on Caesar next to his father. He was grinning—a stupid, foolish grin.

He couldn't help it.

She was *amazing*.

Aria didn't speak, though.

Not to him, anyway.

"My husband will kill you," she told Angelo.

"Yes, well, he's been threatening that for a while," Angelo grumbled. "I have learned to roll with it. Kick the gun over to us, please."

Aria's foot snapped out, and the small handgun slid across the floor before coming to a stop in front of Caesar's leather loafers. "I'll enjoy watching what he does to you, Accardo. Trust that it'll be slow, painful, and you'll wish you were dead long before he lets *me* kill you."

She really did put on a good show.

Even if some of it was a lie.

No wonder Raffe couldn't tell this woman was working to see him dead and cold in the ground. He probably thought she *loved* him.

She didn't.

"Caesar, we need to have a word," Angelo said, never taking his gaze away from Aria, "but first, someone needs to handle *that*. Put her somewhere she can't hurt anyone else ... or something. *Cristo*. She is a *rompicoglioni*—ball-breaker. You know how I feel about those kinds of women."

He did.

Angelo hated them as much as he respected them.

This was going well.

"And hurry up," his father barked, lowering his weapon and turning on his heel to leave the grand entry. "Before she takes another swing at someone else."

Caesar nodded. "I think I can do that."

"This is *not* what I asked for!" The office door slammed shut with a bang the second those words left Angelo's scowling lips. "That woman should be *dead*, not in my fucking home!"

Caesar dropped his form into the leather chair next to the window. A good spot to distract himself by staring out over the yard while he convinced his father this was the better way to go with Aria rather than killing her.

"I think this is better in the grand scheme, actually," Caesar returned. "Think about it."

Angelo huffed, and from the corner of his eye, Caesar watched his father cross his beefy arms over his chest. "I don't have to think about it—we had an agreement. This is a complication I can't afford, and do not need."

"Wrong."

"I swear—"

"You have his wife *alive*," Caesar said. "Before, you were just going to kill her, and be done with it. Claim the kill, and piss him off spectacularly. Drive him into some kind of brilliant violence that would let you kill him and be done with it."

"Yes, because that's *easy*, Caesar! Or have you forgotten that I want to be rid of this shit? They've caused me enough problems, and this would have been the end of it, for Christ's sake."

"Well, that sounds *dull*."

"Two seconds, son. You are *two fucking seconds* away from earning yourself an early grave."

Doubtful.

"We have a bit more insight on Camorra clans now, don't we?" he asked. "You take them down, and five more pop up out of the goddamn ruins. Get rid of him, and his clan is going to have *more* come out on top because of it. And who the fuck do you think they're going to come at because of it? Is that what you want?"

His father paused—*considered.*

Caesar smiled to himself.

"Not particularly," Angelo finally muttered.

"Exactly. Use her to draw him in, and *ruin* him. Make a show of it—they hold their reputation close. Too close, maybe. Make it known the Accardos shouldn't be messed with in any way. Whoever comes out on top of this once it's over will think twice before they come at us again."

Angelo frowned. "And what about *her*?"

Yes.

That …

"Killing her does nothing for your endgame," Caesar said, shrugging. "Killing her when she will have nothing and no one to fall back on would be like pissing on her grave just for the sake of insulting her. What will she have to use to come back on us after this? Nothing. And beyond that, her reputation will be ruined with her clan—to them, that's worse than anything she could do to us, trust that."

Angelo's gaze narrowed. "Is that so?"

"Yes."

"You're asking me to spare the woman."

"I don't see why killing her does you any good."

"Because she is a *problem*."

"But she *won't* be," Caesar countered.

"You do realize I know the amount of times you've gone to that woman—the things you've been doing behind my back. I *know*, son."

"Mmm, you even had pictures, remember?"

Angelo's gaze flashed with a warning.

Careful, dumbass.

His thoughts were a special breed of hell today.

"Camorra isn't like Cosa Nostra," Caesar said, shaking his head, "and just killing them won't drive your point home. If anything, they will rebuild stronger and better, and come at you in a new way because you were stupid enough to let them think death was all they would have to pay for this. That's the thing—they don't fear death. They expect it."

"Even her?" Angelo asked.

Caesar tipped his hand over, saying, "Especially her. You have to humiliate them—drawing her husband in and killing him by tricking and shaming him is the kind of thing that would make them hesitate to attack us again. They would be far more concerned with upholding their image and reputations as a clan."

"You do know that you won't get what you want now—the marriage, I mean. It will go through because of this. We agreed, and you fell through."

A dry, dark chuckle passed Caesar's lips.

"What is so funny?" Angelo asked.

"You were never going to let me out of that marriage, anyway."

Angelo glanced away from Caesar.

He didn't deny it, though.

Because *yeah*, he knew how this game went. Angelo simply forgot Caesar was a far better player in the end.

Shame.

It meant one of them was going to have to lose.

It wouldn't be Caesar.

"But now that the woman is *here* ..." his father said, trailing off with a look in Caesar's direction.

Great.

What now?

FOURTEEN

"YOU'RE LOOKING PLEASED with yourself," Aria mused as Caesar strolled into the library.

He gave the man who had been watching Aria a nod, and the guy quickly darted out of the room, but not before he slammed the door closed behind him. Likely happy to be the hell out of her presence after knowing what she had done to the two men who delivered her to the estate. Caesar locked the door, too.

Oh, good.

Privacy.

Caesar gave his attention back to her—and the glass of liquor Aria was holding. His gaze narrowed a bit at the sight. "And you're looking quite comfortable."

She smiled slyly, and tipped the glass back and forth. He could act pissed all he wanted; she didn't care. She knew full well he enjoyed the little show she had put on when she first arrived. He probably had planned for that, really.

"What good will sitting here staring at old, dusty books do for me? There's not even a *romance* in here, Caesar. I would much rather drink."

Caesar didn't even reply. Strolling across the room, he plucked the glass from her hand, and rested it down on the small wet bar with a little more force than was necessary. Aria had all she could do not to pick it back up—because what the *fuck*—but his hand circling tight around her wrist to keep her still stopped her from doing anything.

"How about no," Caesar uttered darkly. "There's already one woman in this house who is constantly drunk and haunts me regularly. Let's not add a fucking second."

Wait, what?

Aria gave him a second look.

His easy demeanor was gone.

"Are you—"

"What?"

His gaze burned when it landed back on her.

Aria stiffened. "What is your problem?"

She didn't miss the way his jaw tensed, or how his gaze darted away from hers. Something had happened, and he wasn't very pleased about it.

That wasn't a good sign.

"Shouldn't it be me pissed off?" she asked. "You did have random, strange men come into my hotel room, and throw a fucking hood over my head like I was a wild animal."

Caesar's lips twitched with a smirk.

She had the strangest urge to smack it away, or kiss it.

Wow.

"That's because you *are* kind of like a wild animal," he murmured.

"Watch it, tyrant."

"I like it better when you say it in Italian, Aria."

"Too bad."

Caesar sighed, and his grip on her wrist loosened. "Thanks for playing along when you got here—you made for a good show. It was as amusing as I hoped it would be."

Aria gave him a look. "Glad to be of service."

Her tone was cutting.

He didn't miss it.

"Don't be like that, now."

"You're being a bit of an asshole," she countered.

"Force of habit," he replied.

"Then, you get the bitch."

Caesar tipped his head down. "That's fair. I don't get too much control, now, though. Be warned—you're here, so it's all on Angelo to make the calls from now on."

"As long as I don't *die.*"

"Working on keeping that from happening, yeah."

Aria's fingernails dug into the thin skin of his wrist, forcing Caesars gaze to dart quickly to meet hers. "Don't *work* on it—make sure it happens."

In a blink, he was closer.

All in her vision.

Crowding her.

Making it hard to breathe.

She liked it as much as she hated it.

His lips were a breath away from hers when he said, "It won't happen, *bella.*"

"You're distracting."

"And you're dangerous."

Aria shrugged. "Fair trade, isn't it?"

"I haven't decided yet."

She reached up and pressed the pads of her fingers into the tense, furrowed line of his brow to smooth it out. "You're angry. Why?"

"Because you have to stay here. In this mansion. At least, until Angelo says otherwise or chooses to move you to a new location."

She blinked. "Okay."

"No, *not* okay. I have to keep an eye on you—Angelo's demands."

Aria grinned wickedly. "That could be fun."

She was asking for trouble.

Begging for it, really.

Caesar was a fun kind of trouble, though.

Caesar shook his head. "That *means* ... you stay here, and I have to stay here. I don't fucking like this house—I hate it, and the people inside it."

There was something dark in his words.

Something that ached in his tone.

She didn't miss it. They'd had enough conversations for him to let things slip, and she was wondering just how important some of those things were. How much had he told her was tied to this house, and the people inside it?

"Why?" she asked. "Why do you hate it, and *them?*"

Caesar swallowed hard. "Just ... never mind."

"You know you can talk to me about—"

"I don't want to talk," he uttered through clenched teeth.

Yeah, something was *really* wrong. Something that bothered Caesar so much that he couldn't even make an effort to hide it.

"Okay, no talking," she said.

"No talking," he agreed. "Something else is good, though."

"Something like what?"

"Something that would really piss my father off." The words were no sooner out of Caesar's mouth than he kissed her—hard, deep, and fast. Taking away what was left of her air, and making her wet between her thighs when his hand snaked up the skirt of her dress so his fingers could rub along her sex. Groaning against her mouth, he muttered, "Yeah, I really just need to piss him off."

She would have asked *why*.

He was already on his knees. Her panties were already being pulled down. His mouth was already on her pussy.

Jesus Christ.

Aria almost lost her balance when he hooked her leg around his shoulder, and his tongue found that *sweet spot*. If someone was outside in the hallway beyond the library door, they would hear every single fucking hot noise crawling out of her throat.

He had some kind of crazy talent with that tongue of his. It could make her come in less than thirty seconds—faster if he got his fingers working her pussy, too.

His mouth was damn good, though.

Too good, even.

Distracting and delirious.

Caesar was relentless. His mouth drove her wild. His tongue made her *beg*.

Over, and over, and over.

Yeah, she would have asked why.

She *really* didn't care right then.

Three days.

Three long fucking days.

And so far, Aria had only gotten to see one small section of the Accardo estate. Not that she was complaining, but she wasn't used to this. Even as controlled as her life was with Raffe, he never locked her into a single small wing somewhere for days at a time, and refused to allow her to leave.

That was exactly what Angelo Accardo did.

Aria was going stir crazy in every possible way. It didn't matter that she had all she needed between the five rooms she had been provided, or the fact that Caesar brought her food, and kept her company for a good part of the day ... no, it didn't matter.

She hated *not* knowing.

Wondering.

Being out of the fucking loop.

Her husband had to know by now that she was taken—there was no way around it. Raffe was probably in a right fit, but she couldn't plan or prep for whatever move he might make next when she didn't *know* anything.

Yeah, that made her nuts.

Aria had stopped trying to check the door that led out of the small wing because it was locked regardless if Caesar was inside with her, or if she was alone. Thankfully, Angelo had not come to see Aria since her arrival— she didn't think it would end well for the man if he did, considering he'd locked her away like a wild animal.

At least, someone had thought to grab her luggage from the hotel when she was taken. She had clothes. *Decent* clothes that were hers, and weren't someone else's things. That really would have been the icing on this hellish cake.

Aria sipped from a tea that Caesar had brought up to her with her breakfast, and stared at the set of doors from the other end of the hallway. Thick, dark oak doors that she would really like to blow—

The doorknob jiggled, and Aria cocked a brow as the two doors were opened just a sliver. It was enough for a woman to slip in through the cracks before she closed the doors behind her without barely any sound at all.

Wearing a designer dress with black heels, her blonde hair pulled into a simple chignon, and makeup, someone might think this woman was … put together.

Except for the drink in her hand.

It was *ten*.

In the morning.

"Can I help you?" Aria asked.

The woman spun around to face Aria. She only needed a peek at the woman's features to know who she was.

Angelo's wife.

Martina.

Aria had seen enough pictures of the woman gracing the society rags to know it—fifty-three, but lived life like she was in her twenties. Sometimes, she had wondered how appropriate it was for the wife of a Cosa Nostra boss to be pictured regularly hammered, and out on the town. Not all of those pictures in the rags were very flattering, either.

Pictures couldn't be flattering when someone was stumbling drunk, and *looked* like it, too.

"Trying to find a way out?" Martina asked, fiddling with the wine glass in her hand.

Aria lifted her cup of tea. "Enjoying my drink, actually. Shame to waste it when Caesar made sure to make it just the way I liked."

And he even brought it *warm*, too.

Martina's gaze narrowed briefly before her features schooled. She tipped her glass up for another drink of wine, and eyed Aria at the end of the hallway. "I don't see what Angelo is so worried about with *you*—you're not very much to look at, tiny little thing. I doubt you're very dangerous."

"Is that what he told you—that I'm *dangerous?*"

The woman shrugged. "That, and something about Caesar. Thinks he's taken a liking to you."

"Men usually do after they've spent more than five minutes looking at my tits or face."

Martina lifted a brow. "I can't see why. There's nothing interesting to see."

Was that …

Jealousy?

Was this woman jealous because her step-son showed *interest?*

Aria couldn't be sure.

"If your husband told you not to come into my wing—"

"This is *my* home," Martina snapped. "You would do well to

remember that, you little whore."

Ouch.

Martina's outburst came so fast and hateful that Aria could only blink. She suspected it was because of the drink in the woman's hand, and probably the many other drinks she had already had that morning.

Hadn't Caesar said there was already one constantly drunk woman in this house?

Aria suspected she was looking at said woman.

"Point is," Aria murmured, "if your husband told you I am dangerous, you would be wise to heed that warning, Mrs. Accardo."

She sipped on her tea again.

Matrina didn't move.

She was dumb, then. Didn't realize the hell Aria could do to her before she even got the chance to shout for help. She probably snuck up there, and no one was around to hear her. It would be *easy*.

Aria needed to get out of this house alive, though. She didn't think killing this dumb bitch would do that for her.

Shame, really.

"I just had to see for myself," Martina said, finishing off her wine as she turned for the door again, "and I can't say it was worth it."

Again with the nasty comments.

Was that really necessary?

Aria didn't think so.

"Don't come into my wing again," Aria told the woman, "because next time, you won't leave. At least, not looking like you did when you first came in."

Martina glared over her shoulder. "Oh, I won't be back in *here*, but I'm sure we'll see more of each other. Unfortunately. Caesar always gets what he wants in that way."

No, Aria *definitely* heard it that time. It couldn't be missed. The woman was green with it. Her voice was *thick* with it. Martina was jealous all over. Jealous over her step-son, and a *woman*.

It left Aria cold all over.

It left her heart heavy.

Her stomach rolled.

Because *why*?

Aria didn't think she would like the answer to that question. And she suspected ... Caesar might have already told her exactly why, but she hadn't listened—people often didn't when it came to a victim, even if it wasn't intentional.

Or they didn't *want* to hear.

"What, you won't let me play with your little *thing*?" Martina asked her step-son.

Aria, hidden by the shadow that the kitchen entryway provided between the room and the hallway, watched the confusing scene happening down the way about twenty feet. Neither of the two noticed Aria standing there, and she wasn't moving an inch.

She *couldn't*.

The woman was too close to Caesar.

Her gaze was too hazy.

Too drunk.

Too *hurt*.

Like his refusal actually caused the woman pain, and she wanted to show him it, too. She moved slightly closer to her step-son, and reached a hand up.

Caesar hit it away—hard enough for the sound of skin smacking against skin to echo—before her palm could come in contact with him. "Keep your fucking hands to yourself."

"I'll tell your father that you let her out, Caesar."

"Do that. He expected me to, anyway."

Martina huffed. "Why do you have to be like this? There was a time when you *adored* me, you know."

"Is that what you call all of that?" he asked. "Because I would call it something else entirely."

Oh, *God*.

The disgust and hatred colored every word Caesar spat out. He didn't even try to hide it. Martina didn't seem the least bit bothered.

Aria didn't like what she was hearing. She could barely stand what she was *thinking*.

"Play nice," Martina said, her words slurring a bit. "Fine, go play with your little thing alone. I do miss having you around this often, though—I'll mention it to your father. He always gets you to come around more, doesn't he?"

"I would rather chew glass than come here more than I already do. Angelo won't change that, Martina."

The woman pushed away from Caesar with a laugh. "We'll see."

Then, she was gone as she disappeared into a connecting room. Aria stayed in her place just long enough to see Caesar let out a heavy breath, and clench his fists hard at his sides. She quickly slipped back to her spot at the table before he came into the room.

His presence in the space was tangible before he even made a sound or spoke. It was enough to make her heart pick up speed, and for her skin to tingle.

She didn't know *why*.

She just liked it.

"You done?" Caesar asked, rounding the table.

She glanced up at him. "Done what?"

He cocked a brow, and pointed at her plate. "That."

"Oh, yeah."

Fucking smooth.

Caesar didn't say a thing. "What do you want to do next? Have a tour—go piss off Angelo's guards? Feed the ducks?"

"You have ducks here?"

"*He* does. They live in a small pond toward the back of the property."

"Ah."

"Might as well let you stretch your legs."

Sure.

"While the king is away, the prince will play," Aria said in a sing-song fashion.

Had he known she was watching?

Caesar chuckled as he pulled her empty dinner plate away from her. "Something like that—I just thought you might enjoy getting out of that wing for a bit."

"And the fact your father isn't home has nothing to do with it, huh?"

"Oh, yeah. It has everything to do with it."

She laughed.

Caesar shrugged.

As unashamed as ever.

Her amusement died as another thought filtered into her head—one she had been meaning to ask since her encounter with his step-mother the day before.

And where was that vile woman now?

"When did your parents divorce?" she asked.

Caesar stiffened as he lowered his form into the seat next to hers. "They didn't—Catholics don't divorce."

Fair.

"She's passed, then?"

He nodded. "By means of one of the worst sins, should you ask the Church. The priest appealed to the bishop, but uh, he wouldn't bend even a little bit; we couldn't have her funeral at the church, but they did allow her to be buried in the graveyard."

She didn't need to ask what he meant, then.

She knew with those words.

"She killed herself."

Caesar cleared his throat, and reached for the glass of water in front of him. He didn't take a drink, but he did distract himself from needing to look at Aria when he spoke by edging the pad of his fingertip around the rim.

"She fell into a bad depression after losing a pregnancy, and that's what came of it. I was four; Angelo remarried before I turned five."

"To Martina."

His jaw clenched.

His finger froze on the glass.

A fire blazed in his gaze.

"Yeah," he said thickly. "To that thing."

"You don't like her."

"That's not a good enough word for what I feel regarding her, actually. Even hate isn't strong enough, but it works just as well."

"Why?" Aria asked.

Instead of answering her, Caesar asked, "Where's your mother?"

"An incident between two clans killed her. My father never remarried."

He nodded. "Sorry."

"You don't have to apologize. I didn't even know her; I have no memories of her, either."

"Well, then, I'm sorry for that. I remember my mother. Sometimes, I think that fucks me up more than anything else ever did because it's warped in my head now. She chose to leave—I got fed to the wolves. Even if my mother needed help, I just ... blame her."

Hate her, Aria thought. He hated her.

His tone said that without him needing to.

Hated her like he hated most—if not *all*—women.

"The wolves being your step—"

"Is there a reason we're talking about this?" Caesar asked, his tone gruff and strained. "Because I would rather not."

"We can't talk?"

Caesar leaned back in the chair, and glanced up at the ceiling. "My favorite color is red, and I like vintage cars. I enjoy a lot of things, actually, despite what people say about me. It's just that none of the things I enjoy are very moral, or good. Specifically, I make a game out of irritating my father just because I can and that's caused me more trouble than anything else ever has."

He tipped his head to the side like he was considering something as he said, "What else? Oh, I have exactly *two* friends. They're married, by the way. People think I have a kink for fucking married women, but I just tend to like anything I'm not supposed to have. I'm Italian through and through, but I could do without pasta. *Unless*, it was my grandmamma making it from scratch. No one made it like her, but she died from a heart attack last year, so I haven't eaten pasta since. Your turn."

Aria blinked. "To what?"

"Talk. That's what you wanted to do, wasn't it? So, *talk*."

"Actually, I want to talk about Martina, and something you told me in the hotel room—"

His gaze cut to her; sharp as a knife in a blink. "We're not talking about that."

"You don't know what I'm going to say."

Caesar's face smoothed into a mask of stone.

Cold.

Blank.

Distant.

"I know exactly what you're going to say, and we're *not* talking about it," he murmured coolly. Standing from the table, he pulled a phone from his pocket, and set it on the table in front of her. "You're going to be moved to a new location tonight; Angelo's orders."

He rattled off an address.

Another hotel.

One still in Philly, though.

"Let's say," Caesar said, "that *somehow* you got ahold of a phone, and let your husband know you're at said hotel with only a couple of guards. He should probably show up with as few people as possible—preferably alone, but we'll make due. He really won't need more; we won't have an army, and he won't want to make a public scene."

Guilt climbed up Aria's spine.

Caesar wouldn't even look at her, now.

"Caesar, wait—"

He was already turning to leave.

Already done with her.

Already *hurting*.

"I'm done talking," Caesar said, heading for the entryway of the kitchen. "And you have something to do now."

"I'm sorry."

For bring up pain.

For hurting him.

For a lot of things.

She didn't think he was going to respond, but he did. Quietly, as though his words were barely there at all. Like he didn't want her to hear them.

"Don't apologize," he said. "No one else ever has—why should you?"

FIFTEEN

THE COMM BUZZED in Caesar's ear, taking his attention away from where Aria currently sat on the edge of a table in the hotel room. She wasn't talking to him, and he wasn't talking to her. They hadn't said a word to one another since he took her from the locked wing in his father's mansion, drove into the city, and set them up in this hotel for the evening.

He didn't have anything to say—he refused to dredge up old demons to satisfy whatever fucking thing she wanted to know. What good was that going to do for him except hurt him? Hadn't he already been hurt by that shit enough?

That's not what this is about.

Or, it shouldn't be.

She kept staring at him, though, and she wasn't even ashamed to be doing it. It was almost as though she were trying to figure him out—and whatever was going on inside his mind—just by looking at him. Caesar felt like he was a bug under a goddamn microscope, but at the moment, he had more important things to be worried about other than what was going on in Aria's head.

"Three entering the building. Raffe Ferri leading." Cain's voice came through the comm in Caesar's ear with a smooth calmness that he really needed to hear right now. He would much prefer to have his eyes on Raffe from the moment the man came inside the hotel, but that just wasn't going to happen. Cain kept him informed on what was happening, and that would have to be enough for now. "Standby."

"Show time," Caesar murmured to his companion.

Aria heard his words if the stiffening of her back was any indication. "Did he listen to me?"

"He only brought two men—makes three with him. I'd say yes."

Which made this somewhat easier, and probably a hell of a lot faster. Cleaner, too, given the way Cain and his guys would work to pick off Raffe's men either outside of the hotel room, or in the hallways depending on how they chose to try and retrieve the man's wife. Cain and Caesar had a plan, then a backup plan, and another plan just in case.

Nothing was left to chance.

It couldn't be.

Aria nodded, and fingered the hem of her wine-red dress. Other than first thing in the morning when they had woken up in bed together, he had never seen her without her hair and makeup done up to perfection. Today was no exception—except he thought she'd taken a special care to look even more beautiful.

Not for him, certainly.

This was all about the show for her.

She wanted to make a show out of Raffe.

Even through her beauty and carefully kept composure, Caesar found her nerves were still quietly present. He found it in her darting eyes every time she heard the smallest of noise outside the hotel room—the way she'd glance at the door like she was expecting someone to burst through it. He could see it in the small tremor working its way through her fingers even though she tried to hide them by fidgeting with something.

"It'll be fine," Caesar told her.

Aria's gaze cut to him in the corner of the room. He was slightly hidden by the shadows leading into the master bedroom of the large suite. It was a good place for him to stay until he needed to come out of hiding, and do his job where Raffe was concerned. The man wouldn't even know Caesar was coming up behind him if he walked quietly enough.

As for their hotel room, it was the only room on the top floor—a penthouse-style room with several square feet, and a hell of a lot of privacy. The hotel manager had even taken a hefty bribe to ensure his cameras would be shut off for the night, and to—no matter what—keep his employees far away from the top floor.

It was all good news for *them*.

Bad news for Raffe.

"One of Ferri's men is down—stairwell," Cain said through the comm.

Caesar pressed the button to talk back, asking, "Why the stairwell?"

"He directed one there. The other one is with him."

Caesar didn't bother responding. The less communication they had at the moment, the better this would all work out for them. His curiosity ate at him, though. He ignored it by talking to Aria instead despite not wanting to do that very much either.

"How do you think he'll react to all of this?" Caesar asked.

Aria didn't look away from the door. "Badly."

"You asked for a few minutes—what do you plan to do?"

She shrugged the dainty line of her shoulders. "*Hurt him.*"

Ah.

Yeah.

Caesar knew that urge all too well. "Physically, or emotionally?"

"Can't one be nearly the same as the other when done properly?"

"That's fair," he returned.

Aria stared down at her hands. "He's hurt me for long enough; it's my turn, now."

"Who am I to judge? I've spent the last two decades of my life hurting everyone and anyone who I felt deserved it all because of a bitch who wouldn't keep her fucking hands off of me as a kid. You want to hurt him, then go ahead and *hurt* him. Make it worth it; otherwise, you're left with guilt when you don't follow through because maybe you *couldn't*—maybe he didn't deserve it. They all fucking deserve it."

His question sent her questioning gaze flying to him, and she replied, "Not *everyone*, Caesar. They didn't all deserve it. They're not all culprits."

"Maybe not, but they all looked the same to me at the end of the day. The person who didn't wake up down the hall. The bitch that ignored what she saw one night. The family that didn't care enough to notice. The people who saw obvious signs of something being wrong, but chose not to ask or do anything about it because it was fucking inconvenient to their life and business. They may not be identical in appearance, but they are all a similar breed of monster."

"Sor—"

"Don't apologize," he said sharply.

Aria sucked in a quick breath, and nodded before she went back to staring at the door. He was grateful that the comm buzzed in his ear again because it took him away from his darkening thoughts. Something he desperately needed right then.

"They're coming up your way, Caesar," Cain said.

And this was where it got ... well, tricky for a bit. Keeping the cameras off meant for the time it took for Raffe and his—now *one*—man to get up to their floor using the elevator, it was just Caesar and Aria. Cain and his men would take the stairwell to get up to their floor—but would Raffe come in blazing with the man at his side, or alone because he thought he was invincible?

It was hard to say.

Well, not really.

"You're going to hear a gun shot, likely," Caesar said.

Aria's gaze narrowed. "What, why?"

"Cain posted a guard outside the door here. It's to make Raffe think that's who is watching you, and that you're in here alone. We want him to come in without his man, right?"

That was their hope, anyway.

"Oh, yeah, I—"

Pop.

It wasn't entirely silent.

It wasn't loud, either.

The guard's—a disposable man that Angelo could afford to lose— body hitting the door was louder than the gun going off, actually. Silencers worked wonders.

Caesar quickly pressed the comm in his ear, and muttered, "Go time." Then, to Aria, he added, "Smile—this is your show for the next ten or so minutes. And then we end him."

All he got from her was a nod.

That was fine, too.

Caesar's gun was already locked and loaded at his side while in his other hand, he kept a tight grip on a string of razor sharp wire. Just as he expected, Raffe didn't *try* the fucking door to see if it was unlocked—it actually was—he simply kicked it in.

The scene was already set.

The moment that door flew open, there she was for him to see.

Pretty, sweet, and waiting.

Sitting on the edge of a table.

Distracting.

Dangerous.

Divine.

Raffe's gaze was only on his wife—narrowed and angry—he didn't even look around the room when she was the first thing he was able to see. He certainly didn't notice Caesar pushing out of the corner from the shadows, and coming for him.

Caesar tucked his gun into the waistband of his pants, and strung the wire out straight between his two hands. He came up next to Raffe just as the man who had been left in the hall shouted, "What the fuck?"

Raffe's head turned fast.

Too late, though.

Caesar wrapped that wire around the man's throat, twisted hard, and pulled back for all he was worth. Raffe was one hell of a big bastard—at least forty pounds of muscle on Caesar, and a couple of inches, too. And yet, when the unexpected hit, it didn't matter how goddamn big a man was—he still fell like Goliath.

"Fuck—"

Raffe's words were cut off by his back slamming into the floor, and his air rushing out of his body in one hard *whoosh*. Another pop echoed out in the hallway—Caesar's comm buzzed again.

"Last man down," Cain grunted. "Coming in, man."

Good.

Because Caesar could really use some fucking help right about now.

Cain swept into the room, and was fast to tuck his pointed gun away at the sight of Caesar struggling with Raffe to keep the man on the floor. It didn't take long for the two of them to drag the man further away from his currently *smiling* wife.

Raffe was fighting; even as he was dragged across the room to the chair Caesar had set up five feet away at the opposite end of the table Aria was sitting on. He bucked, and kicked, and more. Anything to get away, but it was pointless.

He had no air.

His strength waned fast.

They got him into the chair, and Caesar kept a firm hold on that wire while Cain grabbed the rope that had been sitting underneath it. Less than a minute from the moment Raffe had kicked the door open, he was bound to a chair with a razor sharp wire cutting bleeding lines into his throat.

"Give us a few," Caesar said to his friend when Cain stepped back.

Cain glanced at him. "What?"

Yeah, so that bit hadn't been part of the plan. It was now.

Caesar gestured at the door. "Give us ten minutes—close the door, and keep it that way. Don't come back in until I call for you."

"Caesar—"

"Now, man."

Cain nodded once, and then he was gone, forcing the broken door closed behind him. It was only then that Aria pushed off the side of the table and rounded the front of it, so she could lean against the edge and stare directly at her still-struggling husband.

"Would you let him talk?" she asked quietly.

Caesar shrugged. "Your ears, I guess."

And what he meant by that was—

"Fucking *cagna*," Raffe spat the second Caesar loosened the wire. The man's voice was hoarse, and strained, but it still carried volume and weight. "I will kill you for this, *puttana*! You're going to di—"

Yeah, that was quite enough of that shit.

Caesar tightened the wire again, and instantly shut the man up. He looked to Aria with a sardonic smile. "*My* ears don't care to listen to it, really."

Aria wasn't paying him any mind. She was too busy staring down at her bleeding husband as she came closer. The front of his blazer and silk shirt were soaked in a morbid red from his raw throat. That wire could really do a number on someone.

She crouched down enough to be at eye level with Raffe, and yet, still managed to somehow look graceful doing it.

She really was something else.

"I promised you, didn't I?"

Raffe glared.

Aria smiled. "I did promise you, Raffe. I promised to kill you—after you raped me that first time on our wedding night, I told you this would happen. Don't you remember? I had those diamonds on my neck that you gave me as a gift, and my blood on my thighs. You couldn't even be bothered to take your pants off all the way. You didn't even give me a chance to say yes, not when you just wanted me to say *no*. And you laughed at me when I told you I was going to kill you for doing that to me. You *laughed*."

She did exactly that, then; a dark, bitter laugh escaped her lips, and she looked like the devil rising with her narrowed eyes, and white teeth flashing in her cold smile. She looked like pain and hell was about to come for the man standing in front of her, and Caesar was *most* grateful to not be in her way in that moment.

"You laughed at me while you still had my blood on your cock," Aria murmured, still as cold as ever even as she outed Raffe's torment against her. "I promised this day was going to come—I always keep my promises."

All throughout Aria's tirade, Raffe had continued to struggle against Caesar's hold despite how fucking useless it was. Cain had triple wrapped those ropes around the man's ankles and wrists. He wasn't going *anywhere*.

Glancing down at Raffe, he found the man's face had turned a molten red with his rage and lack of oxygen. Caesar loosened his hold just enough to let the man breathe a bit better, but not enough for him to speak very damn well.

Not that he didn't try.

Sadly.

"*Whore*," Raffe hissed.

Aria cocked a brow. "I guess so, yes. I did enjoy myself throughout this whole thing—managed to find a man who could actually make me *come*."

Caesar grinned, and bent over Raffe so the man could see him pointing at himself. "That'd be me, yeah?"

Rage stared back at Caesar.

It barely even stung.

He couldn't help himself but taunt the man further. Aria *had* wanted to make it hurt, after all. How much worse could it get for a man than to have every ounce of his pride stripped away by the man who had fucked your wife again and *again*?

"And," Caesar said, tugging his tie away from his neck to use it as a makeshift gag for Raffe, "she comes like a dream when she wants it—begs like an angel. Have you ever tasted her after she's been sucking on your cock, and her lips are swollen and hot? *Fuck*, it's like candy."

Tightening that tie hard around Raffe's head, Caesar moved in front of the man, and bent down to be at eye-level with him when Aria stepped back. "She gets tart and hot and *sweet*. It coats your tongue, and you just want to hear her fucking scream for you. She likes it best when you bend her over, and pin her down. But she'll really fucking holler if you—"

Raffe jerked forward in the chair.

Caesar didn't even flinch—no, he *laughed*. "Where the fuck do you think you're going to go, huh?"

He smacked the man's leg with his closed fist.

"You're stuck here, fucker," he added. "Back to that vicious wife of yours, though. Bet you've never got a taste of her from behind, have you? Spread open like a buffet, and shaking while she begs you to stick a finger or two up her ass. Christ, she'll really shout for that. And *damn*, when you choke her ..."

Caesar trailed off with a husky noise, and a shake of his head. "*That's* when she gets really wild. That's when she'll do just about anything for you. That's when her skin gets soft, and hot, and her pussy gets as wet as a fucking lake. It almost feels like she's squeezing your dick so hard, it's going to break off. But you just keep choking and fucking her because that's what she wants—except you don't know that at all, do you? You don't know the kind of woman you had in your bed. Shame, really."

Behind his gag, Raffe shouted and mumbled unintelligible words. Caesar had a mind to tear off the man's gag just to hear his shame and horror—even if the fucker would only try to hide it by cursing and raging—but Aria stopped him with one simple question.

One question that made his dick hard.

That *killed* him instantly.

That drove him crazy.

"Want to see, Raffe?"

Sweet.

Hot.

And yes, *vicious*.

Caesar grinned at the widening of Raffe's eyes, and the way the man's struggles stilled at the seemingly innocent question. And then she asked it again.

"Do you want to see what you've missed?"

"Yes, do you want to see how I can make your wife come with just my fingers, and then how good she looks while she rides my cock?"

Because *fuck yeah*, he was up for that.

All of that.

Raffe shook his head wildly, and behind the gag, Caesar could still hear the man refusing. *No, no, no.* A chant of his refusals that fell on deaf ears—refusals that mixed in with Raffe's desperate, muffled laughter.

Not because he was amused, no.

But because he was stunned.

Because he was horrified.

And *disgusted*.

Good.

That's what he should be.

Standing straight, Caesar said, "I bet this wasn't how you expected this night to go down, was it? Yeah, your wife has been surprising me since the moment I saw her sitting in that club."

Caesar moved to stand beside Aria at the table, but she still didn't look away from Raffe. There was something in her eyes—satisfaction, maybe. *Relief,* no doubt. Maybe she felt like it was almost over, and that's what it was.

He didn't know.

Caesar flashed his hand at Raffe a second before he grazed the back of Aria's bare upper thigh where the skirt of her dress came to rest. "I like these dresses she wears," he told the man, "because it's easy access."

And just like that, Caesar's hand was up Aria's skirt, and he slipped between her thighs. He stroked the curve of her ass first, and then let his knuckles graze her sex overtop the silk panties she wore. She shuddered, and her hands curved tightly around the edge of the table to keep steady, but other than that, she didn't move.

Already, he could feel she was hot, and damp.

"This got you wet?" he asked.

Aria shrugged, still staring at the stunned man a few feet away. "Doesn't it make you a little hot?"

"Well, to be fair, a lot of things do that for me."

Finally, she took her gaze away from Raffe to peer up at Caesar. Her red lips curved into a sensual, sexy smile as she said, "You do that for me."

She could have said that for Raffe.

To piss him off.

To irk him more.

To make this worse.

Except she hadn't—Caesar could hear it in her voice, and see it in the way she stared at him unashamed, and *trusting.* She said it for him, and no one else.

Raffe didn't like that if the way he jerked forward in the chair was any indication. He damn near toppled it over, and his eyes *blazed.*

"Careful," Caesar said, barely passing the man a glance, "or you'll fall over, and have a terrible seat for the show."

Aria's teeth cut into her bottom lip, and she grinned when Caesar let two of his fingers slide beneath the gusset of her panties and thrust into her pussy.

"Tight, hot, and *soaked,*" he murmured. "Show him, *bella donna.* Show him how wet you are, and how much your pussy likes this."

Aria used one hand to pull up her skirt while the other kept her balanced against the table. She tipped her head back, and let out one of those sweet moans he adored so much while his fingers kept working in and out of her sex. It was the sound of her pussy sucking in his fingers that he liked the very most—wet flesh, and that scent.

So distinctly *her.*

He didn't need to check on Raffe to know the man was watching—how could he not when his wife was just feet away being finger-fucked by another man?

How could he do anything else but *watch?*

No, Caesar's attention was all on Aria, now. Like it usually was when he had her breathless, spun, and ready to come for him. Nothing else mattered to him in those moments; only the need to feel her.

"Talk," Caesar ordered, his voice dipping into a lower octave. "Tell me, love."

Aria's green eyes flew wide to find Caesar was slightly bent over her, and staring down at her. He found lust there—swirling in those irises, and blowing her pupils wide. He could feel her orgasm coming in the way her pussy clenched around his fingers as he massaged her G-spot, but he could see it in her eyes, too.

Needy.

High.

So ready.

"*Talk,*" he urged.

"It's so good," she whispered.

"Do you want more?"

"*Please.*"

It was always the sound of her begging that undid him—a simple, single word that could rip away his control. As much as he loved the look of degradation on a woman, he *needed* to hear this far more.

Fast as lightning, his hand came up, and clenched around her throat. Aria sucked in one fast breath, and let out a moan that echoed when he pushed her back to the table, and pinned her there. His fingers stroked deeper, then. They pressed firmer into her G-spot with knowing precision—she was going to come *hard.*

"You'll be so fucking slick for me. Tight as hell when I fill you up, Aria. Don't you want that?"

"*Yes,*" she breathed.

The noise a few feet away picked up. More refusals. More rage. More movement. Caesar only laughed because what did it matter now?

What done was done.

Glancing over his shoulder, he found the red-faced, humiliated man still stuck staring at the show in front of him.

"See this?" Caesar asked, grinning. "This is what *gets her off*—wait until I squeeze that pretty throat a little tighter, and you'll love the way she screams my name." Aria trembled; her legs widened a bit more for him, and her pussy clamped down hard around his fingers. *There it is.* "And if you treat her just right, then you'll learn to love to make her—" Caesar cocked a brow, and his gaze cut back to Aria as he added, *"Come."*

And she did.

Loudly.

Shaking.

Beautiful.

"Caesar."

Her shout reverberated in the room—a breathless, high cry that came off entirely broken, but blissed just the same. He could have stayed like that forever; enjoying the sight of her with her skirt pulled up, and her pussy on display with his wet fingers buried knuckle deep inside.

But *no.*

Now, he needed what *he* wanted.

Pulling his hand from between her legs, Caesar made quick work of yanking her away from the table, and pushing it sideways. Aria moved for him, then, bending over the table so that she faced her husband while he moved in behind her, and spread her legs wide with two slaps of his hands. She was still shaking—her juices slicked down her thighs.

He pulled those panties of hers down just enough to give him access, and then he worked his own pants down over his hips. His length throbbed in his hand, already too fucking hard, and almost painful.

He stroked the head of his cock from the crack of her backside, down to her sex. That first thrust was hard, but he found heaven there, too. Damn—he'd been right. So fucking wet, hot, and tight around him.

Like velvet.

And fire.

Perfect, really.

"Jesus Christ," Caesar grunted.

Aria's fingers gripped tight to the edge of the table when he pulled out, and thrust right back in. Hard enough to send her flying up on her toes in those goddamn heels. *Fuck-me-heels.* They lifted her just enough for him to bend her over and fuck her anywhere.

He was starting to think he wanted to do that forever.

How could he *not?*

"Don't fucking look away," he heard Aria hiss suddenly. "I'm the *whore*, Raffe. Remember? Watch your whore, then."

Damn.

She'd already come, and Caesar could tell *this* time, it wasn't about her coming at all. She just wanted the man who hurt her to see what he didn't have—what he had never been given from her. Even as Caesar's pace became faster, and more brutal, she only begged for more, and urged him on.

Christ.

This woman …

This woman would kill him.

Hurt him.

Defile him.

And he would let her.

Caesar felt that telltale heat in his gut, and the tightening in his balls. It shot to his spine a second before he grabbed tight to Aria's hips and held her there, so he could come as deep as he could get inside her pussy. Though he thought she wouldn't come again, she did in that moment. Softer than before, and with quieter, yet deeper moans—she came with a sob.

The relief was sweet.

But *short*.

They had other business, now.

Hadn't they played enough?

"End him," she whispered, still shaking.

He didn't ask if she was sure.

Not if she wanted to do it.

None of it.

Caesar pulled away from Aria, and tucked himself back into his pants. He moved behind a struggling Raffe as Aria rounded the table. Her skirt was still pulled high, and she kicked those panties away.

Her hand snaked between her thighs where Caesar's come was starting to leak from her cunt. She swiped her fingertips through her pussy as Caesar grabbed hold of the razor wire again, and pulled tight.

Aria kneeled down, and with his come on her fingertips and her gaze cold, she looked like retribution in the *flesh*.

Raffle turned red.

His air was gone.

"I'll see you in hell, Raffe," she said.

Hell was the only thing that was promised for people like them.

"Your father has been notified," Cain said from the doorway.

Caesar passed his friend a look, and then nodded. "Thanks, man."

"We'll have to move again. Get her back to the mansion like your father wants."

Aria looked to Caesar, but he didn't have anything to say. At least, not yet. This hadn't been a part of the plan that he let her in on. Frankly, this wasn't *his* plan to begin with. This was something Angelo demanded.

"Close the door on your way out," Caesar ordered.

"All right."

Then, Cain was gone.

Caesar moved to the wet bar the second they were alone, and poured himself a glass of whiskey. He sipped on it while Aria watched him from the foot of the bed in that way of hers. She was still simmering—still *thinking* too much.

About him.

About his secrets.

About *everything*.

He could tell just by the way she looked at him. He knew that meant she cared—and fuck him, because he'd never had somebody actually give a shit before. They were either too stuck in their own problems to notice he was drowning, or it was inconvenient for them to acknowledge there was a reason why he was the way he was.

That someone *did this* to him.

"Say it again," he said suddenly. "That I can tell you, or talk to you about anything. Tell me you won't use this for something, and—"

"You can. And I won't."

Yeah.

He knew that.

Somehow.

"It started when I was seven," he said quietly, staring down into the amber liquid. "And it continued until just shortly before my sixteenth birthday."

Aria cleared her throat, but he refused to look at her. "That long?"

"Probably would have been longer, but uh, I had a bit more freedom by then and learned how to avoid her as much as I could."

"Oh."

He was grateful she didn't apologize again.

Why should she?

"My father married my mother because she wanted to; he loved her," Caesar said, smiling a bit, "and then she died, so he had to marry again. For his status, and because he had a four year old that apparently needed a mother. He was too busy to notice anything—too busy with his own issues and problems. Still grieving a wife, and trying to do as little as possible with the problematic cunt he married because someone told him he had to. I think that's why she first started to mess with me; it was a way to get closer to him. Angelo paid more attention to me than he did her."

"Jealousy," Aria filled in.

Caesar shrugged. "Call it that if you want, I guess. Martina came to him *already* fucked up. Already had a drinking problem; she even drank when she was pregnant, but she thought nobody noticed. It started with little things. She'd come into the bathroom when I was taking a shower, or walking in on me when I was getting dressed. But she was supposed to be taking care of me, so even though I felt awkward, I didn't know the difference when she started doing other things. And then she'd start coming into my room at night when she was drunk, and ..."

His jaw clenched tight; like his hand around the glass he was holding. "When I was younger, well, it just made me ashamed. What was I supposed to tell people—that my step-mother was telling me this was how you *felt good*? That she made me touch her? And then when I was older ..." He let out a bitter laugh, and shook his head. "Someone rubs on you, and you get fucking hard. You can't control it, even if you don't fucking want it. She used that shit a lot, too.

"All of it," he added, "was just another way for her to hurt my father, I think. Because the more I distanced myself, and worse I became with my behavior or toward him ... the happier she seemed to be. She used sex to hurt him, and in turn, I just wanted to hurt everybody else. I wanted them to feel even a little bit of what I felt like because they didn't know or help me."

"That's not sex, though," Aria whispered. "Sex is supposed to be good, and consensual, and whatever else you want it to be, Caesar, but it's not supposed to be *that*."

Caesar glanced up to find she was staring at him—no pity looked back, though. Just another soul who might possibly be a little broken like he was, but it still wasn't the same. It was enough to make him take notice.

It was *enough*.

"It's not supposed to be that," she repeated.

"Monsters rarely look like monsters."

"I know."

Sometimes, monsters were pretty women with a drinking problem, and an ever-constant presence that he couldn't rid himself of.

Caesar tipped his drink up, and swallowed the rest of the whiskey in one burning pull before he set the glass aside. "Time to get back to hell."

Aria let out a soft sigh. "Hard to believe."

"What is?"

"It's almost done. I'm almost free."

Caesar chuckled darkly.

Didn't she know?

There was only one way his father would let her—and probably *him*—get out of this alive now. And she wasn't going to like it at all.

"You're never going to be free now, Aria."

SIXTEEN

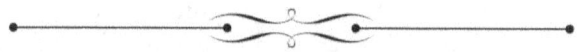

THIS WAS NOT what Aria was expecting.

This was not what she wanted.

This was not the *plan*.

"We go ahead with the original idea for her husband," Angelo said, eyeing Aria from where he sat behind his ostentatious desk. "Send him back to his people with a message—make sure our point is driven home that our organization is not the one they want to mess with, and wipe our hands clean."

"And what of her?" the man sitting in the corner asked.

She thought his name was Christoph—an underboss, or some nonsense, but she couldn't be sure.

Angelo's eagle-eye still hadn't left Aria. "I am undecided."

"We had a—"

"Quiet, Caesar," Angelo muttered, raising a single hand to quiet his son. "You know just as well as I do that deals change all the time in this business."

Beside her, Caesar stiffened. "Only dishonorable men renege on a deal."

The man behind the desk chuckled dryly. "And you would know all about being a dishonorable man, wouldn't you?"

That silenced Caesar *instantly*.

Aria chose to speak, then. "If you don't return me, then they'll raise hell. I guarantee it—given who my father was, and what has happened to my husband, they won't let it rest. Camorra clans aren't the type to shy away from retribution when it comes to something like this."

Angelo raised a single brow. "Even for a woman like *you?*"

"What's that supposed to mean?"

"You know exactly what it means," the man returned easily, smirking just a bit. "You certainly put on a good show, Aria De Rose, but that's all it is. And when someone strips you of the things you use to hide your intentions, the show is no longer *amusing*."

Jesus.

"What's to say she won't come back on us, then?" Angelo asked Caesar, his gaze cutting back to his son lightning fast. "Should we hand her back over as a peace offering like she suggests, then what's to say she won't come back on us for what we've done?"

"You have my word that I won't," Aria said.

Angelo didn't even look at her that time. "Your word is useless, *donna*."

"She did start the war between our organizations," Christoph added. "It's not a stretch to think she might continue it on."

"And that's no good for *us*," Angelo said heavily.

Aria didn't want more fighting.

She didn't need more bloodshed.

None of that was important, now.

She had got what she wanted the second Raffe stopped breathing. She could go back to her life *before* she had become his wife, and regain some semblance of the normalcy she had lost. She could *heal*. Finally, really heal from the hell she had needed to endure.

She didn't want war.

And these men didn't care.

Caesar lifted a single finger high, drawing every eye in the room to his seat beside Aria. "I have another option."

Angelo's lips flattened into a grim line. "I can't say I am particularly interested in hearing it, but go ahead and try me anyway. It can't be any worse than the ones that are already on the table. *Dio* knows we could argue the semantics of this bullshit all night."

"I think you might like this one, actually."

"I rarely like things you do or want, Caesar," Angelo grumbled. "Don't get your hopes up too high."

His father's barely-hidden insults didn't even seem to faze Caesar. It was like they simply rolled off his shoulders with every single one, as though he were used to this, and it had become second nature for him to be the verbal punching bag.

Or maybe …

Shit, maybe he liked this.

Maybe this was part of what made him who he was.

Beyond the rest …

"Do tell," Angelo said, waving a hand dismissively at his son. "Before my patience wanes, and I just take the easy route by killing her."

Aria's spine stiffened like someone had driven a stake into the bone, and forced her to sit a little straighter in the chair. It infuriated her to no end how she could be sitting right there, and yet these men talked as though she wasn't in the room at all. Her opinion—despite having shown her muscle against them at every turn on the streets—counted for absolutely nothing in the grand scheme of things.

She was still *just* a woman.

And women were less than a man.

At least, to these people.

A shame, really.

It was their mistake.

"Well, it *is* something you've wanted for a while," Caesar said. "And you don't need to be rude about it, that's all."

"Caesar, don't test me tonight."

"You're no fun."

"You've made me this way, *figlio*."

"Have I, really?" Caesar asked.

Angelo simply stared at his son.

Caesar looked right back.

"*Get on with it,*" Angelo barked.

"Fine," Caesar said under his breath. And then, louder, "I marry her—she's a widow, and we don't even have to pretend to wait for a period of time like we might if it was another Cosa Nostra woman. She's not Cosa Nostra, but she *is* Italian, and that's what counts to you, isn't it?"

Aria's head snapped to the side, and she stared dumbfounded at Caesar.

No.

He was *not* offering what she thought he was.

He couldn't be …

"Marry her," Angelo echoed.

Caesar nodded once. "And then the Accardo organization can absorb the De Rose Camorra into a faction for our business—the men will either get in line, or they can be killed. Either way, their added business is a win for us. They have a decent territory where their drug trade is strong. A heavy hand in loansharking within Philly. And even a racket in the new development on the west end where those condos are being built for the next five years. Her father knew a guy higher up with the suits—it looks like it'll be a good deal."

Aria was stunned.

Silenced.

Livid.

How did he know all that?

"They're not *made* men," Angelo pointed out, although not unkindly.

It sounded like he was actually fucking considering this.

"They don't have to be made men to work *under* a made man," Caesar returned. "Name one Capo in our family who has a crew made up of entirely made men. Go on—I'll wait. I have all the time in the world tonight, apparently. No better place to be."

He even flicked his hand at his father like he was passing the goddamn torch.

Angelo sighed. "No need; I get your point."

"And should a crew fall to shit, well, the business will still be there at the end of the day," Caesar said, shrugging his Armani covered shoulders.

Like he didn't have a care in the world. Like he wasn't ruining *everything* Aria had worked for. Like he wasn't ripping apart her entire world without even looking at her while he fucking did it!

Inside, she seethed.

Outside, she was a mask of calm.

Life had taught her to be this way.

She didn't know anything different.

Angelo leaned forward at his desk, and rested his elbows along the edge as he steepled his fingers together. Overtop his fingertips, he stared at Caesar for a long while. The room stayed quiet with a tension so thick, it seemed almost suffocating.

Then again, that could have just been her.

And her *rage*.

"That would renege the deal with the Canadian boss," Angelo murmured.

Caesar looked entirely unaffected that statement. Was that was this was? He'd been nailed to the wall with that marriage arrangement, and his way out was using her?

He'd told her that once, hadn't he? This—to be free from that marriage arrangement—was what he needed. His way to freedom was to cage *her*.

"I'll handle the De Rose crew—stay on my side of the city, and out of your hair. Other than tribute once a month, you won't need to see me at all, or have anything to do with me. The trouble will be, essentially, gone. That's what you want the most, isn't it?"

"And you *will* see it through?" Angelo asked, ignoring his son's question altogether. "The marriage, I mean."

Caesar nodded. "I picked it, didn't I?"

"It's true you haven't done that before."

"I keep my word when *I* make it, and not when you do. There's a difference. I will see it through."

Angelo tipped his chin up, and then glanced over at Aria with narrowed eyes. "Well … it seems you've managed to find your way out of yet another one of my arrangements for you, Caesar. I hope this woman is worth the trouble. You won't like what happens if she's not."

She's to stay here until the day you marry—that's my demand. Take it or leave it.

Those parting words of Angelo's before he'd sent them from the office were still echoing in Aria's head like a bad fucking dream—a nightmare that had somehow become her reality. She didn't know how any of this had happened. This was not what was supposed to happen!

She trembled all over. From the five-inch patent leather pumps on her feet to the very top of her head—she vibrated with her rage. How she had managed to hide it for this long, she didn't know. They were just entering the upper, private wing that had become her prison before all that fury she had been holding in finally started to show.

She was going to break her teeth from clenching them so hard. Her nails were breaking the thin skin of her palms because she couldn't unfurrow her fists.

Caesar's hand came to press at her lower back as they stepped through the oak doors leading into the wing, and she *snapped*.

Her hand swung hard, and snapped against his wrist to knock his touch as far away from her body as she could get it. He did *not* get to touch her now.

How dare he?

Spinning in her heels, she faced Caesar and let him see all that anger and betrayal she had been keeping hidden since he decided to open his fucking mouth downstairs. He didn't look the least bit surprised to see how mad she was—if anything, he looked smug.

Too fucking smug.

Too arrogant.

Too cocky.

This man was *too much* of everything!

"You didn't think you would get off scot free after everything, did you?" he asked.

Aria's cheek twitched as she replied, "I thought you understood what I needed—we had a *plan*."

"*You* had a plan. I used what bit of it would work for me, and the rest … well, shit happens. What you need isn't always what everyone else wants. I've been told time and time again that the world rarely revolves around me. Maybe it's a lesson you should learn as well."

Screw him.

"Since when do you give a fuck about everyone else, Caesar?"

His lips curled at the edge—only one side. A sexy, hateful half-smirk that she might have enjoyed seeing any other time. But not right then.

"Low blow," he said.

Oh, he hadn't seen anything yet. She could promise him that, but very little else.

Caesar took one step forward, but Aria refused to let him come closer to her. Not after everything. She took one giant step back. He didn't even seem bothered or offended by it.

"You manipulated me in to making a bigger war with your family—in to killing your father, and your husband. You showed everyone just how vicious and dangerous you can be, *donna*. And what? You thought after all of that, he was going to let you *go*?"

He, she noticed.

Angelo.

Not Caesar, though.

"Killing you would have been the easy choice," Caesar said, "except I had a better option."

"For who?" she asked. "Not for *me*. You've ruined everything, Caesar."

"Have I?"

"How *could* you?"

Caesar grinned. "Stomp your foot, and add in a *how dare you* for good measure, love. It might get you the same result, but you'll look fucking cute doing it."

Fire blazed through her very being—burning through her muscle and sinew with devastating intent. It was going to ruin her like he had, but she would much rather her rage take her down than this man.

He caused her to feel a fury so strong, it nearly knocked the wind out of her. She *cared* for this man—she didn't know when it happened, or why or how. And none of that mattered anymore.

None of it mattered because of this.

Because he betrayed her.

The two stared at one another in silence.

Caesar, unmoved and cold.

Aria, enraged and trembling.

It was a stark contrast, and she was not so distracted that she didn't recognize it for what it was. Both broken, and damaged in ways that would never be repaired. They were two entirely different people who played the most dangerous of games. And at the end of the day, they were still just pawns to one another.

Nothing more, and nothing less.

Caesar forgot, though, how goddamn good Aria could be at this game.

She knew her moves.

She knew *his*.

And she knew how to work them against each other.

"Fuck you," she uttered.

"We've already been there and done that—you're still wet from it, Aria."

Caesar rocked back on his heels with a dark laugh, and turned his back to her. He reached for the handle on the oak doors a second after a knock echoed from the other side. He turned the knob, but just before he opened the doors, he looked back at her.

"A parting gift ... if you want one."

She didn't *care*.

She wanted nothing from him.

Not now.

And yet, when Caesar pulled open the door, there stood someone she did want to see and talk to. Or ... needed to see and talk to after everything.

Nico.

The only person she could actually trust.

"Told you she was alive," Caesar said to Nico.

"Lucky for *you*."

"That is a matter of opinion at the moment."

Nico didn't respond to that at all. He stood with a guard at his back, and his wild gaze darting between Caesar, and her. Nico didn't move an inch until Caesar passed him by, and when he did move it was only to come closer to Aria.

"Behave," Caesar said over his shoulder, "and Nico stays for as long as you want him to. You could use a friend, Aria. Don't be stupid."

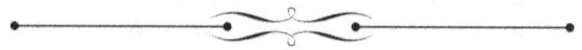

"Ten minutes," Nico murmured.

Aria glanced away from the mirror, and nodded at her friend. "Okay."

She was grateful for his company—he stayed with her in the mansion's wing even when he could have gone home, and filled in the important people with the news of everything that had happened. Instead, he stayed there with her for three days.

So far.

Caesar hadn't come back to the wing since he left that first night, and she wasn't even entirely sure that he was still at the Accardo estate. But she couldn't say for sure. It was a wise move on his part to keep his distance.

Strangely enough, the wing wasn't locked, either. Aria was allowed to leave, and wander the mansion or the grounds without much interference. Although the guard that had accompanied Nico—he called the man an enforcer—was never too far behind when she left the wing.

He didn't speak.

Luckily.

Aria went back to her reflection in the mirror, and smoothed out her white dress. The elbow-length sleeves, and short skirt was both modest, and yet sexy. She'd managed her curls into a thick mane that fell over her shoulders, and halfway down her back. She'd done up her makeup, and wrapped a bracelet of pearls around her wrist.

Simplicity and elegance.

They asked for a De Rose—they got one.

"You don't have to do dinner with them," Nico said. "It was only offered."

She shrugged. "It *was* offered, though. And why not take them up on it?"

If the Accardos wanted to pretty Aria up, and put her on display for their people to show what they had done and what they now had, she was more than willing to play along. At least for the moment, anyway. She couldn't say how long it would last.

"Shame I wasn't invited."

She might think Nico was offended about that if he wasn't *smirking*.

"Cute," she said.

He shrugged.

"Good, you're ready."

In the mirror, Aria saw Nico stiffen. She, too, felt like a rod had been thrust into her spine as she turned to face the man standing in the doorway of the bedroom she'd picked to use. It was the first time she had seen Caesar in days, and yet, he still looked the same.

Like sin, and hell, and the hate in her heart.

He wore one of his tailored, black Armani suits, and Tom Ford loafers. He checked the Rolex on his wrist, and then dragged his fingers through the dark blonde hair on the top of his head. His ice-blue gaze drifted over her, and then to Nico.

"Do you want to come to dinner?" he asked.

Nico's upper lip curled a bit. "Not particularly."

Caesar tipped his head in Aria's direction. "Not even to keep an eye on her?"

"Do you think she needs protecting?"

A laugh answered Nico back.

"Not at all," Caesar murmured. Then, to Aria, he gestured for her to move with a single hand. "Let's go—people are already sitting down to eat, and we don't want to be rude."

Right.

No being rude.

"I promise nothing," Aria said, passing him by in the doorway.

Caesar sighed. "I figured you would say that."

Fifteen guests.

Fifteen faces Aria didn't recognize.

Fifteen people she didn't give a single shit about.

And yet, they couldn't stop staring at *her.*

She had a good mind to give them the show they must have been expecting what with the way they kept watching her like she was some kind of wild animal in a cage. Being their little amusement for the night wasn't even the worst part of this whole goddamn dinner.

No, the worst part was where she was sitting.

At one side, Angelo headed the table as people worked through yet another course of food. At the other end, his horrible, vile wife sat in another captain chair like the queen of the room.

And Aria?

She sat next to the bitch.

Caesar sat directly across from Aria, but for the most part, his attention was on just about anything but her. Small blessings, she supposed. One less thing for her to seethe about right then.

The queen bitch, however, was working on her fifth glass of wine, and already starting to laugh a little too loudly, and slur her words. Despite how pissed Aria was with Caesar, she could tell that the more vocal his step-mother became and the drunker she got, the more uncomfortable he was with his current seat.

He didn't want to be there at all.

Neither did she.

Aira wished—*God,* more than anything, she wished—that Caesar's discomfort didn't affect her. After everything, she shouldn't care about him. Not after what he did, and was still doing.

And yet, she *did.*

She hurt for him.

Fuck him for doing that to her, too.

"And we have good news to share tonight," Angelo said from his spot at the head of the table. Aria hadn't even been listening to the man drone on throughout the dinner, but he had her attention *now.* Especially because he was looking right at her. "As you can see," he added with a gesture at her, "we have an unusual guest at our table tonight. Certainly not one you all expected to see, and yet here she is, as beautiful and docile as ever."

Hesitant chuckles passed over the table. These people had to know that at the very least, she was far from docile. She had more blood on her hands than a lot of these men, likely.

Aria's rage festered a little deeper.

Caesar's gaze drifted to Aria, but he said nothing.

Angelo was still speaking, after all. "We've finally come to an … agreement, we'll say, with the De Rose Camorra. Isn't that right, Aria?"

Her mouth was damn dry.

Her throat protested.

And still, she spoke. "Yes, it is."

Angelo offered her a thin smile. Like he was *praising* her.

Fuck him.

She didn't need it or want it.

Angelo nodded, and wagged one finger between her, and Caesar. "They'll be married within three months—preferably sooner, if I get my way—to solidify this new arrangement we've made. The business will be good, and the streets will be quiet again. I look forward to seeing my son follow through on this agreement."

A quiet laugh echoed from beside Aria.

Martina.

The bitch.

Nasally and slurred, the woman asked, "And do you honestly think Caesar will follow through with this one, Angelo? How many marriages have you tried to arrange for him so far? Five … six? A bit pointless by now, isn't it?"

"Martina," Angelo started.

The woman set her now empty wine glass to the table, and gestured for the bottle that was just out of her reach. It was passed to Aria first, but she hesitated in handing it to the already hammered woman beside her. It wasn't like the cunt needed more alcohol.

"Oh, whatever," Martina said with a wave of her hand, and a higher laugh. "You almost have to feel sorry for any poor woman who gets saddled with Caesar's mess, don't you?"

Martina gave Aria an apologetic smile, and shrugged her velvet covered shoulder, saying, "He'll fuck anything that's warm and wet enough to call his name, sweetheart, and you might as well just accept it now. Everyone at this table has already gone through the rounds."

First, it was disbelief.

It saturated Aria.

Silenced her like it did the table.

And then the fury came.

Fast.

Destructive.

Painful.

That pain was echoed from the man sitting across from Aria—oh, he hid it so well, but Aria could still see it in the dimming of his eyes, and the way he tensed all over.

How dare she?

After everything she did to him … after it all?

"Like you, too, right?" Aria asked softly before she could stop herself.

That silence echoed louder.

175

Sharp as a blade and ready to injure the way this woman had, Aria said, "Like you did to him when he was a boy—how you dishonored him when he was a *child*?"

Martina's gaze cut to Aria and widened.

Fear and anger stared back.

Aria didn't care.

"Deny it," Aria urged a little louder. "I *dare* you."

"*Aria*," Caesar murmured. "That's enough."

She didn't even look at him.

Didn't look at *anyone*.

Except Martina, and her reddening face.

"You're a *stupratore*," Aria said, standing from the table, and still holding the neck of that wine bottle in a death grip she wasn't letting go of. "A *pedofilo*, Martina."

Rapist.

Pedophile.

She'd all but hissed the words, and let them snake down the table like the poison they were.

Like the truth that had to be said.

A truth that had *never* been said.

"*Aria!*"

Caesar's response was a shout this time—thick, and loaded with an ache she hadn't heard from him before. It was too late. She'd already swung that bottle before someone—including the bitch she aimed for—could react.

Green glass shattered over Martina's face, and red wine mixed in with the blood that poured from the woman's busted nose and mouth. Martina's cries for help and pain was a song like no other, but the bitch was going to have to sing it for years before Aria would ever grant her mercy.

Aria wished that was *enough*—*wished* the sight of this woman bleeding and failing to get her arms up to prevent the second hit was enough for Aria to feel even remotely better.

It wasn't.

Nothing short of death would be enough.

Someone did pull Aria away before she landed a third hit—Caesar. His arms wrapped tight around her like a cage, and he pulled her further away from the destruction she had caused. The rest of the guests at the table still seemed too shocked to react, or maybe they didn't know what to do.

What did it matter?

Aria kept fighting regardless of Caesar's efforts, even as she kicked the table, and at the woman stumbling out of her chair while holding her broken and bleeding face. The scars that wine bottle would leave behind would be a nice reminder every time Martina looked in the mirror.

And it still wouldn't be enough.

It was nothing compared to the scars this woman had left behind.

Martina's time would come.

Aria would make sure of it.

Caesar finally dragged Aria out of the dining room, but not before she got the last word in.

"Karma is a bad bitch, but she's never met *me*. Remember that, *cagna*."

SEVENTEEN

ANGELO RAGED ON.

Caesar was numb.

He felt nothing; heard nothing; seen nothing.

"Get rid of that woman! Get rid of her right now!"

His father's words echoed from the dining room he'd just left, but they bounced off his shoulders like rubber bullets missing a target. He could hear footsteps behind him, but no one followed. He figured people were leaving.

That usually happened when a party ended badly.

It was only once they were far enough away from the dining room that he could no longer hear his father's shouts that Caesar finally let Aria go from his hold. He pushed her away from him a few steps, but the woman spun around to face him anyway.

He stilled in place.

Caesar wasn't sure what to say, and he sure as hell didn't know what to expect when she faced him. Maybe haughtiness and anger—those were things Aria knew all too well when she aimed to kill a person.

He found none of that.

Instead, she stared at him silent and resolved—calm, yet still empathetic. The other shit, he might have known how to deal with.

Not this.

"Why did you do that?" he asked quietly.

It was the only thing he could think to say.

"Did you *hear* her?" Aria asked back. "Did you hear the things she said, and how she spoke about you like it was *nothing at all*? Didn't you hear her?"

Caesar blinked.

His step-mother, she meant.

And yes, he had. But this was his whole life in a nutshell. This was the kind of thing he had learned to deal with, or punch back hard when it happened. *That* was how he dealt with this kind of problem.

But *damn.*

How he wished for years that he could have done what Aria just had. That somehow, the shame he constantly felt would lift just enough for him to speak the fuck up, and do *something*. That it wouldn't terrify him more than anything in life ever had just to point at the bitch who molested him for years and say what she did.

Except he couldn't.

He didn't want to be weak.

Didn't want to be shamed.

Could *not* be disbelieved.

"I'm *not* going to apologize for that," Aria said when Caesar stayed silent. "She deserved a hell of a lot more than what I did tonight."

"She does," he agreed.

Aria's brow furrowed. "I ..."

"What?"

"You don't seem angry. I'm not sure where to go from here."

Caesar managed a smile, as faint as it was. "Was that what you were expecting—my anger? Is that why you did it ... to piss me off?"

Aria's head snapped up at that statement. "No."

"Don't act like it would be a far stretch for me to think that, Aria. We both know you're willing to use whatever you have at your disposal to get what you want from someone."

"Except that's not what this was."

Yeah, he could tell.

"And yet, you're still going to get something you want," Caesar said dryly.

And he would be left dealing with the aftermath here.

Something he'd been dreading for a lifetime.

"What is it that you think I want?" Aria asked.

Wasn't it obvious?

"Not to be here," Caesar said. "Let's go find your friend while we still have time to."

The mansion had quickly emptied of guests—other than a couple of stragglers, but those were people Caesar expected to find when he finally made his way to his father's office upstairs. For once, Angelo didn't sit behind his desk. Instead, he stood by the windows and stared out over his property.

His underboss, Christoph, was in the midst of pouring two glasses of whiskey when Caesar came through the doorway. One of which he handed to the organization's consigliere, Davide. His half-brother, Daniele, sat in a chair closer to their father.

No one noticed him standing there.

It was strange.

It felt insulting.

His whole life had been people overlooking things that should have been noticed. At the very least, someone should have thought to *ask*.

No one ever had.

None of these people, anyway.

Christoph glanced up from his drink, asking, "Angelo, do you want a drink?"

"Not right now," Angelo replied, glancing over his shoulder. It was then that his gaze landed on Caesar. There was no sympathy in his father's eyes, but the rage was gone, too. Angelo looked entirely done with the day. "There you are—come in, and we'll have a chat."

Yes, a *chat*.

That was a funny way to describe discussing what had happened.

All things considered ...

Caesar only came far enough into the office to pass the threshold of the door. Right then, he didn't want to be any closer to these people. He didn't like the way their gazes drifted to him, and then lingered a beat too long.

He was the troublemaker.

A sinner.

The *issue*.

He caused problems because that gave people enough shit to focus on where he was concerned. It was what they could always expect from him— guaranteed.

Now ... *now* they were looking for something else.

And he hated that.

Angelo turned away from the window, and sighed. "Where is the woman?"

"She has a name," Caesar said, knowing exactly who his father was referring to. "And she's gone. I sent her away with someone I picked—not *your* guard—and the man from her family."

Angelo's expression hardened. "You sent her away."

"You said to be rid of her. Did you want her to stay?"

"I meant I wanted her—"

"Dead," Caesar interrupted coolly. "Yeah, I figured that, but it's not going to happen. I made an agreement, and I intend to see it through."

His father scoffed, and wagged a finger at him. "Come on, now, *figlio*. I'm sure you don't need me to tell you why you won't be marrying that woman after tonight. You can't honestly expect me to allow a marriage between you and her after the things she said, and what she did to my wife."

Silence echoed in the room.

Thick.

Brutal.

And *suffocating.*

No one said a fucking thing. No one even wanted to look in Caesar's direction, but he was used to that. Usually for different reasons, sure, but he was coming to find it really wasn't all that foreign to him.

"And what about what your wife did to me for years?" Caesar asked. "Doesn't she have to answer for that?"

He said the words easily. Far easier than he thought he would when the day finally came for him to open up his mouth, and say something about Martina's abuse.

"That's a *lie!*" Daniele was up out of his chair in an instant, and looking like he might come Caesar's way any second. His fists clenched at his sides in tight, shaking balls, and his gaze burned with every ounce of hatred he had always felt for his older brother. "My mother would never—"

"Why," Caesar asked, "because she never did it to you?"

Daniele snapped back like Caesar had punched him from all the way across the room. The two stared at each other for a long while, but Caesar really didn't give a shit about his half-brother. Or what the man thought about the things he had learned.

It wasn't about Daniele.

It never was.

"Because she never climbed into your bed when you were a kid," Caesar continued, refusing to be silenced by *anyone,* "you feel safe enough to say it didn't happen, right?"

"My mother loved you," Daniele snapped, "and you've been nothing but horrible to her, Caesar. Everyone knows it. Everyone has fucking seen it."

"But did you ever wonder why?"

Daniele's gaze narrowed. "I—"

"Never cared to *ask.* Yeah, I got it."

With a nod, Caesar turned back to his father. Angelo looked even more passive than he had before. Like none of this was surprising, and he'd heard it all before.

Caesar knew then.

He *knew.*

Everyone else in the room was in various states of shock, or disgust. Maybe because they hadn't known, or they didn't want to believe.

"It's never a woman, right?" Caesar asked his father. "We always just assume it's a man."

Angelo's shoulders relaxed a bit. "Son—"

"When did you know?"

"I can't say I *knew.*"

"You did," Caesar said confidently. "I can tell you did. So, when?"

Angelo cleared his throat, and gestured with a hand at the other men in the room. The three men were quick to scatter, and close the office door behind them as they went on their way. It was only once the two of them were alone that his father turned to him again.

"You were ten," Angelo said, "and one of the maids you took a fancy to had found something in your room as she was cleaning. Something of Martina's—I don't remember what it was now, but she mentioned she was concerned, and it wasn't the first time someone had said something."

His father fixed a cufflink on his shirt. "And then again when you were fourteen, we were having a Christmas party, and one of my men happened to see Martina … crowding you in a hallway, but he didn't say anything else. They were things that didn't draw my concern, Caesar. It could have been a lot of things—she drank too much, and got a little too handsy. She was your step-mother; her things could be excused if they were found in your room. I never thought to look at something like that until you were far older, and by then, you were gone out of the house and it didn't matter."

Caesar laughed.

Hard.

Bitter.

And entirely dark.

"*It didn't matter?*"

Angelo tipped his chin up at Caesar's words. "No, I—"

"It didn't matter?" Caesar scoffed, and shook his head. "No, what you mean to say was it wouldn't be *convenient* for you, and who you are to *know* that your son was being sexually abused by your fucking wife!"

His father said nothing.

He didn't even try to deny it.

And suddenly, things made so much more sense to him.

It all came in with a clarity so sharp, it hurt his mind.

"That's why," Caesar said quietly.

Angelo raised a brow. "Why, what?"

"All these years. Everything I did that you excused, or covered up, or overlooked. All the times I broke every rule that could have justified you putting me in a grave—the way I've dishonored our name time and time again. Despite all the things I have done, and the ways I've hurt people you care about … *this is why.*"

"Son," Angelo started to say.

"Because you felt guilty," Caesar continued, uncaring about what he had to say. "You felt guilty about what she had done, and what you knew. And *this* was your way of apologizing or making it up to me?"

Caesar laughed again, and pointed a finger at his father. "I don't want your fucking apologies, Angelo. I want you to give me what I want *now*. After everything, you owe me."

Once again, Angelo said nothing.

And once again, he didn't deny it.

Cain was sitting on the front stoop of the unfamiliar home when Caesar pulled his Corvette into the driveway. He expected to see more vehicles there—surely Aria would have made some calls the moment she was returned to her house, but it didn't look like she had done that.

Stepping out of the car, Caesar stared up at the inky sky. Dotted with faint stars, the blackened canvas matched his mind right about then.

He was pissed.

Hurt.

Standing on unsteady ground.

His usual go-to when he felt like this was to act out—hurt someone back just because he could. Because they never cared enough to know he was hurting.

Caesar went and sat down with his friend on the step instead. "I'm surprised she doesn't have a whole army here."

Cain shrugged. "She went in and cooked food, actually."

"Huh."

"Her friend—Nico—left about an hour ago."

Caesar nodded. "He's not half bad. Less violent and unpredictable than Aria is, anyway. Pretty sure that's a mark in his favor."

"He's not us, either."

"Yeah, well … depending on who the *us* is in that statement, he might be a hell of a lot better regardless of where he comes from."

At that statement, Cain stiffened a bit beside Caesar. He'd been there at the dinner—he would have heard the things that were said.

Wordlessly, Cain's hand struck out, and landed on Caesar's forearm. He squeezed tight, but said nothing. He didn't need to say anything. The action, and the support, was clear enough. Caesar was grateful.

"It's fine," Caesar muttered.

"I don't think it is, man."

"I've handled it."

"But have you handled it *well?*" Cain returned.

"Probably not."

Cain sighed. "I know people might say shit or assume whatever based on what they think they know about you …"

Caesar chuckled under his breath. "They've been doing that for years, anyway."

"Right—true. I got you, though."

He glanced over at his friend.

Cain just shrugged.

"Yeah, I know. Say hi to your wife for me when you get home. She's probably ... concerned."

"Gina always worries about you. Don't know *why*."

Caesar laughed. "Yeah, me either."

Cain clapped Caesar hard on the shoulder as he stood. "Speaking of Gina, though. She would like her, you know. Aria, I mean."

"You think?"

"Hell, Gina likes anybody that can fuck shit up."

"Yeah, Aria is good at that."

To say the least ...

"We'll get this figured out," Cain said as he moved down the steps. "We always do."

"I don't think we'll have to do too much, actually," Caesar replied. "Everything is about to change, now."

Cain simply gave him a look over his shoulder, silently questioning without actually asking out loud. Caesar grinned back, saying nothing.

It was what he did.

He was who he was.

"He's known for years."

Aria looked up over the tarts she was currently sprinkling with powdered sugar, and found Caesar standing in her kitchen entryway. He could have taken the time to appreciate her house, and the way it was decorated, but he had a lot of shit on his mind.

Too much, really.

"Who?" she asked, setting her utensils aside.

"My father."

Aria placed her hands to the island, and considered his words for a moment. "Are you sure—"

"Absolutely."

"My initial reaction is to apologize."

"Please don't," Caesar murmured. "Actually, let's talk about something else."

Aria nodded. "Okay—why did you send me here?"

"Because this is your home, isn't it?"

"It is, but that doesn't explain anything, Caesar."

"Do you not want to be here?"

"I have always wanted to be here."

He gestured at the room. "Here you are."

"Yes, *alone*. Minus you."

"And you'll remain that way. No guards—no men of ours stepping in on your business. You're free to do what you want until we see this agreement of ours through."

She stiffened, then.

He didn't miss it.

"The marriage, you mean," she said quietly.

Caesar shrugged. "What else?"

"I thought—"

"What, that because I let you come home and be comfortable that the deal was done? I don't go back on my word. There's still something I need, after all, and you can get it for me."

Aria blinked.

Her anger was a slow simmer in those green eyes.

Getting hotter by the second.

"Would I be so bad?" he asked. "We get along well enough when we're not trying to kill each other, and it's not like you don't enjoy being on your back for me."

Her cheeks pinked, but she only asked, "To marry?"

"Exactly that."

"You're trapping me. It's not by choice. There's the difference."

Caesar sighed. "For one's freedom, someone else always has to sacrifice. I'm sure you know that well, considering everything you've done to get to this point."

Aria's jaw clenched. "That doesn't mean—"

"You know, when I have a night like tonight, the first thing I do is … something destructive. Usually to someone else, although I have been known to go out and fuck myself up nearly beyond repair, too. I just want to forget; I don't want to feel, or think. It's easier. I get pissed off, and I need to distribute it elsewhere, so I don't implode on myself."

"Your point?"

Simple, really.

"I *know* I could get that with you right now if I just pushed you the right way."

"You mean *fuck* me?"

Caesar gave her a pointed look.

"Is that an *offer*?" she asked when he said nothing.

"I didn't say that."

"Good because the answer is no."

"Ever?" he asked innocently.

Aria narrowed her eyes. "Not tonight."

"So, even though you want to kill me a little bit, we're still good to fuck is what—"

"*Not tonight.* And not when you're feeling like you do right now. At least give me the respect of not using me like some object to make yourself feel better because you don't want to deal with your issues, Caesar."

Fair point.

"I'll take the couch," he said, "because I still don't have a place to live since your husband burned it to the ground, I don't want to grab a hotel, and I am not going back to the mansion."

"You can take the bed with me."

Lady's choice.

Who was he to argue?

"Have a tart," Aria said waving at the sweets in front of her. "They're my specialty."

He arched a brow, and gazed at the sweets. "Did you poison them?"

She smiled. "You know me better than that—nothing is ever as it appears, and I don't do *simple* when I want someone to die."

Truth.

He ate a tart.

It was good, too.

And not poisoned.

EIGHTEEN

A LOT OF things were not supposed to happen in this plan of hers. From the moment Aria had started to work out exactly how she was going to free herself from the marriage to Raffe, and take over her father's Camorra in the process, she had a clear goal.

One path.

One road to travel.

One prize at the end.

And sure, she had sought out Caesar specifically because she figured—given the things that were widely known about him and his family—he would be an easy way in to cause problems, and someone she was capable of manipulating.

He had been exactly that. He'd also ended up being far more to her, too.

Aria had not been prepared for him, or the hurricane he would be once he swept into her life. She'd expected a man—like every other man she'd encountered—but he hadn't been *that* kind of man at all.

He'd been *this* man.

This broken, beautiful man.

This wounded soul.

And yet, he went beyond even those things.

He was *more*.

He was the kind of man that even when she wanted nothing more than to kill him for the things he had done, she still wanted to see him sleeping in her bed.

What was she to do with that?

Aria hugged the Afghan blanket tighter around her shoulders, and stared at the sleeping man from her position across the room. She'd gotten up an hour ago when the sunlight first peeked through the window shades, but found herself drawn back to the bedroom despite *everything*.

Why?

Because a part of her wanted this man. Somehow, she had grown to care for him in all their vileness, and hurt. It was never more apparent to her than when she drifted back to the bedroom, and sat in the corner chair simply so that she could watch him sleep.

In his dreams, Caesar was at peace. He didn't move, or want to hurt. He was relaxed, and even boyish in his features. Nothing like the sharp-edged, dangerous man he could be when his eyes were open, and his mind was ready to find the next thing to attack.

And even when he was like that, she enjoyed him, too.

Wanted that, too.

Aria knew it, then. She knew what it was that had wrapped its way around her heart like a fist squeezing the organ with a tight grip, and refusing to let her go. She knew because nothing in her life had ever quite had this sort of effect on her, and no one probably ever would again.

That terrified her.

Amazed her.

In everything they had done to one another, and within all the destruction they had caused, she *loved* him.

How, and why, and *when*.

Those were the things she didn't know.

Didn't understand.

And she didn't know what to do about it.

The peace written in the hard, handsome lines of Caesar's features were quick to leave as his eyes opened, and he stared directly at the window where the light was shining in. He took a moment, and blinked awake fully.

Aria didn't move. "Sleep well?"

Rolling to his back on the bed, Caesar scrubbed his hands down over his face, and stared at her from the bed. "It's only reality where my nightmares visit me."

Yeah, she bet.

She knew that well.

Now, though, it was time to get back to that reality.

To life.

To her *plan*.

"I was thinking about what you said last night," she murmured.

Caesar stretched his arms over his head, showing off his muscular, naked chest without even realizing how damn good he looked. And fuck him for doing it, too. He probably did know how he looked; he just didn't care of the effect it had on women.

"About what, specifically?"

"The marriage."

His right eyebrow arched, and he passed her another look. "Go on."

Now or never.

She could give them what they both wanted.

He had to let her, though.

Setting her half-empty mug of coffee on the stand next to the chair, Aria stood, and dropped the blanket. Caesar's gaze drifted over the silk baby doll nightie she'd slipped on the night before to sleep in, and then traveled down her bare legs. Once she was close enough for him to touch, he reached out a hand and did just that, stroking a single palm along the curve of her thigh down to her knee.

His touch burned her.

In the *best* way.

"You seem … more pleasant this morning," he noted, glancing up at her.

Aria nodded. "You don't give me much of a choice."

"That so?"

"Very much."

"Or are you trying to get something from me?" he asked.

Aria grinned.

He knew her so well.

Kind of.

"I'm not being nice because I want something," Aria told him, reaching out to run her fingers through the longer bit of hair at the top of his head. "I don't need to be nice to get what I want, Caesar."

"Mmm, good."

"Good?"

"That's what I said, *donna*. What do you want, then?"

"To talk about something."

Caesar made a face. "Fine, but first I get what I want, and then you."

"And what do you want?"

The words were barely out of Aria's mouth before she found herself yanked to the bed, and pulled on top of Caesar. His hands cupped her face, and pulled her in close for a kiss that took her breath away. The kiss—like him—was fierce, and hot, and *violent*.

Dangerous, too.

A war between two people, but the only kind that wouldn't end in bloodshed between them.

Murmuring against her lips, Caesar said, "You said *no* to last night. It's not last night—it's today. And feel, I woke up ready for you, love."

Goddamn him.

He was right.

About *both* things.

He flexed his hips upward, and it caused the hard length of his erection to grind against her sex through the thin silk covering her sensitive spot. A small moan escaped her lips before she could even think to try and stop it.

Not that she wanted to.

Caesar's hands moved to her ass, and squeezed tight enough for it to ache. He dragged her body against his again, and chuckled when she shivered in his hold.

"Don't you want a taste?" he asked.

"How is fucking me the first thing on your mind this morning?"

His blue eyes found hers. "Because it's easy. Everything else is hard."

Oh.

She pressed a quick kiss to his mouth, and then let her lips travel down over his jaw, chest, and lower. Her hands slipped beneath the boxer-briefs he'd slept in, and pushed them down just enough to free his cock. Thick, hard, and warm in her palms, she stroked him as she shifted lower, too. Her gaze darted up to find he was staring down at her with a smirk lingering at the corners of his lips.

"Get that cock in your mouth, Aria," he said gruffly.

She didn't even want to refuse.

The silken flesh of his cock met the roughness of her tongue when she swallowed his length in one pull. All the way down to the base—his thick groan echoed in her ears. She could feel the pulse of his heartbeat in his shaft, and the shudder working its way through his body.

She didn't tense when his fingers threaded into her hair, and held her down on his cock as his hips flexed upward. Her throat constricted from the action, but she relaxed. He never pushed too far—never hurt her.

"*Fuck*, just like that," he murmured. "Get me nice and wet for you, my girl."

And then his hands loosened their hold just enough for her to move. She raked her fingernails down his chest and stomach as she sucked him off. Every single noise that crawled out of his mouth was a dangerous sound for her.

Dangerous for her heart

For her body.

For *everything.*

"Shit, get up here."

His sharp words were quickly followed by him yanking her up from his lap, and pulling her back onto his lap. Those deft hands of his had her panties swept to the side in no time at all, and then he was grabbing her hips, and tugging her down.

Onto him.

All nine inches.

Filling her full.

Stretching her open.

It really was the best feeling first thing in the morning.

Below her, she watched Caesar's eyes close as his fingers dug in tighter to her hips, and held her in place on his cock. She felt his length jerk inside her pussy—once, and then twice. His hips flexed upward, and he hit *that spot.*

It made her bite her lip, and moan.

"You always make music for me," he murmured, eyes still closed.

"And what does that make you—the composer?"

190

"As long as I'm the only one *composing* in you."

Aria laughed.

Caesar's eyes opened, then, all stormy-blue again and burrowing into her. "Not funny."

"No, it isn't."

"*And?*"

"And it's only you."

"Better be."

His statement was punctuated by one of his hands traveling around to smack her ass, and then grab tight to the same spot. His fingers skimmed further around her backside until she could feel just the tip massaging the tight entrance back there.

It sent a shock of pleasure rushing through her blood. And then a hard jolt of need when that finger slipped into her ass after a few small circles to get her relaxed, and ready.

"Jesus Christ," she breathed. "What if I wanted more of that?"

Caesar flashed a grin. "I would ask if you had lube."

"In the nightstand."

"Then, I would tell you to bend over."

"Would you?" she asked sweetly.

Anticipation curled through her gut.

Hot, and heavy.

Lingering, and sweet.

"*Bend over.*"

God, yes.

She was fast to climb off of him, and despite how empty she felt without him between her thighs, the second she was on her knees, and holding onto the curved edge of the headboard, it didn't even matter. He was behind her again—already had that small bottle of lube in his hands.

The cool, slick liquid dropped between the crack of her ass, and then his fingers were there, too. One sliding into her ass, and then a second. The third came with a bite of pain, but it was gone quickly enough. His hot mouth came down to kiss the swell of her ass as he fucked her with his fingers, and then his teeth bit into the same spot.

Pleasure.

And *pain.*

A delicate balance.

A lot like *them.*

The sounds that escaped her as he worked her ass, and praised her with dark whispers were raw. Climbing out from deep within her chest, and showing just how much she *needed* what he was giving to her.

Then, his fingers were gone.

"Breathe," he said, his palm sliding up her spine as the head of his cock pressed against her ass. "Just keep breathing."

She was high.

Or, it sure felt like it.

Aria had all she could do not to bear down when he first started working his cock into her ass—thicker, and longer than his fingers, it stretched her in a more painful way. But with every teasing lick of pain, bliss soon followed, in the way he touched her, or even his fingers between her thighs circling her clit. His lips kissing the back of her neck, or the way his body fit tight like a glove against hers.

"Oh, my God," she whined.

It took one hard pull of her hips, and he was buried in her ass all the way to the base of his cock. The ache that settled deep inside her core was unlike anything, but it quickly turned into something else entirely as he started to pull out slowly.

Like his cock was hitting untouched nerves.

Dragging against every *good* spot she had.

Caesar was slow, and careful. Gentle strokes that filled her full, and then pulled right back out again. It drove her crazy—she just wanted *more*.

"Please fuck me," Aria breathed, resting her cheek against the curved edge of the bed. "Fuck my ass, and make me feel *good*. Please."

Caesar's fingers pressed hard enough into her hips to leave bruises behind. His next thrust hesitated, and she knew she had him. Instead of another slow flex of his hips, he fucked her hard enough to make her whine. He didn't slow between one thrust, and the next. Her words and moans melted into the same fucking sound.

Something wild.

Something *raw*.

Caesar leaned over her, and tangled one of his hands into her hair. His lips were at her ear, and he fucked her harder. "You better give it to me if you want me to come in your ass, *donna*. Give me what's mine—come for me."

It was the way he pulled her hair, how hard he pounded into her ass from behind, and the circling of his fingertips against her clit that threw her over the edge. She went numb all over but for the pleasure slicing through her body.

She heard nothing but him.

Felt only *him*.

He didn't slow even as she came—if anything, her orgasm spurred him on to fuck her harder, and faster. She was just coming down from her high when she felt his last deep, jerky thrusts, and then he spilled inside her.

He came with a groan of her name.

Her name.

And it sounded like *God* on his lips.

Except it was her fucking name.

It was only when he'd pulled away from her, and those gentle hands of his were brushing the hair away from her face that she spoke again.

"My turn," she murmured.

"Mmm, for what?" he asked.

"To get what I want—let me apologize."

Caesar stilled. "I beg your pardon?"

"To your father, I mean. If we're going to see this through, then issues between him and I won't do us any good. Let me apologize to him privately for what happened, and then we can go from there."

"Aria—"

"Please?"

She only ever needed to say that one word to get what she wanted. At least, when it came to Caesar.

This time was no exception.

Apparently, Angelo preferred to take his late breakfast in a small enclosed porch on the east side of his home. It allowed him to overlook the property, and gave him some semblance of privacy with only one wall of windows to stare out of.

Or, that's what Caesar explained.

Just outside the porch, frosted glass covered the French doors leading to where Angelo was currently eating.

"Just you," the enforcer said when she gestured for Nico to follow.

Aria frowned, and glanced at Caesar for an answer. "What, I can't have my right-hand man with me?"

"His rules. You asked for this."

She had.

"Fine," Aria said, rolling her eyes. "We *were* checked, though. I don't have anything to hurt him, and neither does Nico."

Caesar shrugged. "His rules."

"It'll be fine," Nico murmured. "I'll be right here when you're done."

She didn't doubt it.

Caesar, on the other hand, leaned back against the wall, and gave her a look. "Don't antagonize him—we're hanging by a very thin thread here."

Right.

"Antagonizing him is the last thing on my mind," she assured.

It wasn't a lie.

Caesar nodded at the doors. "Go ahead. We'll be here."

Aria grabbed the handles on the French doors, and pulled them down. Pushing the doors open, music filtered through the space. Italian opera, it sounded like.

Jesus, she hated that garbage.

It wasn't important.

At the other end of the room, Angelo sat at a table near the windows. A small, two person dinette set that gave him the perfect position to see everything. He didn't even pass her a glance as she closed the doors behind her with one last look at Caesar and Nico. As she crossed the room with quiet steps, her heels still clacked against the tiles.

In front of him, Angelo had a full spread of food.

Eggs, bacon, bagels, and more.

Anything he wanted.

Currently, he was buttering a bagel.

Aria came to a stop two feet away from the table, and waited. Angelo didn't keep her waiting for long—he gestured with the butter knife in his hand at the seat across from his at the small dining set. Once she had joined him at the table, Angelo tapped the edge of his butter knife against an empty coffee mug.

"Make yourself something to drink," he said, "if you think we're going to be here a while."

"I don't know that I will, actually."

The man's dark eyes lifted, and landed on her with a heavy weight. She could tell he was unhappy—he didn't like her, and she didn't even wonder why. After everything she had done to him, she suspected it was only because of his son that he allowed her to be in his presence.

"Then, what are you here for?" Angelo asked gruffly. "I was told you wanted to apologize."

Aria nodded. "That's what I said."

"Get on with it, then. Kind of pointless, though."

The song changed on the small radio behind Angelo, and he set the butter knife down on the table before turning around to increase the volume just enough to make Aria smile.

Every move was a mistake. Setting the knife down. Turning his back on her.

Assuming shit about her.

Why did they keep underestimating her? Why did they think they could trust her?

Angelo turned back around in his seat, but it was too late for him. Aria had snatched up that butter knife, and swung hard the second she had the chance. It embedded deep into the side of his neck—right into the major artery—and she was quick to grab the bagel on the plate when Angelo's mouth opened to shout. She shoved that hard piece of warm bread deep

194

into his mouth, and yanked the knife out.

Blood went *everywhere*.

On her.

The table.

The windows.

Warm, and sticky, and *crimson*.

He'd bleed out in minutes, and no one would know a thing. Even if someone did come in, it was already too late to save him.

The music was turned up just enough that Angelo's choking gurgles could barely be heard even standing right next to him. He almost tipped over the table as he fell to the tiles, and blood pooled all around him.

His eyes stared up at her wide and stunned. She smiled down at him as she began to make a coffee with the bloodstained cup.

"There was really only one way for this to end," Aria said quietly. "Me, or Caesar. One of us was going to have to go so that the other could get what we wanted. That couldn't happen, and so I figured out another way to give us both what we want. What was one more death, Angelo? He'll understand why I had to lie and hurt him one more time."

She was sure he would.

That didn't mean Caesar would *like* it.

"I did come to apologize," she said, tipping a spoonful of sugar into her coffee cup. "I'm sorry you'll never get the chance to ask your son for forgiveness. I don't think he would have given it to you anyway. Die knowing that, Angelo. It's what you deserve."

Aria, like she had just before she first entered the enclosed porch, took a deep breath, and then pulled open the doors. As promised, Nico and Caesar were still waiting for her right where they had been standing when she left.

The enforcer was directly across from the doors.

He saw her first.

Saw the blood first.

"What the fu—"

All eyes were on her, then.

She imagined she was quite a sight.

Aria smiled at the man. "There was a *little* accident."

She barely got out of the way before the enforcer rushed the room, and the doors automatically closed behind him. Nico made a noise under his breath, but Aria simply flicked a hand at him as if to dismiss whatever concerns were about to fly out of his mouth.

She turned to Caesar.

He was waiting with a *smile*.

"Now we both get what we want," she told him. "You're free—no marriage, no rules. And so am I. You shouldn't have trusted me again."

His striking features turned almost playful in his grin.

She didn't know what to make of it, or him.

"Wrong," Caesar murmured, "I trusted you to do *exactly* what you did, Aria. See, you taught me a new trick, *donna*. You thought I didn't know what would happen the second you got him alone? I knew. I don't have to plan my own moves when it comes to you, I only have to plan for what I expect you to do when something happens, and work accordingly. I would thank you for removing my last problem, but I don't think you want me to."

She stared at him.

Stunned.

Unsure.

Amazed.

"Well done," she said.

Caesar nodded. "A bit of a shame, isn't it, my girl?"

"What is?"

"All we've done to one another. Every cut we made. And though I hate you for a lot of things, still, I somehow love you."

Her heart stopped.

She swore it did.

Spattered with his father's blood; knowing she lied to him again; manipulating him one last time to get what she wanted.

All those things …

He still said, *I love you.*

"Why?" she asked. "Why do you love me?"

"Because you're amazing, and you're everything I can't have. After everything we've done, it could never work. We're not healthy. This isn't that kind of good, Aria."

She was scared.

That terrified her.

Because what if he was right? What if like everything and everyone else the two of them had touched on their way to the top, they were ruined now, too?

"You should probably go," Caesar said, "I have a problem to handle, and you don't want to be here when the shit really hits the fan."

That was his goodbye.

He couldn't even say it.

She didn't want him to.

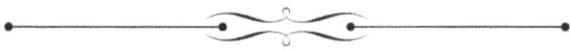

One week passed.

And then two.

Aria fought tooth and fucking nail to get her life—and the Camorra clan that had been left in utter chaos—back to some semblance of their *normal*.

And yet, it was everything but.

Her people, still unknowing of everything she had done to get them to the place they were now, wanted action and retribution against the Accardo family.

For Raffe, for her father, and even for her.

Retribution she wouldn't give.

Action she wouldn't take.

She was being challenged at every turn. She hadn't expected it to be easy. She didn't think it would be this hard, either.

Life in Camorra as a woman had always been a little too fucking suffocating. And even now, it was just as horrible, only maybe worse given her position. They were looking for a reason to discard her—something to give them any reason at all to replace her.

And she understood why.

She would do it, too, if needed.

Mostly, she was just unhappy.

And *lonely*.

Nico dropped onto the couch beside her, and handed Aria a mug of coffee. "You look sad."

"I am," she said quietly.

"Why? Don't you have everything you want, now?"

Almost.

Mae clicked her tongue, drawing their attention to where she was sketching with a pad and charcoal next to the window. "She won't even smile for *me*, Nico."

Aria did smile at that. "I always smile for you, Mae."

More so, now.

Her sister-in-law—Mae would always be family regardless if her useless brother was dead or not—had the chance to do whatever she wanted. *Be* whatever she wanted to be, now. Aria was going to keep working to make sure the girl could do exactly that from here on out.

Including keeping control of the Camorra.

Mae would not be someone's pawn.

"Okay," Mae corrected, giving Nico a look, "but she doesn't smile as much for me."

"Mmm," Nico hummed. "Sad thing, that is."

Fucking Nico.

"I miss him," Aria admitted.

The first time she had willingly admitted it.

Mae passed Aria a look—her newest confidant next to Nico. It was best she have both a male and female with her at all times so that her behavior and actions couldn't be questioned. They needed to be people Camorra respected and trusted. Mae and Nico were both of those things, thankfully.

Nico sighed. "This was not a part of the plan."

"No, it wasn't."

Mae glanced over her sketchpad. "Does he—this *Caesar*—have the kind of face I can draw?"

Aria wet her lips, and nodded. "He has a beautiful face. Handsome and haunted."

"*Oh*, I like him already."

Nico, on the other hand, was still on their previous conversation. "What are you going to do now? About him, I mean."

"Let him bury his father," she told her friend, "and have his time."

After everything, Caesar deserved that. He didn't need her there to do it. Even if she needed him.

Hell, he might not even want her at all.

She would understand that, too.

NINETEEN

THIS WAS NOT how you thought it would end between us, did you, Papa?

That question lingered heavily in the back of Caesar's mind as he stood at the very edge of his father's grave. He was so close to the six-foot hole that the toes of his loafers hung over the edge, and dirt crumbled down onto the black casket from his weight.

Still, he didn't move.

Not as the priest did his business, and said his prayers. Not as the people came to say goodbye. And not as the first shovelful of dirt was tossed down.

You always thought you would be burying me, didn't you, Papa?

It was funny to him that in his mind, he referred to his father the way he had when he was just a young boy. As his *papa*, and not Angelo, or the bastard, like he had been using for the last several years.

On the outside, Caesar was sure he seemed disconnected from the funeral and burial to anyone watching. He made the bare minimum effort to do anything when it came to this day. He'd picked the church, and the burial plot for his father's sake, but very little else. He left those details up to whoever wanted a say, and stepped way back.

Things were good once, weren't they, Papa?

Back when he was little.

And Angelo cared.

Before *Martina*.

Caesar sucked in a deep breath, and finally looked away from the casket scattered with dirt on the top six feet down. He looked up instead—at the bright blue sky, and the fluffy clouds rolling overhead. Heat bore down on him, but he barely felt it even under his black three-piece suit when he was too busy feeling everything else.

God picked a good day for you to say goodbye, didn't he, Papa?

It was just too bad that Caesar had said his goodbyes years ago. He'd said goodbye to the man his father once was, and to the things that could have been. He'd said goodbye to a lot of things, and today, he felt almost nothing for this.

He felt things, sure.

Too many things.

Not for *this*.

"You couldn't even give me *this*, could you?"

Caesar's vision blurred as he looked away from the bright sky to acknowledge the person speaking to him. He had to give it a second to adjust from the sunlight, but he wished he had just kept staring at the sky when he realized who was standing on the other side of the grave *glaring* at him.

Martina.

She was a mess.

Her dress crumbled.

Face streaked with tears.

Makeup ruined.

Heels caked in mud.

Drunk.

Caesar was at a point where he no longer wanted to even share the same air as this woman—but he wasn't at a place where he could correct that issue for himself just yet. Oh, soon, sure. Not quite yet.

"What couldn't I *do* for you?" Caesar asked. "Don't you think I've done enough for you, Martina? Don't you think you've taken enough from me?"

Everything.

She'd taken everything.

His mother's place.

His father.

His trust in women.

Any love he might feel for his family.

His virginity.

Innocence.

Happiness.

This bitch and everything she had done to him turned Caesar into someone he might not have been, otherwise. And for the most part, he had learned to love this person staring back at him in the mirror.

He was who he was.

Nothing was ever that easy, either.

He thought it was kind of like grief—it sure felt a hell of a lot like it. He was grieving a man he could have been, and a life he could have had if she had not abused him for years. It was only *now* that he was finally starting to see how much her misdeeds and wrongdoings had shaped and affected him.

And she wanted something from him? After everything she did, this *thing* had the audacity to think she could demand anything from him?

It was infuriating.

Hilarious.

And entirely sad.

"Go crawl back into your hole, Martina," Caesar muttered, his attention going back to his father's grave. "No one cares to hear whatever problems you've got with me today. Add them to the list—I hear Cain keeps one just in case I ever want to go back to it."

His step-mother huffed.

"No, *this*!" she shrieked.

Her voice grated on Caesar's nerves.

"This grave," Martina continued in that shrill way. "You had to bury him next to *her*. You couldn't even give me that, Caesar!"

Ah, *yes*.

His one of two requests for this event.

Next to the church, he'd picked the grave for his father. Angelo had never said where he wanted to be buried should he die, and it hadn't been in the man's Last Will and Testament, either. This spot seemed like the perfect place.

Next to Caesar's mother, *Isabella*.

Angelo would like that.

Turning on his heels, Caesar moved to step back on the path. But not before he called over his shoulder to Martina, saying, "It seemed appropriate that he be buried next to the only woman he ever loved, doesn't it? You've lived for two decades knowing you were a replacement— I'm sure you can manage for a few more hours."

That should have been a warning for her.

She should have *heard* him.

Martina only shrieked at him again.

Stupid woman.

Caesar flashed the woman who stepped out behind her desk a smile even as she put her hand up to try and stop him from entering the elevator.

"I'm sorry, sir, but you can't—"

"Oh, they're expecting me," he returned easily. "No worries."

They being the made men of the Accardo Cosa Nostra.

And *they* weren't actually expecting him at all.

Cain rushed to get inside the elevator as well before the doors could close—giving his friend a fucking side-eye the whole time. "Slow down."

"Keep up," he countered.

"That's fair."

The elevator jerked as it moved up fifteen fucking floors without stopping once. Who thought it was good to have a meeting between made men in a hotel where not only did *Caesar* know the owner, but said owner was also very open to being paid the fuck off?

Stupid men did so.

That's who.

Of course, it hadn't only been the owner of the hotel who let Caesar in on this little meeting that was happening, but he confirmed it. Caesar would deal with the person who did tell him at a later date—*if* he felt like it.

"You could do this another way," Cain said.

Caesar shook his head. "There is no other way."

And even if there was, this was what he wanted to do.

"And besides, do you think Angelo's old consigliere and underboss gathered the rest of the made men of the family here because they were going to talk about a *party*?" Caesar scoffed. "No, and there was a reason why you and I were not invited to this, too. While we're waiting to get up there, let's take a fucking bet on how long you think they would let the two of us live before someone whacked us. It'll be fun—you go first."

"Fuck off."

Caesar shrugged. "Your loss."

The elevator jerked one last time, dinged, and then the door opened to expose a long hallway. There was only one penthouse suite on the top floor, and it was way down the hall. He did a cursory check of the hallway before he stepped out of the elevator, and Cain followed behind. Caesar pulled out his gun, and checked the clip before making sure the safety was off, and it was ready to fire.

He wasn't fucking around.

They hadn't, after all.

At the room door, the two men stopped.

"Should we knock, or ...?" Cain asked.

"Fuck knocking. I am beyond that."

He was so beyond any and all politeness at this point.

Rearing back, Caesar let his booted—*God*, he missed his loafers—foot smash into the wood just below the doorknob. Wood cracked and splintered, but the door swung open with a bang. Sure enough, every made man of the Accardo organization that had not at all been expecting Caesar or Cain to show up stood from the table in a rush.

They couldn't get on their feet fast enough.

They were already too late.

Caesar lifted his gun, aimed, and *fired*.

Davide, Angelo's consigliere before his death, took a bullet right to the forehead. It sent the man flying back from the head of the table, and crashing into the glass stand behind him. Knickknacks and shards went flying—the dead man's body lie bleeding on the floor.

Cain already had his gun up, and he took his shot, too. Like his friend, he didn't miss when he aimed for Angelo's old underboss, Christoph. He blew the side of the man's head out, and made quite a mess on the far wall when it became splattered with Christoph's brain matter.

Caesar lowered his gun.

All eyes were on them, now.

He smiled. "Now, who thought they could have a meeting without inviting us?" he asked the silent room.

Gazes darted around.

These men looked like they wanted to *bolt*.

Caesar passed a cursory nod to the one man who had actually filled him in on this meeting that was to take place right after Angelo's funeral that afternoon.

Daniele.

He wasn't sure if his half-brother was trying to save his own skin, or he was feeling some kind of guilt about everything that had happened. It really didn't matter at the end of the day. What was important was that Caesar would not be letting any fucking man make a plan on his life like he was just going to stand there and *take it*.

Even if that meant hurting them.

Or taking over the organization.

Maybe killing a few.

Whatever it took—here he fucking was.

Caesar moved around the table as Cain stayed in his position with his gun aimed and ready. He took the seat that Davide had first been sitting in, but not before he kicked the dead man's leg out of the way, so he could roll the chair back in its proper place.

Sitting down at the head of the table, Caesar moved it closer and gave another one of his brilliant, cocky smiles to the dumbfounded men. He set his gun to the table, and then gestured with a single finger at the men, saying, "There seems to be some kind of confusion about what's going to happen to me from here on out, but that's okay. I'm here to correct any kind of misconception you all have. Shall we get started—do any of you want to go first, or should I?"

The men stayed silent.

Caesar figured that.

It was kind of hard to find the balls to talk when there was a gun pointed at you, and the man you were planning to kill just foiled everything you were working for.

Karma really was beautiful.

Leaning back in the chair to appear more relaxed, Caesar folded his arms over his chest, and eyed each of the men individually. "You know, I could go through each one of you, and humiliate you with different things. Which of your wives or daughters I've had the pleasure of bending over some variation of a flat surface—hell, Micky, I didn't even need a flat surface for your wife, did I? Ever get the back of your Mercedes cleaned?"

The Capo in question turned cherry red from Caesar's statement.

Caesar laughed, and nodded. "Yeah, see, we could do that whole thing. And I could explain to each and every single one of you how you've all been dishonored in some way by me, but I don't think we need to do that. You are *all* compromised, though. And unless you want those details to leave this room—see, I have more than just memories when it comes to the shit I've done because I've been waiting for this day—we're going to sit here, and have a nice conversation about how I plan to take over this family, and what I want to do with it."

Dead stares.

Clenched jaws.

Shaking fists.

Their rage was palpable.

And he ate that shit for breakfast.

"Thing is," Caesar continued, "for every one of you that speaks out here, Cain is going to drop you. He and I can leave this room alone, and begin the process of rebuilding this organization, or you can all make it a bit easier on us. Keep standing if you've got something to say, or sit your asses down if you want to let *me* talk. Go ahead and choose—I'll wait."

"You cock—"

Pop.

Caesar felt the splatter of blood drops hit his cheek when Cain turned his gun on Micky, and pulled the trigger. The back spray was a *bitch.*

Shaking his head, Caesar wiped at the blood on his cheek, and likely just smeared it. "All right, that's one. Who wants to be next? We've got all day."

Three men sat, including Daniele.

Two stayed standing.

Hard way it is.

His father's office wasn't as dreadful as it had been when the man was alive. He used to hate coming here—it could fucking induce walking nightmares, really. Yet, there he stood just hours after regaining control of an organization his father's father had helped build for years, and he felt nothing but calm.

It was strange.

But he wasn't complaining.

Moving behind the desk, Caesar pulled the chair out, and dropped into it unceremoniously. He had always hated this desk because it was huge, and terribly ostentatious. What kind of man needed a desk this big?

One trying to make up for something.

He still didn't *like* it.

He simply respected it.

The phone in his pocket buzzed—Cain, likely, asking if he was done or if he was ready for the cleaner to come in and fix whatever hell he caused. Caesar slipped his hand in his pocket, and silenced the phone for a moment.

He needed to be alone.

To *think*.

Or at least until—

"W-what … Angelo?"

Caesar's gaze drifted to the drunk woman stumbling past the office's oak doors. Her hazy gaze, messy appearance, and missteps told him she had been drinking a hell of a lot since the funeral that morning. Martina looked like she was one good breath away from falling over, and dying of alcohol poisoning.

Too bad for her.

That would be an easy way to go.

Caesar wasn't about to give this woman *easy*.

Her gaze narrowed as she blinked, and came closer to where Caesar sat behind the desk. She wasn't seeing him—that he could tell. Her words only confirmed it further.

"Why won't you come to bed, Angelo?"

Caesar didn't speak, simply tipped his head to the side, and watched her come closer. How she was even staying upright, he didn't know. At least, she had managed to throw on something for bed even if it was *just* a silk robe. God knew he'd seen enough of her nakedness over the years—not by his choice, obviously—but he kept his stare strictly to her face. She had nothing he wanted to see, anyway.

Martina rounded the edge of the desk, and used a shaky fingertip to trace the corner as she said, "You're still angry with me, aren't you?"

He refused to speak.

Not until he was ready.

She made him ready with her next words.

"You know how Caesar is," she mumbled, staring at the floor like some poor, wounded animal in need of healing. "He made a bigger deal out of what happened than what it actually was—I only ever *loved* him."

Caesar snapped out of the chair in a flash, and had Martina's throat in his hands before she even understood what was happening. He slammed her down on the desk, and squeezed her throat for all she was worth. Despite the rage swimming in his bloodstream, and the absolute fury he felt at just having to even touch this woman to *kill* her, his face and voice remained cool, and calm.

"Loved?" Caesar asked. "That's what you call *love*?"

He knew love.

He knew it from his mother.

And from the way he felt without Aria despite ... *everything*. He was so lonely without her, and he wasn't even sure when that had happened. All he knew was that she was every single thing that made him question who he was, and he thought he could be better.

For her ... for Aria, he could be *better*.

He knew love.

And what this woman had done to him was not it.

Martina's eyes widened, and her face reddened with the lack of oxygen. Oh, sure, she tried to fight but, in her drunkenness, it was pointless. He could have eased up and let the bitch talk—try to find another way out of this—but he didn't care to hear her excuses.

He didn't want an apology.

Not from her.

"Enjoy your place in hell," Caesar murmured.

He didn't let Martina see his anger, or the pain she caused him for all those years in her final moments. He made sure all she saw was his cold face until the last second, and he didn't let go of her throat until he couldn't feel a fucking heartbeat racing under his palms anymore.

And it was only when he did finally let her go that all those emotions came rushing in like a tidal wave ready to devastate and destroy him. Like a jackhammer pounding against his chest; the grief, anger, and pain swelled and spread.

He couldn't breathe.

And his body *hurt*.

His mind felt broken.

And his heart ached.

He'd killed his monster; his demon was gone.

And he was still ruined.

He was still shattered glass standing there looking at her body—made up of fractured pieces, sharpened edges, and he couldn't be made right again.

He was never going to be right again.

He couldn't be.

It was then that he finally cried.

After all these years ...

It was then that he finally broke.

TWENTY

"SIMONE IS VERY angry," Mae whispered as she slid into the kitchen. "And he's got the rest of them in an uproar."

Aria's irritation level spiked higher, but she managed to keep her cool. "Is that so?"

"What is his *problem?*"

"Me," she said simply.

What else?

Aria had always known that she was going to need to take care of Simone Bruno at one point or another—she had known it from the very first time he tried to act against her after her father had been sent to prison. She'd hoped she could hold off on removing his little problem for as long as possible. He was a good earner for their Camorra, and he controlled a great portion of the loansharking business that kept them in the green more often than not.

But that just wasn't the case anymore.

His time had run out.

Aria had to handle him now—later was no longer an option—because if she didn't, then Simone was going to continue to rally the rest of the Camorra men against Aria until he staged a fucking coup. And then there she would be ... fucked.

Everything she worked for would be gone.

She would not let that happen.

Not for a *man.*

"I'll bring in the food," Mae said.

Aria shook her head—her sister-in-law didn't need to see what was going to come next. Mae was still untouched by a lot of dirtiness in this life, and Aria wanted to keep it that way for as long as she possibly could for the girl.

Life would teach her soon enough.

It always did.

"How about you head upstairs, and just stay there until Nico or I call for you," Aria suggested, not even posing it as a question. "That would be better."

Mae shrugged. "You sure?"

"I might make a bit of a mess."

Probably would.

Aria had her taste for violence, after all.

She couldn't change.

Mae nodded. "Okay, then."

Aria waited for her sister-in-law to leave the kitchen through the back entrance, and then she grabbed the paring knife she had been using to peel potatoes on the island. Slipping the blade up the sleeve of her blouse where it couldn't be seen, she moved to the main entryway, and listened to the conversation happening just beyond the threshold.

"And she has *no* guards," Simone barked.

"She has me, and Mae," Nico returned. "One of us is always with her."

"*Always?*"

"Are you questioning my intent with Aria? Or Mae's standing? I don't take kindly to that, Simone. Watch your step."

"She acts like a free woman!"

"Because she *is*," Nico snapped back.

"She may be a widow, but Camorra still expects—"

"Too much," Aria said, stepping out from the entryway so that the rest of the room could see her. This dinner was far smaller than it might have been, but she only extended the invitation to a select few. Unfortunately for him, Simone had been one. "Camorra expects too much from a woman— we give and give and give, but you only take. When do you give back to me, Simone?"

The man's eyes blazed. "You know very well what is expected of you, Aria."

Yes.

For her to be *perfect*.

Unsullied.

Reputable.

Everything.

And it was too much.

"Look at all I have done for this clan," Aria murmured, waving a hand at the room. "We have the territory we fought for, and the money to do whatever we want with it. We have control, and *power*. Everything *men* didn't give you. A woman did. And what do you give me in return, Simone?"

"I—"

"You give me disrespect, and hatefulness. You shame me behind my back, and dirty my name. My *name*. The one and only thing I was allowed to keep in this fucking life, and you dishonor it every single time you open your mouth."

Simone didn't move from his chair even as Aria came closer. After all that she had done, and every move she had made, these men still thought to underestimate her. For no other reason than she was a woman, and they were men.

Stupid men.

"Since you like my name so much," Aria said, stopping just two feet away from Simone's seat when he turned to face her properly, "then you won't mind saying it."

"Wha—"

"*Say it.*"

Simone's jaw clenched. "Aria—there, happy?"

"My last name. Say it. You do it every day. The *De Rose* bitch. The De Rose whore. *Say it*, Simone. It's your mantra now, isn't it? Don't open your mouth again unless you're going to say what I want you to, otherwise, I will really make this hurt."

He stayed quiet.

But it didn't last long.

"De Rose," he uttered.

That paring knife slid down from her sleeve, and the handle fit perfectly into her palm. She struck out with a fast swipe of her arm, and the blade came across Simone's throat with a deep slice as she said, "And you can die with my name in your mouth, too."

Blood arched.

Hit the ceiling.

Her.

Jesus.

She really did hate the mess.

Aria let out a sigh, and tossed the paring knife to the table even as Simone continued bleeding out, and gurgling in a morbid way. She was done with him, and moving on to the rest of the foolish idiots at her table. "Anyone else?"

Silence answered her back.

She was so damn tired.

This work was exhausting.

They exhausted her.

Aria waved a hand at the mess. "Someone clean this—I have far better things to do."

She was back in the kitchen, and staring out the large windows when Nico finally came after her. He said nothing as he slid in beside her, and watched the birds pecking at the seeds she had left out for them the day before.

"You usually have more patience than that for Simone," he noted.

Aria shrugged. "He had to go."

"Fair enough, but in a way that ruined the rug I know you went to the Maldives to buy?"

She made a noise under her breath. "So, I'm a little touchy."

"Is this still about him?"

Caesar, Nico meant.

"It's always about him now," she admitted.

Even when his name wasn't on her lips …

Even when he wasn't there …

Even when she was alone …

It was still about him, and how empty she was now.

"I waited—it's been a week since he buried his father," she said. "He's made no effort to contact me, Nico. I think … everything I did was just too much."

Maybe she'd lost her chance.

Another sacrifice to add to the growing pile.

"Or maybe it's time for you to make another move," her friend suggested.

"I don't—"

"Anything can be fixed, Aria. You just have to hit restart."

She did like that idea.

"Restart it is, then."

Aria never once considered that she would return to Lucifer's Den, and yet, here she was. Right back at the beginning again—trying to find her magical do-over. The restart button that would fix all of her wrongs … or some of them, anyway.

His eyes were on her the moment she stepped through the doors that led into what the patrons affectionately dubbed *Hell*. The private area for anything and everything. The very place where she had approached Caesar the first time.

She didn't wear gold this time around.

She wore *red*.

Her curls were up instead of down.

Her makeup was simple.

Her heels still sky-high.

And yes, she could feel Caesar *staring*.

She found him easily enough in his usual spot, and her men trailed behind at a safe distance to give her the illusion of privacy. She had no choice but to bring them along considering how fine of a line she was still walking with them.

They gave her room to breathe.

But not *too* much.

Lest she get cocky with it.

As handsome as ever, and dangerous for her heart, Caesar looked like every woman's walking wet dream in his dark, three-piece suit, gold rings on every finger, and one loafer resting on his bent knee. He seemed relaxed on the velvet couch with his arm tossed over the back, but those stormy-blue eyes of his showed all the emotions he felt as he stared at her.

She saw what he didn't show to others.

"Have you found someone interesting?" she asked as she sat across from him.

For the first time since she entered the club, Caesar's gaze drifted away from her to survey the floor. Quietly, he replied, "No, I haven't."

Curiosity got the better of her.

"At all?"

His stare was back on her—heavy and hot—in a blink. "If you're asking me if I've found a woman who is interesting enough to make me want to fuck her and kill her; or if I've found one that looks and sounds like an angel, but fucks and kills like a devil; or if a woman could even remotely make me as crazy, and hard, and irritated as you do—no, I have not."

Aria smiled a bit.

She didn't even hide it.

"That's a shame," she murmured.

"It really is. I can't even try to fuck my way out of this mood. I can't get hard."

"Ouch."

Caesar's gaze darted to her men fifteen feet away. "Why are they here?"

"They have to be—business, that's all."

"Oh, you're here for business?"

"Is that what you want me to be here for, Caesar?"

His calm expression was gone, then, and replaced by something far darker and dangerous. "Haven't I given you everything you wanted? The streets, and territory—all of that. You have it. What business is left, *donna*?"

He had done all of that.

"You forgot one thing," she said.

"And what is that?"

"Us."

Caesar stiffened a bit, and let out a long exhale. "I haven't *forgotten* anything."

She heard the heat in his words.

The *ache*.

"Do you really love me?" she asked softly.

It was only the subtle turn of his head that let her know he was staring at her again—that, and the way her skin tingled. "How can I not—you didn't give me a choice, and I don't know whether to love you for that, or

211

hate you. And it's not even your fault. It's me. It'll always be me, Aria."

He thought he was broken.

She knew he was just … *bent.*

"I miss you," Aria said, offering the words freely.

Caesar's head did snap to the side that time—he didn't even try to hide his staring. "Do you?"

"Every day."

"Say it again."

Aria grinned, and gave him a look. *"Mi manchi, il mio tiranno."*

I miss you, my tyrant.

She found comfort and warmth and a strangely familiar love in the blues of his eyes when they finally met hers. She found something she hadn't even been looking for—he was not the only one who walked into this with one thing on their mind, and walked away with something else entirely in their heart.

"I've done everything I needed, and I have everything I wanted," Aria said. "Everything to be free, and to have my life back. And somehow, I'm alone now because I'm not with you."

Caesar set his foot to the floor, and leaned closer as he hooked a finger for her to come nearer to him, too. He didn't speak again until their lips were just a breath apart, and the only thing she could see was him.

Here's that restart you wanted.

"I could fix that for you," he murmured.

"My loneliness?"

"I could fix it … on one condition."

"And what is that?"

"That you won't ever leave."

Aria stilled, taking in his words.

He'd been wounded so much; left behind far too many times. The forgotten one; his life nothing more than a throwaway.

Trouble and *bad* and *awful* they called him.

And worse were the people who could be blamed for that abandonment and fear he had about loving someone, or wanting to keep her with him. People who should have loved him, and yet, they either hurt him, or overlooked what was hurting him.

A shame, really.

"I will always stay, but …"

"Mmm, what?"

She smiled. "I keep my last name no matter what."

Caesar chuckled darkly. *"Donna,* I will take your fucking last name if you want me to. I don't care."

So be it.

"Deal," she whispered.

His mouth—that searing kiss she adored—was on hers before the word even passed her lips. And it was everything she had hoped for.

She learned then that hope was not always for the weak. Sometimes, hope was what came through when faith failed.

EPILOGUE

Six months later ...

ARIA WAS ALWAYS on her best behavior when Caesar had her bent over something, and filled full of his cock, fingers, or any one of her favorite toys. Like a cat being stroked just the right way, her body trembled, her claws retracted, and she was terribly sweet.

From the way her come tasted in his mouth.

To the heat of her skin.

And even her cries.

Like this?

She was at her *best*.

Caesar tightened the leather belt around her throat just a fraction of a millimeter, and felt her pussy clench just the way he liked around his dick. Should anyone else get too close to her throat, and Aria was quick to strike them down no matter the reason. She wouldn't even let someone put a necklace around her throat.

Him, though?

She woke him up with his belt in her hands like an offering, and a pretty little smile that said she was ready for fun. And her kind of fun was always worth getting up early for.

"Oh, my God ... *please*."

Her begging was raspy, now.

She was almost out of air.

Nearly ready to come again.

She was sweat-slicked, exhausted, and shaking like a leaf. Nothing turned her on more than the red handprints currently painting her ass, or the streaks of his come already sprayed across her back.

Filthy.

Wild.

Wonderful.

He was just about ready to blow again, too.

Shit.

"If you keep tightening those muscles like that," he warned.

Aria laughed.

High.

Breathless.

Spun.

"Just fucking do it already," she goaded. *"Make me come, Caesar."*

They called him the tyrant.

She was just as bad.

He loved it.

His thrusts came harder then—a brutal pace he knew she was going to feel for the rest of the day. And Jesus ... he wanted her to feel it. As she slipped on white lingerie that he would tear off later, and had her face painted and her hair done in soft curls. As her gown was slipped over her body, and she was waiting behind Cathedral doors for them to open to their forever.

He wanted her to *feel him.*

Her words—still airless and struggling from the belt tight around her throat—melted together in a slur of bliss as she came harder than before.

Please, and *fuck,* and *love you, love you.*

She'd feel him.

He'd hear *her.*

"Still resentful about this, I see," the woman across the room noted.

Caesar eyed the pencil skirt—modest with only a slit to her knee—and the pale pink silk blouse his therapist was wearing today. Unlike him in his flashy Rolex, Italian leather loafers, and a custom fit Armani suit, she dressed in a simple, understated way. As though she didn't want to draw attention to herself, but especially not when she was in a session with a patient. She didn't want to be a distraction. Even her pinned back hair and face clean fresh, sparingly-applied makeup was minimalist, and easy.

Over the rim of her thin-framed pink glasses, she asked, "Do you have something to share, Caesar?"

"Yes."

"Do tell."

"Why did Aria pick you for me, Amber?"

The therapist smiled a bit—not *a lot,* mind, but just enough to let him know there was a reason his wife-to-be had picked this woman when she made her demand for this whole shit-show.

So, yeah, maybe he was a little resentful.

Still.

Caesar kept his end of the bargain, though. He came when he was supposed to, and never missed an appointment. He would clear his schedule for two days every week just to make sure he was here like he needed to be.

He *did it.*

Because Aria asked him to—*wanted* him to.

And fucking really … because he needed to.

Resentful, sure.

It was still good for him.

"Why do you think your fiancée picked me out of the hundreds of capable therapists in this city, Caesar?"

"I hate when people answer a question with another question," he muttered.

Amber cocked a single brow high, and smiled in that condescending way of hers. "And yet, when you are on that couch and in this office, you wield very little power, Caesar. You are the patient, and I am the therapist. I don't answer to you—that's not how this works."

That right there.

"That's why she picked you," Caesar murmured.

His therapist nodded. "I thought you might say something else, actually. Considering …"

"Like what?"

"Like maybe she picked me because you think she doesn't trust you."

Caesar tipped his head to the side, and narrowed his eyes. "Why, because you're a beautiful woman that I might notice, and so, I wouldn't be able to control my need to manipulate and abuse the situation with sex like I usually do?"

"That is your typical style, isn't it?"

Is, he noticed.

Not *was.*

Caesar's jaw clenched, but he checked the urge to lash out with something that would cut the woman down. She hadn't said directly that was why, simply that it would make sense if that's what *he* thought was the reason why.

"Aria trusts me," he finally said.

Tightly.

Roughly.

Strained.

Amber didn't miss it. "But do *you?* Do you trust yourself? Do you find yourself wanting to strike out at those around you in a familiar, comforting way because it's how you have always handled situations? Do you still want to hurt and manipulate with sex because that's what your step-mother taught you sex was best used for—to cause pain, or to control? To be your *weapon,* Caesar? Do you?"

Jesus.

"Getting right to the point today, aren't you?" he asked thickly.

"I think today is the best time for it."

216

His lips flattened into a grim line. It was the only way he thought he might be able to keep himself from talking. It didn't matter, because in typical Caesar fashion, his words slipped out anyway right along with his anger.

"You thought that on my *wedding day* it would be best to talk about how my step-mother sexually abused me for years?" It was slightly easier to say those words, now. He didn't feel the same sting of shame that he once had, but he wasn't going to tell every fucker that crossed his path, either. Leaning forward in the chair, Caesar steepled his fingers, and stared hard at the woman ten feet away with her legs crossed, and her face an impassive mask of calm. "Why today, of all days, would I want to dig into that again?"

"Because don't you deserve to know—and Aria, too—whether or not you still go into every intimate moment with her believing sex is tainted, Caesar? That sex is not about relief, or connection, or a baser need, but rather, an action you use to sedate the shame your step-mother made you feel, or even the weapon you can use to hurt someone else with? Don't *you* deserve to know that? Wasn't that the agreement between you and her—to talk about this?"

In a roundabout way.

Sort of.

Aria was every reason he was sitting in this office. And their wedding day was every single fucking reason he agreed to do this, too.

He couldn't forget it.

Not even if he tried.

"Marry me," he'd whispered against her lips. Because how could he not want to marry this insane, beautiful, sinful woman?

"Marry me," he'd demanded with his fingers stuffed deep into her cunt, and his hand tight around her throat. Because how could he pretend like she didn't own all the good and terrible pieces of him?

"Fucking marry me," he'd said roughly when she came for a fifth time, sobbing through the rushes, and shaking just the way he liked. Because when had he ever believed that he could live a day without her when today he'd woken up feeling like she'd been there his whole damn life?

Caesar expected that yes to come easily. Especially when he and Aria were like this—the very best of them was like this. Sex, and sin, and them. He expected her yes to burst from her lipstick-smeared red lips because he loved her, and she loved him.

Even if they were still figuring that love thing out.

She surprised him.

Like this, he was the one with all the power. She never let him believe differently inside their private moments, but fuck him if she wasn't so damn good at pretending, too. He controlled, and she bent to his demands. It was the only time he did get her so compliant and sweet.

And fucking still …

Still she managed to turn the tables.
She was always doing that to him.
"Marry me, mia cara donna."
Breathless, trembling, and barely able to breathe with his hand still tight around
her throat, she whispered, "On one condition, il mio tiranno."

This was the condition.

This therapy.

This couch.

This woman.

Twice a week, it never failed, even on his goddamn wedding day because that was just how the fucking appointments landed. It didn't matter. He still needed to come, and face this woman for at least an hour. He had to spill his darkest secrets, and bare his tar-black soul.

It hurt.

It was vicious.

It left him *raw*.

Caesar told Amber things he had only ever told Aria, but here, it was different. Here, he had no relationship with his therapist that muddied up the waters. Here, he was not fucking her or loving her like he did Aria.

"I know Aria trusts me," Caesar said, coming back into their earlier conversation again. "And that's why I come here, Amber. I *did* this for her—I continue to come for me. I don't think for one second that a couple of months of this is going to rewire the shit in my brain that's made me the way I am."

"But?" his therapist pressed.

"But here I am—I want to be here."

Even if it was his fucking wedding day.

Even if he could be doing literally anything else.

Here he was.

Amber set her paper pad and pen aside before folding her hands in her lap. "And on my other question—what do you have to say for that?"

Caesar sighed, and rested back in the chair. "What, how I go into sex with her?"

"That, yes. And how you still view it—is it still inherently shameful for you, or to be used as a way to harm someone else even if you're doing *none* of those things during sex?"

"You are getting close to my line."

His one *do not cross* in all of this was Aria.

And sex *with* her.

He didn't—and would *not*—bring their sex life into this fucking mess. He had brought their sexual activities into his mess more than enough, and it wasn't going to happen again.

"Caesar, you know that's not what I'm asking," Amber said.

"Maybe not, but it feels like it."

"Give me an answer, Caesar. So, then you can go into today and beyond this day *knowing*. And maybe you can feel like Aria knows it, too."

Fine.

"She doesn't let me do that—there's no option for it."

"How so?"

Because Aria was smart, and just as manipulative as he was on her *worst* days. The difference between him and her was that she could use her abilities for good whereas he had only used his for bad things.

She wouldn't fuck him if he was angry—wouldn't let him touch her beyond a kiss, or something just as innocent on the days he was sharp, and jagged like broken glass ready to cut someone who came too close. She wouldn't let him take her when his moods were bleak, or worse, when he went into one of his spells with someone else.

She wouldn't let him use her.

Not to feel better, or to redirect his need to hurt someone by doing something else with her. Not to distract himself, or even to divert *her*.

No, Aria was too good for that.

She forced Caesar to reevaluate, figure out another way to handle whatever the issue was, and then come back to her when it was good again. Never once did she allow him to use her sexually in lieu of that, though.

"Every moment of me and her is always just *me and her*," Caesar said, unwilling to explain it much more than those words. "That's how she wants this—that's what I like. There's no underlying shit to it; I'm not out for anything but what she's giving me in that moment."

Sure, they were still dirty.

They still fucked raw.

It was great.

But that's *all* it was.

That, and love.

Amber nodded, and picked up her paper pad and pen again. "Good. Now, how's work?"

Just like that, they were onto something else.

He glanced at the clock.

Five hours to go.

Five hours, and Aria was all *his*.

The murmurings in the pews of Cathedral Basilica of Saints Peter and Paul quieted as Caesar and Cain stood at the end of the white satin aisle runner. Gazes—many of those they recognized; guests specially chosen for this day—turned on the two men, although they lingered more on Caesar.

He expected that—a new boss was always being sized up by those around him. Even if it was his fucking wedding day.

The church had been decorated in variances of white and soft lavender. Ropes of delicate tulle connected each pew with a bushel of white roses and purple lilacs holding it all together. He wasn't one to notice decoration, but Aria had worked particularly hard on every little detail for this day, so he didn't mind taking a moment to appreciate all her work.

Every bit of it.

"You ready?" Cain asked beside him.

Caesar nodded to his best friend. "Never been more ready, man."

Cain's large hand landed hard to Caesar's back. "Let's get this party started, then."

The two headed up the aisle, and while Cain stopped to say hello to a scant few guests, Caesar didn't once stop until he was standing on the bottom step of the altar. His friend joined his side just as the priest came out in all his white and golden robes to stand behind the two.

"How was your penance, Caesar?"

Caesar scowled.

Beside him, Cain smirked.

The asshole.

"It went well, Father," he replied.

The priest nodded. "Better to go into a day like today fresh and clean, wouldn't you say?"

"Sure."

That was a demand of the Bishop, and the church's requirements when it came to marrying a couple. Alongside months' long couple's classes, both Caesar and Aria had been made to do confession with their priest before the ceremony could begin.

It wasn't like he could say *no.*

It'd been … hell, five years since he last confessed. It still felt like nothing had changed even as he had slipped into the confessional room, and took a seat across from his priest ready to admit to his transgressions with a promise not to repeat them.

Some sins, he wouldn't commit again. Others … well, that was between him, his wife, and God.

Made men were made for life.

Well, Caesar didn't believe for a second that a few Hail Marys and all the other prayers he had been made to recite for his latest sins were going to change very much between him and God. A prayer wasn't going to get him any closer to heaven.

It had always been a delicate relationship.

At best.

Besides, he always found heaven somewhere else. Now, he found that blissful, wonderful place between Aria's thighs.

Caesar grinned to himself.

Maybe he wasn't all that different. Maybe he hadn't changed *too* much. He was just a different breed of sinner, now.

The church quieted again when the creak of an opening door echoed down the aisle. Caesar hadn't even taken his gaze away from those doors at the back of the church from the moment he came to stand on the altar—he felt like he'd been waiting for this day for *far* too long.

He was done waiting.

And so was she.

There she stood just beyond the open doors in an off-white gown that hugged every single one of her curves, and teased him from fifty feet away. Decorated in lace and pearls, the dress she picked to wear for this day was perfect, daring, and everything he expected. Strapless with a neckline just low enough to be suggestive, yet modest enough to keep the priest from grumbling, it fit Aria like a glove.

Yet, it was still enough to take his breath away. Always keeping him on his toes. He looked forward to that happening for the rest of his goddamn life.

How could he not?

Now that she was there—and *almost* with him—Caesar had the strangest urge to bolt down the aisle and grab his soon-to-be wife. Even as the people stood in the church to begin the procession of her walk, he had to beat down the urge to go and walk with her.

She wanted to walk alone. She wanted to come to him willingly.

She had her reasons.

He let her have them.

This love and marriage and life thing was supposed to be all about compromise, anyway. Wasn't it?

Their procession and wedding party was small. So small, in fact, that they didn't even have one to begin with. He had Cain to stand for him, and sign the necessary documents, but even then, he could have made his best man sit for the majority of the ceremony. Aria had done that for the person she chose to be her witness.

There was no ring bearer to walk.

No flower girl.

No *people.*

Just her.

And him waiting at the end.

Time stood still for Caesar in the seconds it took for Aria to come down the aisle, and meet him at the end. Cain took her bouquet of white roses and lilac accents, and set it aside so that Caesar could finally get her hands in his.

Jesus.

He felt so much better when he was holding her.

He was *him* again like this.

Always, with her.

Her off-white lace veil crowned her face and curls like a halo of delicate perfection. There was nothing hiding her dark eyes and red smile from his view, and he loved it.

Adored that this was how she'd chosen to present herself. She was not some present for him to unwrap—she'd already given him the gift of her a long time ago.

"*Ti amo*," she whispered before the priest could begin.

Caesar grinned. "*Sempre*, Aria."

It was the one thing he knew for sure.

The one thing he believed in until the end of time.

Them.

And his vows would be a reflection of that—his vows would be the truth, so help him fucking God; his truth hadn't killed him.

Somehow.

His truth just loved him.

His vows were for her; because of her: *And I will love you until my last breath the way I should have loved you from my very first.*

It was his promise to her.

No matter what, Caesar would keep it.

A NOTE!

I went into this book without really knowing *who* Caesar and Aria were beyond the skin-deep, surface things. I knew their issues, and how they came to be. But I wasn't far enough into their minds to really *get it*. And then when I was, what I found terrified me.

There has never been characters in my backlist more broken than these two … and I love them for it. I love them for being survivors, but also villains. Because they are that, too. And if you have made it this far, you've probably realized that as much as these two are the hero and heroine of their own story, they are also very much their own villains, too. But for every villain, there is someone who made them that way. It's a good lesson to remember.

Thank you to all the ladies who helped with this book. Proofing, editing, London for the cover, and more. It means the world.

To my hubby who gave me *that look* when I mentioned Caesar was a survivor of childhood sexual abuse, and he never even thought to question me on whether I was sure this was a road I wanted to go down. Of course, it was, he knew. These stories need told, too. Thank you, D. My biggest fan from the jump, babe.

And to my readers—thank you for coming on this journey with me. It's less fun when I'm doing it alone; you all make it far better.

Hugs, loves.

Bethany-Kris

ABOUT THE AUTHOR

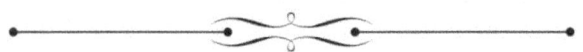

Bethany-Kris is a Canadian author, lover of much, and mother to four young sons, one cat, and three dogs. A small town in Eastern Canada where she was born and raised is where she has always called home. With her boys under her feet, a snuggling cat, barking dogs, and a spouse calling over his shoulder, she is nearly always writing something ... when she can find the time.

Find Bethany-Kris at her:

Website: www.bethanykris.com
Blog: www.bethanykris.blogspot.com
Facebook: www.facebook.com/bethanykriswrites
Twitter: @BethanyKris
Instagram: www.instagram.com/bethany.kris
Pinterest: www.pinterest.com/bethanykris

Sign up to Bethany-Kris's New Release Newsletter here: http://eepurl.com/bf9lzD.

OTHER BOOKS

John + Siena

Loyalty
Disgrace

Cross + Catherine

Always
Revere
Unruly
The Companion

Guzzi Duet

Unraveled, Book One
Entangled, Book Two

DeLuca Duet

Waste of Worth: Part One
Worth of Waste: Part Two

Standalone Titles

Effortless
Inflict
Cozen
Captivated
Dishonored

Donati Bloodlines

Thin Lies
Thin Lines
Thin Lives
Behind the Bloodlines
The Complete Trilogy

Filthy Marcellos

Antony
Lucian
Giovanni
Dante
Legacy
A Very Marcello Christmas
The Complete Collection

Seasons of Betrayal

Where the Sun Hides
Where the Snow Falls
Where the Wind Whispers
Seasons: The Complete Seasons of Betrayal Series

Gun Moll Trilogy

Gun Moll
Gangster Moll
Madame Moll

The Chicago War

Deathless & Divided
Reckless & Ruined
Scarless & Sacred
Breathless & Bloodstained
The Complete Series

The Russian Guns

The Arrangement
The Life
The Score
Demyan & Ana
Shattered
The Jersey Vignettes

Find more on Bethany-Kris's website at www.bethanykris.com.

www.ingramcontent.com/pod-product-compliance
Lightning Source LLC
Chambersburg PA
CBHW072353020726
47506CB00004B/1096